D0424135

4305 7096

WILLOW ASTER

This book is a work of fiction. Names, characters, places, and incidents are either the product of the author's imagination or are used fictitiously. Any resemblance to actual persons, living or dead, business establishments, events, or locales is coincidental.

No part of this book may be reproduced, scanned, or distributed in any printed or electronic form without permission. Please do not participate in or encourage piracy of copyrighted materials in violation of the author's rights. Purchase only authorized editions.

Photograph by Aaron Cota
Model: Jeanette Abell
Cover Design by Blade
Formatting by Jovana Shirley, Unforeseen Editing,
www.unforeseenediting.com

Copyright © 2015 Willow Aster
All rights reserved.
ISBN: 1516979141
ISBN-13: 978-1516979141

Dedicated to my loves who I know would
Drop everything, anytime, no matter what, if I said I needed you.
You've done it countless times,
And I will always be grateful, each and every time.

PROLOGUE

My first telescope was not much more than glorified binoculars, but I faked stargazing long enough that my parents finally bought the one I really wanted. Guilt could do that. And money. My parents would buy anything just to avoid seeing me. I didn't care. It gave me more time to peek in his window.

With acres between our houses, I never had to worry that he would see me.

The second telescope really worked. I could see the smallest details in his room, right down to the red stain on his carpet from a spilled drink. He was only able to get half of the stain out of his carpet, and eventually, he put a bean bag over the spot.

I watched him come in after school, take his shirt off, and play his guitar for hours. He had a blue electric guitar and a dark brown acoustic that sat in the corner. A keyboard was on the other side of the room.

I saw the way he threw things in his garbage can from across the room, making 90% of the shots.

Sometimes his sister came in his room, and those days were especially lonely. Every now and then I could make out what they were saying, but it usually just reiterated how alone I really was.

I subtly followed him at school. He was popular and funny and so cute it made my stomach fall every time I thought of him.

He was perfect. And perfect for me. He just didn't know it yet.

A few things happened in our sophomore year that changed everything.

We finally met. I made sure I brushed my hair until it was shiny that morning, put on my favorite blue shirt that matched my eyes, and scheduled an 'accidental' run-in with him after gym.

I played that conversation over and over in my mind for years.

"Oh, sorry," he said, reaching down to pick up my book. "Here you go." He stood back up and looked me over. "Hey, I've seen you around. How's it going?"

I stared at him, speechless, until his smile grew. I cleared my throat. "Hi," was all I was able to utter.

"Ah, we've got a shy one here," he said kindly.

I knew I would love him forever.

"I'm Beckham." He gave a wave and leaned closer to me. "You have killer eyes—they're so blue. Colorful hair, too." He nodded. "Bold. What would you call that?" He pointed to my hair.

"Thanks. Cotton candy," I whispered and then giggled. I quickly stopped when he smiled.

We stood there staring at each other for a moment.

"Well, I'll see ya," he said and was off before I could catch my breath.

From then on, every time he saw me in the hall, he waved. I kicked myself every night for not saying more, not making more of an effort. I was working up my nerve to speak to him, practicing daily in the mirror. Trying my best to not stutter or blush or do anything other than make smart conversation.

And then it all went to hell.

A tour bus began to park in his yard. I knew his family was talented. They'd done music in L.A. for a long time. I started looking into it online and finally one night, on an entertainment blog, my digging paid off. The Woods family had gotten a recording deal and were going on a huge tour.

Before I knew it, his room was practically empty and everything changed. Once they left, they didn't come back, or at least not to that house. Beckham Woods blew up and left me in the dust.

I failed all my classes that year, dropped out of school, and began to plot how I'd cross paths with Beckham again.

ARCH

It was true lust the moment he saw her.

He had hoped to avoid the audition, altogether, but once he walked into the auditorium and saw her, he was transfixed. Tall, lean, with legs that seemed endless, and blonde hair piled on top of her head, other dancers surrounded her, but even the spotlight seemed captivated by only her. Every movement she made possessed the music. From one song to the next, he watched as she was completely enraptured by the rhythm. The girl could move.

"I don't care who you pick—they all look good. But you have to keep that one." Beckham tapped the choreographer's notes on number four.

"Oh, that's a given." Anthony rolled his eyes. "She could make even you look like you know what you're doing."

"Watch it." Beckham tweaked Anthony's fedora so it fell over his eyes.

"Trying to do a job here," Anthony said as dramatically as he could, which was extremely dramatic.

Beckham stood watching the dancers until Anthony raised his hand and told them to stop. He thanked them and called the next group auditioning. Beckham had seen enough; he usually avoided the whole scene until he knew who Anthony had chosen. Extra guards were stationed all over the theater, and each dancer had been instructed to only speak to Anthony if they had any hopes of being part of the tour. No autographs from Beckham would be given, no pictures, no exceptions. So far, only one girl had tried to get past a guard backstage and she had been escorted out.

Beckham walked to the back of the theater and went to the green room, still thinking about the girl. She made him want to forget the man he'd become. Just a year ago he would have made sure he got her into his bed. A girl who could move like that. Hell. The things he could do with her. He contemplated going back in the auditorium to see if Anthony would have her dance again, but didn't even want to let himself get into that line of thinking.

They'd been in San Diego for two days, trying a different talent pool for this tour. He had holed up in the theater or on the bus during the day, avoiding the crowds that seemed to be multiplying at their hotel. This would be an intense tour, and if he had anything to say about it, the last he'd ever do again. As much as he loved singing for thousands every night to packed-out stadiums, after multiple world tours and dozens of shorter runs, he was ready for a break. A long break. A *forever* break. Not exactly the right way to be thinking before the stringent rehearsal schedule began in a couple of weeks.

Grabbing his sunglasses and ball cap, he walked back into the hall. A little boy who looked around 4 or 5 with curly brown hair had materialized in the short time he'd been in the room. Beckham wondered how he'd gotten through security, but he didn't mind him being back there. He wasn't bothering anyone. He was playing with a ball on the floor and didn't look up until Beckham was standing right by him.

"Hey there. Whatcha playin'?"

"My mom says I can't talk to strangers," he lisped all his S's, "but I know who you are, so I guess it's okay."

"Well, she's right. Is she here?"

The little boy nodded and then a smile took over his face. And Beckham was finished, done for, smitten.

"Wanna play jacks?"

He showed Beckham the metal pieces he'd been squeezing in each hand. The ball went bouncing out of one hand and Beckham leaned down and caught it on its bounce up.

"Sure. I haven't played with jacks since I was little—I never see kids play it anymore."

"I do. All the time. Mom says I have a 'diction." He caught the ball Beckham bounced his way.

"Hmm, well an addiction to jacks wouldn't be the worst thing, I don't suppose. So, I'm Beckham, and who are you?"

"I'm George."

"Really? George? Like Curious George?"

He laughed. "No, I'm Harry."

"Harry. Oh, okay. So which is it? George or Harry?"

"I'm Mavid!"

"Mavid? Is that even a name?"

"Nooooo, you're crazy. Mavid's not a name."

"You're starting to look like a Mavid, actually. I can see it now."

That wiped the grin off his face. "I do not. Take that back."

Beckham held both hands up. "Whoa, dude. Just playing the game here."

The little boy laughed. "Just kiddin'. Whoa, dude, loosen up." He looked at Beckham then and stood up. "And you can call me Leo."

Leo, or whatever his name really was, looked so stinkin' cute, Beckham couldn't wipe the grin off his face. He could hang with this guy a few more minutes before getting some air. In fact, maybe he'd just skip going out.

"You got any whiskey sours?"

Hearing that come out of his mouth, especially with the lisp of all lisps, was too much. Beckham's laugh echoed through the corridor.

"Where have you heard about whiskey sours?"

"I heard my mom saying that's her favorite drink. Joey says it's a girly drink. Mom also likes marragritas sometimes."

"Marragritas ... oh yeah, I like those too."

"You know my mom?"

"I don't think so."

"Well, she knows *you*." He mimed the words of Beckham's song that was still coming from the auditorium and knew every word. "My mom listens to you all the time."

"Ahh, that's nice of her. Maybe I can meet your parents. Where are they, anyway?"

They were just coming to the side doors of the auditorium. "Getting work done. I'm supposed to stay right here and not move an inch. I went and came right back though." He said it like Beckham might tell on him.

"Hey, I think they'd understand you getting a drink. No worries."

The door opened and a cute blonde came out. She gave a startled look to Beckham and then to Leo, and back to Beckham.

"Sorry I was gone that long, Leo." She shuffled nervously behind Leo.

Beckham smiled, trying to make her more comfortable. She didn't crack a smile; in fact, her eyes just grew larger as she stared at him. The kid's mom seemed a little uptight. Not exactly what he was expecting with such a cool kid.

"It's okay," Leo lifted his thumb toward Beckham, "he kept me company."

Just then Jodi, one of Anthony's assistants, stuck her head out and said, "Beck—Anthony's wondering if you can take a look at a small group he's put together, since you're still here…" She smiled, knowing he was trying to escape.

"Ohhhkay," he dragged it out, "I guess I can do that." He looked back at Leo and the girl. "You're welcome to come into the auditorium..."

"Oh, that's okay. We're good here," she responded quickly.

Leo shrugged and with a smile he walked to Beckham and held out his hand. Beckham gave him a firm handshake. "Thanks for playin'."

"Well, thank you, Mavid … I mean, Leo." This got a laugh out of the little boy. "It sure was great to meet you." Beckham walked to the doors and gave Leo another wave before going inside. *What a fun kid*, he thought. *Manners, too.*

When he entered the auditorium, the tension in the air was thick. The room had cleared out, with nine still on the stage.

Anthony motioned him over. "I think I'm ready to call it but wanted to see if you agree with the three that I want to cut."

"K, man. Let's do it."

Anthony turned on the music and for the first song, they all did the routine Anthony had shown them. On the second song, they each had about twenty seconds to freestyle.

Anthony and Beckham talked it out and were in agreement with every dancer. There were three that just didn't have the same deep groove that the rest did. And six who were so tight, you could feel every pulse of the song. And then, the girl, she was the one all eyes would gravitate toward. She just had *it*.

"I'm thinking that girl for the solos, mirroring you," Anthony said. He turned on a slower song and yelled, "Roxie Taylor, show me what you can do on this one."

Beckham nodded, unable to take his eyes off her.

Sensuality oozed out of her when she moved. More than being sexy, it was the emotion she provoked with her movements. She *became* every word of the song. It was impossible to not be mesmerized watching her. Graceful, but funky. Fluid and strong, even in the more intense moments of the song.

Beckham forced his mouth closed when the song ended. Roxie stood up straight then, and for the first time, looked self-conscious.

"Excellent! Okay, everyone, I think we've seen what we need to see. We'll discuss things and get back to you within a few days. If you don't hear from us, thanks for trying out ... maybe we'll see you again in the future."

Beckham cringed. This was why he didn't like to be here for this part. He didn't want to feel bad for the ones who were let go.

"Just a reminder, for those of you who are selected— we will begin two months of rehearsals in L.A. in a month from now. We expect you to be ready to work hard. No distractions. Also—make sure you're able to survive being on a crowded tour bus with people you don't know ... for long, exhausting months at a time. You think you want this now, but imagine if you don't like someone, the close space, the exhaustion, the wear and tear on your body. Be sure about this before we call to tell you you're selected. Otherwise, your future career as a backup dancer is already over."

"Okay, Anthony, enough," Beckham muttered.

With a clap and a complete change of tone, Anthony said, "All right, folks! We'll see some of you in a month!" He turned to Beckham and raised an eyebrow. "What?" he challenged.

"No one will want to do it after that little speech."

Anthony waved his hand, openly scoffing Beckham. "Please. Everyone dreams of touring with you. And dancers are all about torturing themselves. Trust me, my little speech just made them want this all the more."

Beckham smirked. "Whatever you say."

He turned around to leave and saw his manager, Nate, walking toward him. It had to be important for him to show up during tryouts.

They did their usual half-shake, half-hug greeting.

"What's going on, man? You've got my attention, showing up here," Beckham said.

"I want to throw something by you, an opportunity ... something we need to act on quickly."

Beckham frowned and nodded. "Of course. Lay it on me."

Nate tilted his head to the side, motioning for Beckham to follow. They walked through the doors and into the back halls of the auditorium. To his disappointment, Leo was long gone. He wished he'd thought to invite his family to the San Diego show. It would be the end of the tour before they were back through, but still, it would have been fun to see the little guy again.

Beckham took the lead when they got toward the green room and offered Nate a bottled water once they stepped inside.

Nate took it and launched right into what was on his mind.

"I think you've met Donny Carter before, right? Made his career when he signed J. Eliot. I think he might have wanted to manage your family way back when."

"Name sounds familiar," Beckham said.

"Well, he just found out he has cancer and is retiring. It's bad, really bad." Nate shook his head. "Such a shame. Anyway, he called to see if I'd take over his client."

Beckham nodded and waited, confused about what that had to do with him.

"His client is Ian Sterling." Nate leaned back and smiled a slow grin.

Beckham perked up. Ian Sterling was someone he had long admired. He was a true artist—with the pipes, songwriting, and unparalleled guitar skills to back it up. Beckham had seen him play before Ian became well-known, in a little bar in San Francisco, and it had inspired him during a time when he was pretty numb. Earlier this year Ian had taken the Grammy home for Best Album of the Year, and Beckham thought no one deserved it more.

"Bad news for Ian is that Donny completely botched Ian's tour. I mean really—he screwed up. I don't know why he didn't call sooner, but he's obviously had a lot on his mind." Nate lifted his eyebrows and let out a deep breath. "He feels awful about it. Ian has been top-notch about the whole thing, but bottom line is, the guy is now free for the next year, when he was supposed to have a huge tour of his own all lined up."

Beckham and Nate stared at each other, both their minds racing with the possibilities.

"What are we waiting for?" Beckham asked. "Let's make him an offer he can't refuse."

Roxie redid her messy bun and then cursed under her breath when the ponytail holder snapped and left her hair hanging in her face. It reached her waist and was so heavy she usually kept it pulled back when she danced. Already sweating from the audition, she wished for the zillionth time that she'd cut it off at the beginning of summer. Her sister, Chloe, had talked her out of it, saying she looked like a giraffe when her hair was short. Roxie had subtly given her the finger, since the one time she'd ever had her hair short, she'd gotten knocked up, and Chloe had teased her mercilessly then too. Also, Leo was in the room at the time and nothing got past him. She'd made the mistake of saying *shit* in front of him weeks before and he was still giving her grief over that one. The last thing she needed was for him to give the bird to everyone at Northridge

Baptist Pre-K, not to mention getting all curious about his dad. He seemed to be fine, for now, without one. Her brother, Joey, had been amazing with Leo, so had her dad. No need to complicate things with another man.

She dug in her bag for another ponytail holder and just as she rounded the corner, she found one and piled her hair back on top of her head. Ah, it helped immediately. She needed to get out of there before she saw anyone up close and personal.

"Over here, Mom!" Leo was hidden away, sitting exactly where she'd left him. It didn't look like he'd moved an inch.

"Hey, bud. Thanks for being so patient. Where's Aunt Chloe?"

"Bathroom," he pointed at the door next to him, "right in there."

"You should have gone with her."

"Gross, Mom."

"You know I don't like you being by yourself—you-" She laughed in mid-sentence. "Don't you give me the stink eye. Come on, let's get out of here. You ready for some ice cream?" She leaned over and kissed him on the forehead and helped him put everything in his backpack.

"Can I have three scoops this time?"

"Uh, wow, really? Are you gonna be a hyper mess if I say yes?"

"No?" He looked at her, unsure of what to say.

Roxie laughed and messed up his hair. "You know what? Yes. I can't believe how long you waited on me. You deserve at least three scoops."

Leo's eyes lit up. "Cotton candy, strawberry, and blueberry cheesecake."

Roxie crinkled up her nose. "Can your belly survive that?"

"It certainly can."

"Are you absolutely certain, with all certainty, that it certainly can?"

Leo raised his eyebrows. "I'm certain," he said.

Chloe walked out of the restroom and her eyes widened when she saw Roxie. "I didn't leave him long, just a few minutes. I told him to yell or bite if anyone came near him."

Roxie rolled her eyes. "He should have gone in there with you. Someone could have snatched him up. Look how cute he is."

It was Chloe's turn to groan at Roxie. She was a little over the top sometimes. "Come on, Rox, there are guards at every door. No one would be able to take him."

As they pushed the theater doors, an unseasonably hot wind attacked them. They walked to the car and Roxie started it before Leo and Chloe got in, cranking the air conditioner to full blast. The ice cream shop was just around the corner and when they walked in, Leo started humming. The kid lived for ice cream.

When they had their heaping cones, they sat down and started eating it as fast as they could before it melted.

"Did you see him?" Chloe whispered to Roxie when Leo got up to throw away his napkin.

"No, I made it a point to not look for him, actually," Roxie whispered back. "I didn't want to screw up my audition, you know?"

Chloe nodded. Her eyes searched Roxie's, but she didn't say anything for a long time. When they were on their way back out the door to head home, she spoke again.

"What are you gonna do if they call, Roxie?"

Roxie sighed. It was a waste of time to even think about that. They wouldn't be calling, and if by some crazy stroke of luck they did, she hadn't figured out yet how she could actually do it.

"I'm not gonna get the job, Chloe." She shook her head. "You know I have the worst luck ever..." her voice trailed off quietly.

Roxie got on the highway and crept slowly in the rush-hour traffic. She looked in the rearview mirror at Leo, who was holding the good fight of staying awake, just barely.

"You were there a long time. They must have liked something they saw. Rox, you're an incredible dancer," she said quietly. "I think you need to think about what will happen if they call you back." Chloe poked Roxie in the arm for emphasis.

"There's no way I can do it!" She softened her tone when she saw the concern in Chloe's eyes. "I don't know why I went—I think I just needed to see if I still have what it takes." She adjusted the air and sighed. "If they *do* call back, which they won't, I'll know to pursue opening the studio. That's what I've always wanted to do anyway. It would make today worth the stress, don't you think? And Mom and Dad might finally get behind the idea if they hear I was good enough to tour with Beckham Woods."

"You don't need to teach yet. Save that for later. People need to be seeing *you* out there, dancing the way only you know how," Chloe argued.

"I found out today how long the tour really is, Chloe." She swallowed hard, needing to have a good cry. "They're going pretty much non-stop for almost a *year*, not to mention the months of rehearsals in L.A. I'm sure there are breaks here and there, but ... a *year.*"

Chloe groaned and stared out her window for a long time. Both of them had one person on their minds: Leo. When they turned onto their street, she looked at Roxie again.

"Rox ... I'm ready for you to start living for *you* again. I hoped this was the start of that."

"And it is. I've known for a while that I can't keep living like I have been. Coming to the tryouts and making it to the last round ... it helped more than I can say. It was worth it for me, just to get that far, because now I know I have to get back to what I love—but I have to do it the right way. Doing whatever I want had to end when I got knocked up," Roxie whispered under her breath, but Chloe heard every word.

"Moms have lives too!" Chloe cried.

Leo piped up out of his stupor. "Moms have lives too! Moms have—how many lives you think you got, Mama?"

Chloe grinned. "See? They do!"

"Shall I make a bumper sticker with that on it, Chlo-bo?" Roxie snapped back and got out of the car, giving her door a good slam.

"Oh, cut the shit already!" Chloe yelled back and then clamped her hand over her mouth, cringing when Leo hopped out of the car.

Leo's eyes got wide. "Aunt Chloe said *shit*. I thought we couldn't say *shit*."

Of course he could say that perfectly.

"We can't, Leo. Aunt Chloe just let it slip on *accident*." Roxie's eyes narrowed on Chloe.

"It sounded like she could say it. Why we can't say *shit*?" Leo looked between his mom and aunt, confused.

"Just stop already," Roxie said.

"I'm sorry, Leo. I've gotta watch my mouth," Chloe said and mouthed 'sorry' to Roxie, but her shit-eating grin wasn't convincing.

The next morning at ten, Roxie was just finishing up on a loan at work when her cell phone rang. She checked to see the time of her next appointment and picked up the phone.

"BB Credit Union, this is Roxie. How can I help you?"

"I ... must have the wrong number. Wait, did you say this was Roxie?"

"Oh sorry, habit ... yes, this is Roxie." Roxie tucked her cell under her ear and rolled her eyes at herself. Of course, her work phone started ringing then, just to nail the point home that she was an idiot.

16

"This is Anthony Douglas, Beckham Woods' choreographer. How's it goin'?"

"Uh, I'm good. How about you?"

"Great. Listen, you *really* impressed us with your audition yesterday."

Anthony sounded so sincere, Roxie had to sit up a little straighter in her rolling chair.

"Thank you."

"I was seeing here that you've been dancing practically your whole life, but on your resume, I'm not seeing a lot to show for that. However, I would have never known by the way you dance. Were you just being modest? Do you teach in a studio or something like that?"

"I've taken a lot of classes and dance every chance I get, but no, I don't teach anywhere. I have a boring 9 to 5 job." Roxie laughed awkwardly.

"Well, that would normally scare me off, but I've never seen someone catch on so quickly to my routine OR someone who seemed so completely comfortable on stage. You've got quite a gift, girl."

Anthony sounded like a friend she'd like to keep. Too bad he was going to hate her soon.

"Thank you so much." She bit her lip hard to see if this was really happening. Ouch. It was.

"Beckham specifically asked that you be invited on his tour. He saw you yesterday and you knock-"

"What? He was there? I ... didn't see him."

"Oh yeah, he was there. We couldn't take our eyes off you, hon. He thinks you're perfect for this and so do I. In fact, I'm already envisioning featuring you with Beckham on a few of his slower tunes. He's 6'2" ... you're 5'9", 5'10"? Perfect proportionally to work next to him."

She knew that.

"The thing is-" she started.

"I'd like to fly you out by October 12th, so you're ready to begin rehearsal the next morning. We'll be in L.A. until December 20th and then off for about a week and a half before Christmas and just before the New Year. We'll start back up with a final week of rehearsals on the 2nd and our first performance will be the 5th. I can fax over the schedule, if you'd like ... or email, whichever you'd prefer." He finally stopped to take a breath and Roxie put her head in her hands. "Make sure you're conditioned between now and then. Even if you're dancing a lot now, it'll be a grueling schedule. Do you have any questions for me?" he asked.

"See, the thing is, I have..." The words seemed to lodge in her throat. She coughed and then a lunatic took over her brain. "Can you email the schedule and all the details?"

"Absolutely. I'll do that right now. Anything else?"

"No, not that I can think of," she lied.

"I'll email the contract and terms of the salary along with the schedule."

"S-sounds good," she stuttered.

She hung up the phone and looked around at her co-workers, answering phones and working with customers, and thought about how her whole life could change. Two minutes later, she opened up her email. The first page she saw took all the air right out of her body.

Actually it was just one line: $1,000 per show for 120 shows, $500 per rehearsal, and a $100 per diem each day on the tour.

She tapped the numbers quickly into her calculator and put her fist against her mouth to stay quiet when the amount came up: $184,500.

Everything blurred and all the sound in the credit union was swallowed up. Roxie was worthless the rest of the day. Her mind had already landed on the figure that was more than she could even wrap her mind around. Really, even if it had been half of that, she would have been heavily swayed. With a little boy to raise and no winning lottery ticket, she couldn't imagine any single mom passing up that money.

2 EXODUS

Ian looked at his two girls snuggled up on the plush rug in the living room, sound asleep. Their little one was the perfect mini replica of her mama. They both took his breath away. As always, when he looked at Sparrow and their daughter, Journey, his heart picked up and lit into a cadence he'd based many songs on—his muses, both of them.

His fingers latched onto his hair and he pulled until he realized what he was doing. Sparrow told him all the time that his hair would fall out if he kept it up. He didn't want to be old *and* bald for his gorgeous wife. If his hair was going—which, truthfully, it didn't seem to be in any danger of quite yet—he wanted it to be from Sparrow yanking on it when he was deep inside her.

He ran his hand across his face instead, trying to quell the anxiety that had been in his chest since he'd spoken to Donny. He'd known deep down something wasn't right; Donny had been avoiding meeting him in person for the last three months. Ian had attributed it to both their schedules, but when he pressed *again* to meet and talk about the tour, Donny finally came clean. Donny had stage IV cancer.

Ian spent the first week after hearing the news devastated about Donny. They'd only worked together a couple of years, but had gotten close in that amount of time. Donny had been really good to him.

What Ian hadn't known until today, was that Donny only came partially clean. The tour was off. Donny admitted that he'd hoped he could still work it out, but now knew that wasn't realistic. Everything Ian thought was already set in stone, wasn't. Donny had fired the tour manager months ago and tried to do it all on his own. 'One last gift to Ian' that hadn't worked out. At all.

He couldn't be upset with Donny—it was minuscule compared to his friend being so sick—but it did mean he'd have to figure out what to do next. The lease on their house was up the same date as the 'tour' was scheduled to start. He'd also worked on a surprise for Sparrow that he hadn't planned on showing her until a few days before they went on the road, but now he was regretting the whole thing.

Sparrow's eyes opened and shifted to his. She stayed completely still, so she wouldn't wake up Journey.

"You okay?" she mouthed. "Donny?"

He nodded and swallowed hard. "I saw him," he whispered. He shook his head and bit the inside of his cheek, looking away.

Sparrow carefully moved Journey's arm and leg off of her and stood up. She looked at the mantle, making sure the monitor was on. She walked toward him and took his hand, leading him to their bedroom.

Ian pushed the door behind him but didn't close it all the way. They'd be able to hear the little one crawling when she woke up. She was nearly seven months, but Journey had inherited her mom's long legs and her—as Sparrow put it—'complete lack of gracefulness'. Sparrow couldn't help it if occasionally her feet got ahead of her. And even if nothing stood in her way, Journey seemed able to make a racket when she went mobile.

Sparrow turned and wound her hands around the back of his neck, studying his face.

"I'm worried about you," she said. "This with Donny and leaving soon ... the stress of moving everything into storage. It's a lot."

"It is. And there's more. I'll tell you all about it, but right now I just want to sink into you and not think about anything else."

Her eyes widened and then she smiled, pressing closer to him

He kissed down her neck and whispered: "How long do you think we have?" He lifted her short skirt and had the tiny scrap of lace underneath pulled off before she even answered.

"Maybe a half hour," she whispered, unbuttoning his jeans and moving his boxer briefs down, as she took hold of him.

"Oh, you're not messing around," he said, grinning.

"Neither are you, apparently." She smirked, her hands cool on his hot skin.

His fingers dipped inside her, one at a time. "What's got you all worked up, baby?"

She shifted her hips toward his hand, greedy.

"You," she purred.

He had barely moved his fingers aside and inched into her, making contact with his favorite place on earth, when the sounds of their monkey crawler came barreling down the hall toward them.

Sparrow's legs unwrapped from his waist, and he was hanging in the cold air, hurriedly pushing himself back into his boxer briefs, all in split seconds.

When Journey pushed through the door, looking for them, they were both grinning at her.

"Dadadadada," Journey chanted, crawling toward him.

"Pumpkin! Prettiest little cock-block I ever did see," Ian cooed at her, picking her up and hugging her.

"Ian!" Sparrow smoothed her skirt down and turned pink.

He loved making her blush more than anything. He tried to get her good and flustered at least twice a day.

"Just telling it like it is," he said. "She doesn't know yet how she's making her daddy suffer."

"And hopefully she won't ever figure it out," Sparrow mumbled, nuzzling into Journey's chubby baby neck.

Ian blew a raspberry on Journey's cheek and the sound of her laughing made them all laugh. He sighed a long sigh when he stopped laughing, some of the heaviness coming back to him.

Sparrow touched his cheek. "Come tell me about it while I make dinner."

He nodded and then took her hand from his cheek and kissed it. "Okay. And I intend to finish what I started as soon as the little blue-baller goes to bed tonight."

Sparrow groaned and her eyes narrowed, her cheeks doing their thing.

"You need to get out of the naughty name-calling habit right now," she said.

He laughed and she growled, which only made him laugh harder.

Journey wiggled out of his arms when she heard the phone ringing and scuttled over to try and pick it up. He hadn't even remembered where he'd left it, but his daughter had a keen sense of where the cell phone was at all times. It was just out of her reach, so Ian grabbed it and thanked her for finding it before she took it too hard that it wasn't in her little hands.

She didn't care that he'd thanked her—her lower lip stuck out and instant tears filled her eyes. He tried saying 'hewwo' before he answered, to distract her. Sometimes that made her laugh, but this time it wasn't working. Something like 'Heww-lo' came out when he pressed talk. Sparrow giggled as she picked up Journey.

"Hello. Am I speaking to the Sexiest Man Alive?" The guy started laughing midway through his sentence.

"Uh..." Ian paused. "Who's callin'?" *People* had crowned him with that doozie last December and it never failed to embarrass him.

"Sorry, Beckham Woods calling. I hope you don't mind—my manager got your number from Donny..."

"Holy hell. Of course I don't mind. You're Beckham Fu-rickin' Woods." He'd tried desperately to clean up his mouth, especially since Journey was born, but holy shit he had a rock star on the phone. "I think you might have been elected Sexiest Man Alive a few dozen times yourself."

Beckham's laugh came through much louder than his voice.

"Time to pass along the title to someone more deserving, Ian Fu-rickin' Sterling," he said, the smile still in his voice. "I've admired your music for a long time. Saw you in San Francisco once before you got all big and famous."

"What an honor, man. You're as good as it gets. I've been a fan of yours forever ... hoped we'd meet one of these days."

"Well, that's what I'm calling about, kind of. Actually a lot more than that, but..." Beckham cleared his throat.

Ian thought he sounded a little nervous. This might be the weirdest day he'd had in a long time.

"Listen, I want you to be completely honest, and say no if it doesn't sound like something you'd want to do, but ... I'm wondering if you'd consider touring with me. I heard about your tour being canceled and I know that's pretty much the worst thing that can happen to a working musician. Your band, and wife, daughter ... whoever you need to bring—they're all welcome to come. I've been wanting to do something different for a long time, and the thought of you on this tour makes it actually sound interesting. Fun, even. We could go a variety of ways. Split the time right down the middle, or integrate into each other's sets ... I'm open to anything."

It was quiet for a moment.

"I'm speechless," Ian finally said. "It sounds ... amazing. When are you heading out?"

"Rehearsals start just a month from now—mid-October. We tour January 5th to December 6th."

"I can't ... believe this. Thank you, first of all. Thanks for even considering having me along. I'd love to do it. I'll talk it over with my wife—but I'm sure she'll be behind it all the way. I was just getting ready to tell her about ours being off, so this will help ease the blow, *considerably*."

"Great! Think it over and let me know when you decide."

"Will do. Thanks again."

"If you do this I'll be thanking *you*. I hope it works out."

The next month for Beckham would consist of guest hosting on *Saturday Night Live* and all the top late night talk shows, as well as *The Ellen Show*. Beckham always played his part so well. Smile in place, humor intact, charismatic bachelor: check. Ever since he'd stopped drinking and using, life had gotten easier in some ways but more exhausting in others. It wasn't really drudgery for some of the interviews—Fallon and Ellen were two of his favorite people. And he'd gotten a few Emmys from hosting *SNL*, so it felt like a party now every time he was on the show. But there was something missing, and it wasn't just getting sloshed.

He'd had an awakening one morning after tossing three girls out of his bed. He'd been so high, he didn't even know where they'd come from, and in the light of day, they looked worse than he felt. Disgusted with himself, he checked himself into Hazelden and got clean. He was lucky: he hadn't had any relapses and besides missing Jameson, he'd not really had the pull back to it that most of his friends did. It probably helped that he'd lost some friends in the process. The only problem was that his whole lifestyle worked so much better being intoxicated. It dulled the pain and made him feel like he could do anything—like sing for thousands each night in packed-out stadiums.

Off of it all and clean for one year and two months, lately Beckham just wanted to be done. To walk away from his career and have a quiet life somewhere in Italy or Tennessee. Since he was from Tennessee, that probably ruled out a quiet life there. Italy would have to do.

He'd already had a successful nearly twenty-year career. Starting out singing with his family's band as a kid, and finally building a solo career that he could continue living off of for a lifetime and then some, he was set. His last recording project had gone platinum, being touted as the groundbreaking album of the decade. And just a year shy of thirty. If he quit in a year, he could still go out on top.

Of course, he hadn't told this to anyone.

He was excited for what he was secretly thinking of as his last year on the road. And the thought of Ian on the tour made everything sound a thousand times more appealing. The tour felt manageable and was going to be his best yet. Beckham knew he was finally healthy enough to pull it off.

His phone rang the next day, after his morning run.

"I'm in," Ian said.

After at least ten minutes of excited conversation, they agreed to meet the next day at Ian's house.

"Come over before we get serious about packing," Ian warned. "This place is about to be turned upside down."

Ian opened the door before Beckham even knocked, giving him the bro handshake-hug like they'd been friends forever. And maybe they had. There was none of that awkwardness of first time meetings, no uncertainty. Ian was hilarious and straightforward, and just being around him felt like relief for Beckham. He needed real, down-to-earth people in his life.

They were on their second cup of coffee when a dark-haired angel walked through the house, her curly hair trailing into the V of her shirt, her shorts making it hard to resist staring at those perfect legs. Beckham swallowed and glanced at Ian, who smirked at him.

"I know, my wife's hot. I can't even take it half the time and I live with her. Go ahead and catch your breath there, Beck."

Beckham watched Ian look at his wife, who had turned red and looked like she was about to kill him. He swallowed hard again, waiting for the fireworks.

But she just turned and smiled at him. "Hi, I'm Sparrow. Please don't listen to his nonsense. He has this disease that makes him speak without thinking."

Beckham shook her hand and smiled. "Can't fault the man for telling the truth."

Ian's laugh bounced off the kitchen walls. He grabbed Beckham's shoulder and squeezed. "I like you, man."

They pulled out the guitars after they'd talked a while and then the friendship was officially established. All track of time was lost.

Beckham and Ian got together a few times a week, planning the show. Beckham wanted it to feel like a mutual collaboration—not just his thing, but the two of them working together throughout the evening. They would sing a few songs together, Ian would be featured on the guitar through several of Beckham's songs, and Beckham had gotten Anthony to do choreography for some of Ian's songs.

Ian agreed to do the talk show circuit with Beckham, surprising audiences midway through Beckham's interviews. It was a huge hit. The two of them had such an easy rapport with each other that talk began circulating about them doing a movie together.

Ian would miss the first week or two of rehearsals while they finished packing and moving, but besides the songs with Beckham, he and his band were ready. They had already been practicing for the past few months.

Rehearsals would begin the next morning and Beckham was ready. In addition to doing vocal exercises every day to keep his voice in shape, he had a trainer who kicked his ass every day. They switched it up, running through Griffith Park, Sepulveda Basin, Malibu Creek State Park, and every now and then, Runyon Canyon Park. If they went to the same place two days in a row, fans magically appeared, no matter how remote the trail.

For someone trying to clean up his act, the girls were probably the hardest vice. For years he'd had bad habits and girls were at the top of the list. It was just so convenient. And numbing—something he'd needed to be since ... the very first time he'd had sex. There were always girls, women of all ages, ready and willing to do whatever he wanted. And he'd obliged far too many. Being at Hazelden had helped him see that his problem in that area was possibly even bigger than the drugs, since he had relapsed a few times in the past year plus. He spoke to his AA sponsor, Troi, a few times a week. He'd also told Nate and Anthony he needed to be accountable to them. Thanks to them, it had been a long time since he'd relapsed. After witnessing a rockbottom fallout during a girl-crazed weekend, far too much press, and seeing how it was messing with Beckham's mind to be such a sleaze-bag, they knew he had to get a grip. They took the job seriously and checked in with him, especially if they saw him spending too much time with a groupie.

Just a little longer and maybe he could find a nice, *normal* girl. As much as he missed sex, and fuck him, he *missed* it, all the weirdos out there had significantly helped to cure him. If there were even any normal girls still out there ... Beckham wasn't sure anymore. He'd gotten to know Sparrow better over the last few weeks, and she made him hope that there could be a nice, beautiful woman out there for him too. She was exceptionally rare, though, anyone could see that. He really didn't have time for a real relationship anyway, so he might as well keep clean. Otherwise, a nice girl would want nothing to do with *him*.

He found his thoughts straying to Roxie Taylor once more—something that happened frequently during the month since he'd seen her—and knowing that she was a possible problem for him, he gave Nate a call. Nate picked up on the first ring.

"You ready to work like a madman?" was the first thing out of Nate's mouth.

"You know I am." Beckham laughed. "I just need to mention something..."

"What's up?"

"Well, there's this dancer coming on the tour. She ... she might be enough to make me get off my sabbatical."

"What's her name? I'll make sure we keep her as far from you as possible offstage."

Beckham stretched one arm over his head and paused for a minute too long.

"You still there, buddy?"

Beckham squeezed his eyes shut and ran a hand slowly over his face. "You know what? I don't want to call any attention to her. I'll be fine. Hey—got another call coming in ... I'll touch base with you tonight."

"Beck, just tell me her-"

Beckham clicked his phone off and ignored the guilt rising in his chest. *You got this. You're gonna be too busy to even think straight, much less to get in trouble with Roxie Taylor.*

He ran an extra two miles and felt slightly less conflicted afterward.

Beckham didn't feel like going home yet. He'd decided to put his house on the market as soon as he got back from the tour. When he was in town he avoided going home until he was just too tired to stay out anymore. Not a good sign. The walls seemed to close in on him there.

He had a meeting with Anthony to discuss the next morning's rehearsals and pulled into their favorite sushi place with five minutes to spare. Anthony was sitting at their usual table, enjoying a drink. When he saw Beckham walking toward him, he guzzled the drink and looked like he wished he could hide the evidence.

"You can drink around me, Anthony." Beckham laughed. "How many times am I gonna have to say it before you believe me?"

Anthony flipped back the strip of blue hair hanging in his eyes. "I'm just looking out for you, hon. I don't want to make it worse for you. You're early." He stood and gave Beckham a huge hug.

Anthony was a frontal hugger. Beckham wasn't really, but he'd given up avoiding them. He slapped Anthony awkwardly on the back as they both sat down.

"I put in an order already—we can let our waiter know if you want to try something new," Anthony said briskly. He flipped open his iPad and turned it so Beckham could see the schedule. "I've fixed it since we last spoke. I've moved up "Shadows" and pushed back learning the routine for "Right Here"—I *think* it will work out better."

Beckham looked over the song list for the week and swiped the calendar to see the next week. He nodded. "I like that. I think it will be good to get an easy song underway and then focus on the harder ones ... looks good."

"I've also added a section you haven't seen yet to "Woman" and a tiny thing to "Driven" ... I hope Roxie Taylor is ready to work hard." Anthony grinned.

"You're adding to her list? She's already dancing a *lot*." Beckham once again squelched down any alarm and nodded. "I think she can probably handle it, from what we saw anyway. I guess if she's not up to all of it, we can switch her out for Vanessa."

"I hope she'll be up for it. I'm counting on her to knock my socks off like she did at tryouts."

Beckham was certain she would knock *his* socks off, even if she wasn't quite up for all that Anthony had planned for her.

"I think we'll have time to be on our game before Ian comes to rehearsals, too, which is good." Anthony got dreamy-eyed every time he mentioned Ian.

"You might have to tone down the lust a notch with Ian. He's a very happily married man," Beckham teased.

Anthony feigned shock. "Moi? Lust over Ian Sterling? Damn. Impossible to tone down. That man's hot enough to turn anybody."

Beckham shook his head and laughed. "He's safe with me."

"You say that now..."

Beckham shot his straw paper into Anthony's nose, which shut him up. The sushi came and it looked like enough for at least four people. They started eating and didn't talk until the sushi was gone. Anthony had never gone so long without talking.

Before the green tea ice cream came, Anthony showed him a few more details about how the rehearsals needed to go. Anthony had been with him from the beginning of his solo career. Beckham trusted him implicitly, which was irreplaceable in this business.

"It's gonna be a good one. Thanks for working so hard on this," Beckham said earnestly to Anthony. "Couldn't do it without you."

"We all know you couldn't," Anthony agreed with a smirk. He took a bite of ice cream. "I'm ending things with David tonight," he said softly.

"*What?* Why?" Beckham set his spoon down and stared at Anthony.

"I found proof that he was cheating on me with that stylist over on Rodeo. I've wondered for a while if he was cheating and just didn't want to believe it. Apparently seven years meant nothing to him. I thought I could forgive him, but ... I just don't think I can." Anthony shrugged.

"Seven years. I'm so sorry. That's ten times longer than any relationship I've ever had," Beckham admitted. "You gonna be all right? Does he know?"

"I will be. And I doubt he sees this coming. The bastard is nothing if not an egotistical son of a bitch." He groaned. "This tour has the best timing ever," Anthony said with tears in his eyes. He shook his head and squared his shoulders, wiping his eyes. "I'll be fine. I'll probably be meaner than a snake for a few weeks."

They laughed, knowing he was telling the truth.

3 BEND

When Roxie tucked Leo into bed that night, he reached up and pushed her hair back from her face. "Mom? Will everyone forget me at school since I won't be there?"

Roxie leaned her forehead onto his, causing all her hair to fall forward again. He pushed it back again and kept holding onto the sides of her face.

"I don't know, Leo. We're on an adventure now. I'm sure you'll go back to Northridge eventually, but you didn't really need pre-K anyway. You're so smart." She gave his nose a little tug and he smiled sleepily. "You'll spend lots of time with Aunt Chloe ... and me ... and a new place! Aren't you excited?"

"I didn't like it at Norfridge much anyway. But I will miss Uncle Joey and Grammie and Gramps and Nick and Stephanie ... am I gonna see them again?"

She felt a shot of guilt to be taking him away from his family and friends.

"Of course you'll see Uncle Joey and Grammie and Gramps again. I don't know about Nick and Stephanie ... but you'll make lots of new friends here, too."

He patted her face like that was a good enough answer for him.

"Uncle Joey says he'll come see us sometime. You think he will?"

"If he said so, then he will," Roxie promised. "Do you like our new place?"

They both looked around his room, mostly bare still, but with a few of his toys.

"It's not like my room at *home*," he said sadly.

"I know, little man. It will take some getting used to, but this is what we need to do for now. You and Aunt Chloe will do lots of fun things while I'm at work, and whenever I get time off, I will be here as much as I can. And we'll be going to lots of fun places we've never been before…" She leaned down and held him tight, her heart squeezing shut at the times she would have to be gone from him too. It killed her to think of being apart, and she had to keep reminding herself of all the positives. "I love you, son. Close your eyes now and get some sleep. We've had a long day."

"Love you, Mommy," Leo said as his eyes closed.

She watched as he fell asleep. He was so beautiful. It was in these moments that she allowed herself to think about his daddy. He looked so much like him.

This better be worth it, Roxie thought as she got up and switched on Leo's nightlight. They'd certainly all sacrificed a lot to give it a try. After being offered a spot on the tour, she and Chloe had gotten out their calendars, opened up Google maps, and tried to figure out a way. It took days of hashing it out, to settle on all the easiest places for Chloe and Leo to meet her on the tour. They'd also needed to move to L.A. for the practicality during rehearsals, and also the better airfares. Her parents were harder to convince, but even they didn't think she could let the opportunity pass without trying.

She and Chloe found a place to rent in Glendale through Craigslist … not the safest way to look for a place to live, but it was cheaper and faster than the regular route. It was actually a decent-sized guest house in the back of a nice home, so they didn't even have to worry about being too loud. Jill and Eddie, a couple in their forties with no kids, were happy to get the extra income. They didn't really need the money to survive, so they were flexible. The best part about the place was that it was within ten minutes drive of the sound stage where she'd be rehearsing every day. She'd been warned by Jill, though, that a ten-minute drive could take forty-five minutes during bad L.A. traffic.

Roxie walked into the kitchen, where Chloe was unpacking one of the last boxes. Roxie unpacked glasses and set them in the tiny dishwasher, so they'd be ready to use.

"You think this is gonna work?" she asked Chloe.

Chloe smiled at her. "I love our little place!" she said, excitedly. "I think it will be perfect for us. Don't you?"

"I just want you to be sure you're up for this. You're taking on a lot. You know that, right?" She put her arm around Chloe and leaned her head on her sister's shoulder.

"I know. I'm not gonna back out now. This is important. You need this, Roxie. I'm so happy you're going for it! And you're helping me too. I really needed this push to get away from Alex."

Chloe's eyes filled with tears and Roxie squeezed her tighter.

"I'm proud of my sister. He never deserved you." She pulled her head up and looked in Chloe's eyes. "Thank you for making this happen. I couldn't do it without you, Chlobo." Roxie sniffed and pulled away before the tears started falling. "Just promise you'll tell me if it ever becomes too much."

"You don't need to worry. I love that boy in there and am so excited that we're gonna spend so much time together. I need this as much as you do." Chloe wiped her eyes with the back of her hand. *"And,"* her voice brightened, "we'll finally have some money, instead of barely scraping by all the time. You'll get all kinds of exposure, dancing for Beckham Woods. This is what you've always wanted! Be excited about it!" Chloe, the eternal optimist, could cheerlead a cadaver into a frenzy.

Roxie hugged her tight and resisted all the what ifs that were parading around in her head. For all of Chloe's optimism, Roxie had always made sure to cover the logical, or even worst-case scenario train of thought … someone had to do it. She guessed it was from being the oldest of three kids. Chloe was four years younger than Roxie. She was the baby, most popular of everything, homecoming queen. Joey was between the girls and the boy her parents had always wanted. They thought he could do no wrong. He was actually pretty great, too, given how spoiled he'd been. Roxie was only good at one thing: dancing. Until her pregnancy topsy-turvied her world and she'd had to make the decision to be a good mother, too.

She had to force herself go to bed. Well, Chloe actually did, reminding her that she'd wreck her first day at work if she was too tired. Surprisingly, she slept and woke up almost looking forward to the day. *Almost*, with a large side of terror.

Instead of the typical dance studio, rehearsals were held in a large warehouse that had been gutted and fit to the tour's specifications. There were portable stages that had been made for the tour and then a separate room for warm-ups. The details had all been emailed the week before, and Roxie was shocked that it looked even better than she'd expected. The only other person in the room was one of the other dancers. He walked over and held his hand out.

"Justin Rodriquez," he said. "Haven't seen you on the circuit before."

"I'm new," she said, shaking his hand. "Roxie."

He checked her out. *Straight*, Roxie filed away. She tugged on her long T-shirt and thought about putting her sweatshirt back on, but someone else came in, distracting them both with her high-pitched squeal.

"Hi!" She went straight for Roxie. "I'm Vanessa! So excited you're here! I knew you'd make it!" A walking exclamation point. When she reached Roxie, she hugged her. "Remember me?"

Roxie nodded and grinned. Vanessa had been very helpful the day of auditions. She'd been on tour with Beckham before and loved sharing all the information with anyone who would listen. She was so nice, though, it was hard to not like her.

"Roxie, right?" she asked as she pulled away.

Roxie cleared her throat. "Yeah," she croaked out. "Good to see you."

"And can you believe Ian Sterling will be on this tour too? How cool is that? I couldn't believe it when I heard!" Vanessa kept going.

"Yeah! So cool," Roxie added weakly. She couldn't believe it about Ian Sterling either—when they'd heard the news, she and Chloe had danced around the house for a solid fifteen minutes. She just wasn't very good with meeting new people.

"Justin…" Vanessa said in a voice a hundred times cooler than the one she'd used with Roxie.

Justin leaned over to hug her and where her hug for Roxie had been bear-like, she stood limp as he wrapped his arms around her.

"Oh come on, Nessa, don't be like that," he crooned.

Vanessa rolled her eyes. "Let go of me, Justin."

Ew, ouch. Icicles dripped off her words now. Roxie decided she *really* liked this girl.

They could hear commotion outside the room. Roxie recognized Anthony's voice. He came in with the other three dancers.

"Oh lookie, we have everybody," he said with a clap. "Does everyone know everyone?" He quickly introduced Brooke, Brad and Shelton and greeted Roxie, Justin and Vanessa. "Okay! Everyone ready?" He walked over to the stereo and turned it on.

Beckham was nowhere in sight and Roxie was so relieved she felt a rush of adrenalin.

"I'm not gonna waste time talking about what we're gonna be doing over the next couple of months. It will be too overwhelming if I do. I'll only say that I'm gonna work your asses off and you better deliver." He raised an eyebrow and looked each one of them in the eye. "Line up, we'll start with a couple warm-ups and then get to work."

For the next three hours they moved without stopping. Anthony yelled a lot, but the guy was such a good dancer that everyone wanted to work hard to please him. They hadn't done a full routine yet, just some exercises and dances that helped them learn to move together as a group.

When they broke for lunch, Roxie called to check on Leo. She'd planned on going to see him for lunch, but it had been catered in, and she thought it would look rude for her to bail on the first day.

"Whatcha doin'?" she asked when he said hello.

"Auntie and I are at the park!" he yelled.

Roxie held the phone away from her ear and grinned. "Oh good! Well, have so much fun! I'll see you tonight at dinnertime, okay?"

"Love you, Mom!" He hung up before she could say it back.

She found everyone at a big round table, piled her plate and sat between Brooke and Brad.

"Eat much?" Brad said when he saw her plate.

She shrugged. "I burn it fast. Starve much?" She stared at his plate.

"It's hard work to look this good," Brad said, lifting his shirt and doing a stomach roll.

Roxie smirked. "Define *good*."

Justin laughed. "*Oh*! Zing!"

Brad looked wounded for a minute and then started laughing too. "I know I shouldn't, but I like you." He moaned. "I always like the mean ones."

Everyone laughed, including Roxie. She leaned her shoulder into his. "Maybe we can have Anthony work it in the program." She lifted her shirt and rolled her stomach so fast, they all yelled.

That's when Beckham decided to show up.

Beckham couldn't take his eyes off of Roxie. Her bare stomach rippled as she did things superior to any belly dancer. Brad was trying to keep up with her, but Beckham barely saw him. His eyes landed on her chiseled stomach and couldn't budge. And her laugh. God. She made his chest and stomach clench, along with other body parts.

He walked over to the table and laughed along with everyone else. When they noticed him standing there, it went silent, fast. Shit. It was enough to get a complex. He put on a cocky smile and nodded at Roxie.

"Do that wearing a bikini, and you're hired!" he said with a laugh.

Fuck! Why the hell did that come out of his mouth? His first time speaking to her and he acted like a creeper? Everyone laughed. Except Roxie. She went completely still and her red cupid's bow lips tightened into a scowl. She pulled down her shirt and pushed back from the table. The other dancers were too busy staring at Beckham to even notice Roxie walking out of the room.

"Excuse me," he said to the table and got out of there.

He looked both ways and saw her at the end of the hall to the right, either headed for the restroom or the practice room.

"Roxie! Wait up!"

She turned around and looked tempted to keep walking.

He jogged up to her and put a hand on her arm. She quickly pulled away. For a moment, he couldn't even think straight. Wow, she was hostile.

"I'm really sorry. I don't know why I said that. It just ... was stupid." He paused, not sure what else to say, since she wasn't saying anything. "Roxie, right?"

She looked everywhere but in his eyes. He blinked and inched closer, thinking he saw tears in her eyes. Shit—had he really upset her that much?

"Look, please. Forgive me. What can I do to make it up to you?" he asked when she still wasn't speaking. "Dinner?"

She snorted. "That's how you fix everything, isn't it? You think you can say anything and everyone just bends. 'Oh Beckham Woods, you're so *hilarious*! Everything you say and do is *so* fabulous! Let me just bask in your presence!' Uh, no, thank you very much to dinner." She slapped her hand over her mouth and stared at him.

The seconds pulsed in the air like bullets hitting their target. She turned suddenly and practically ran away.

Beckham was so stunned, he didn't move until Anthony came down the hall with everyone else.

"You gonna stick around?" Anthony asked as he was passing Beckham.

Beckham had planned to say something to the group—to welcome them and thank them for committing to the tour—but he was so confused by what had happened with Roxie that he shook his head.

"I'm gonna head back home. Thanks for being here," he said to the dancers. "I ... well, I'll see you later in the week. Don't let Anthony be too hard on ya!" He tried to sound light, but knew he just needed to get out of there before he could screw things up further.

He sped home in his Jag, winding around the hills faster than he should. He was so angry with himself, but the more he thought about it, the more he resented Roxie's attitude. What the hell? He hadn't really done anything that awful. The whole thing was just embarrassing.

When he got home, he walked into the kitchen and grabbed a bottled water. He'd rather have a Jameson and Coke right now, but he'd settle for safe. Damn Roxie. She'd already made him want to cave on two of his vices and they'd barely spoken.

He picked up the phone and called Anthony. He knew his phone was off, but he wanted Anthony to hear the message as soon as he was done with rehearsals.

"Hey, Anthony. I need to talk to you about Roxie Taylor. I'm thinking Vanessa might be a better fit for the sets with me. I got Roxie all worked up today ... and I just don't see us having much chemistry when it comes down to it."

He knew that was a lie. She might not feel it, but even as much as she had humiliated him, he still wanted to wrap his hands all over her body.

"Anyway ... think about it. I'd be more comfortable. Vanessa and I have worked well together before—it wouldn't be as far of a stretch."

He hung up and felt better, but knew he had another call to make. She answered on the first ring.

"Hi, honey. How did it go today?"

"Hey, Ma. I left early. I'll go back in a couple days. They don't really need me yet. Anthony's got it."

"Okay, well, do you want to come over for supper tonight?"

His mom had her southern accent still, and nobody anywhere did good southern food like her. He always felt his accent slide on just a little more when he talked to her.

"That's just what I need, Ma. When you want me?"

"You know you can come over whenever you feel like it," she said.

"How 'bout I get a few things done around here and then I'll be over. Is Sierra there?"

"Sure is. She'll be glad to see you. Come on."

He hung up with her and felt better yet. Time with his mom and sister always did him good. His dad had passed away a little over five years ago, with no warning. It had shaken their whole world. A seemingly healthy man, he'd had a heart attack in his sleep and died instantly. Nothing would ever be quite the same without his dad. It was part of the reason Beckham was anxious to be done with all the traveling—he knew his mom and sister needed him around more.

When his dad died, months went by that he barely came out of the stupor. His mom and sister didn't talk about it much anymore, but when they did, they always bawled. He never wanted to put them through that again, and he hoped one day he could make up for the time they'd lost.

He planned to talk them into Italy when the time came. It wouldn't be that hard—they'd gone to Italy a handful of times together and always talked about what it'd be like to live there. The slower pace of life sounded better all the time.

When he got to the house later that afternoon, he ran up the steps and walked right inside.

"I'm home. Anybody here?" he hollered.

"Back here, honey," his mom called.

His sister stepped out of the kitchen and came walking toward him. "Hey, stranger. How are ya?"

"Better now. It's been a long day," he admitted.

"Well, come on. Once Ma found out you were coming, she put together a feast. You'd almost think you were her favorite or something."

"No, the daughter always trumps, you know that."

She scrunched up her nose. "Is that how it works? You better tell Ma that."

Sierra was a few years older than him and they'd always been close. She teased him about being the favorite, but she had always been so proud of him. He'd tried every tour to convince her to come sing backup with him, but she wasn't interested. When they finished their family traveling days, she was *done*. She didn't want to see the inside of another tour bus.

"I need you to get her to stop trying to set me up. I don't need a hipster musician. That's all she wants to set me up with? Give me a nerd any day!"

"Shut up. That's so offensive!" Beckham jabbed her in the side. "I resemble that!"

She groaned. "You know you're a nerd in sheep's clothing. All this hip rock star vibe thing you got going … I know you're just a nerd begging to be loved."

He gave her another good jab until she slapped his hand and tattled.

"MA! Beckham is picking on me!" she hollered.

"Oh, please." He did it again just to annoy her. "Sierra's calling me names," he yelled, laughing and backing away as Sierra tried to pinch him.

Their mom came out with an apron on, wiping her hands on it. "There you are. Have you two already started? Come on, set the table, B. It's almost ready."

And just like that Beckham felt himself again. Well, almost.

"Please go on tour with me this year. Please, Sierra. I need you. Please." He clasped his hands together and got on his knees, following her like that all the way to the kitchen.

"What is your problem?" she laughed. "I'm too old for tours. I have a good job, thank you."

"Don't you miss singing? It's in your blood. I know you miss it."

"Occasionally, I do … but not enough to get in a bus with all your crazy entourage. That time in Japan cured me. Your fans are cuh-razy. No, thank you."

Twice today I've been rebuffed with fake politeness, he thought and then shook his head. Roxie wasn't going to bust his good mood. They started eating and he was still on the topic.

"Did I mention Ian Sterling is going?"

"NO, you didn't tell me!" Her eyes were huge. "You should have opened with that."

"Oh, even I knew that, honey. It's been all over the place, for the last month." Their mom lowered her head, but her eyes were still on Sierra. "You should turn on your TV once in a while."

"Ian Sterling." Sierra breathed his name.

Beckham snorted. "No hip musician for you, my ass."

She rolled her eyes. "He's different."

"Um, yeah," he said sarcastically. "Actually, you're right, he is. I like him a lot. So come on. You'll like his wife too. And you'd learn the material like that." Beckham snapped his fingers. "I've got great singers, but it wouldn't be like it is with you…"

The thought of having her with him made everything seem so much better.

"I'm gonna tell you two something and don't you dare breathe a word of it to anyone. Not even yourself," Beckham whispered.

"Oh gawd, you've always been so dramatic," Sierra said.

"I'm retiring. This might be my last year—hell, I *want* it to be my last tour. I'm ready to be done. I'm almost at the end of my contract and I know they think I'm going to stay with the label, but I haven't signed anything and I'm not going to. I want us to move somewhere very far from L.A. at the end of next year … Italy, perhaps?" He wiggled his eyebrows at his mother. "I'm walking away." He picked up his fork and dug into the food, feeling better than he had in a long time. "I'd like you to be there with me, Sierra."

Neither of them said anything for a few minutes. They looked at him like he'd just bombed a country.

"Well, say something!"

They both started talking at once.

"That is the best news."

"I'm so glad! It's time. I mean, I know you love it, but we miss you."

"You can focus on starting a family!"

"Even if you go back to it later, you need a break!"

And on and on it went.

Beckham laughed and put another pork chop on his plate. He intended to eat whatever he wanted for one more night. It wouldn't be like this once he was rehearsing.

"Okay, I'll come," Sierra said quietly at first, and then louder, "I'll do it!"

"Really? You will?"

She nodded.

"Yes! Thank you! This is great. You have about two weeks to learn the material backwards and forwards. And then vocal work will be going on at the same time as the dance rehearsals. We'll combine you guys in a few weeks."

"I know it pretty well already," she said. "I'll just need to break it to the office that I'm leaving." She shrugged. "Honestly, I was ready for a change anyway."

She took a sip of wine and stared into space, a smile faintly touching her lips. He groaned, hoping his entourage wouldn't embarrass themselves too badly over Ian.

4 FAINT

She stuck a tack through the forehead of every person involved. *Stick, prick, blood.* She grinned. If it were only that easy.

There were only a few backup singers. His sister was the only new one. She touched the hair on Sierra's picture and repositioned the tack so it looked like a hair barrette instead of a colorful ball in her forehead. Better. The sister was safe.

Ian Sterling and his wife and daughter were surprises she hadn't seen coming. She had them on the wall, but they didn't really seem threatening. From what she could tell, they were so wrapped up in each other, they wouldn't stand in her way of getting to Beckham.

The dancers. She ticked off their names. Memorization had always come easy for her. There were two who had toured with him before, so that left two less to worry about. She repositioned the tacks on Justin and Vanessa's heads. Brad and Shelton, too. They were gay and wouldn't get in her way. Without question, Beckham was damn straight.

That left the last two: Brooke and Roxie. She left their pins right where they were and studied the pictures intently. Brooke was the prettier of the two, with black hair and porcelain skin. But there was something appealing about Roxie. Almost magnetic. Her thick, waist-length blonde hair made you want to pull it and her eyes looked deep blue-green innocent. She also had an ass that would probably be insured by the time the tour was over. Brooke was beautiful, but Roxie was sexier ... by far. She tried to look at them through Beckham's eyes and see what he would see in both of them.

Roxie. She would have to watch that one.

She stepped back to look at her walls. The maps were ready. Each of Beckham's tour stops were marked on a huge map that covered a wall. The other two walls she'd been adding to for years, clipping her favorite shots of Beckham Woods. Some she'd printed from the Internet, some she'd clipped from magazines, most of them she'd taken of him herself. Those were her favorites.

The final wall was anyone who might get in her way. She belonged with Beckham. There was no doubt that she would have him.

Red X's were drawn through Josephine Sales, Genny Freeman, and Bethany Cook—girls he'd dated. She kept watch on them every now and then to see if they were still in contact, but they seemed to have all moved on from each other.

There was one girl he'd met in rehab that she'd followed for weeks after he got out. He contacted the girl and went out with her once. She might have seen to it that the girl got reacquainted with her little buddy, heroin.

But that could never be pinned on her.

Stick, prick, blood. She grinned. It really was that easy.

5 MIGRATE

Ian poked his head into the rehearsal room and watched for a few minutes before he saw a place in the back where he could sit unnoticed. Beckham had given him the security code, but Ian wasn't expected to come in for another week at least. He was stunned by the whole set-up. The dancers were unbelievable. He'd done a lot of rehearsals and traveling—short tours and an extended tour—and liked to think he did things with excellence, but he'd never been part of something as big as this. This tour was a *production*, far better than anything he and Donny could have dreamed up on their own. He couldn't wait for Sparrow to see all of it. She would freak.

When he realized Beckham wasn't coming in, he went out the same way he came in—secretly. He walked outside, dialing Beckham before he reached the car. He looked around, feeling the hairs on the back of his neck stick up ... the way he usually knew he was being watched. Then again, he felt that way pretty much all the time now when he was out and about in L.A., and unfortunately, it was usually true. He hoped he hadn't been followed. Beckham wanted to keep this location private as long as they could.

He looked around one more time but didn't see anyone. Beckham answered just as he got in his car.

"I stopped by the warehouse," he said. "Thought I might see you here."

"Ahh, not yet. I dropped in the other day, but I probably won't go in until later this week. I don't want to make them too uncomfortable when they're still learning the material."

"They're looking pretty damn phenomenal," Ian said.

"Good, right?"

"Better than that," he said. "There's one that seemed like she could teach the whole group. Anthony kept having her demonstrate. She's got it down, backwards and forwards."

Beckham groaned. "That's Roxie. She's gonna be the end of me."

Ian laughed. "Oh, it's like that, huh. This is gonna be *so fun.*"

"Shut up."

"Okay, touchy."

"Hey, baby, come take a ride with me."

Sparrow looked up from the book she was reading. He was glad she'd listened to him and taken a break from packing while he was gone.

She managed to scrunch her nose and smile at the same time. "Journey's right here. We can't have sex right now." The last three words were not even whispered, but mouthed.

He leaned down and kissed her nose. "I meant a ride in the car, but I like your idea so much better."

"Oh!" Her eyes twinkled as her smile brightened. "Where are we going? We still have a lot to do…"

"Not today we don't. I want to take my girls out. Come on. I need to show you something."

He looked over at Journey, who had a cloth book in her mouth, her bib soaked with drool. He raised an eyebrow to Sparrow.

"She's eating books. Are you really okay with that?"

"When you say it like that, no."

She leveled him with her eyes, and he flinched, throwing his hands up.

"Everything is going in her mouth today. At least it's not a copy of *Gone With the Wind* or something," she said.

"Good point. I guess we've got to let her normal-ness come out every once in a while. She can't be perfect *all* the time. I think she should be allowed to have at it with the book." He nodded gravely.

She smiled up at him, and her head tilted to the side as she studied him. "Do you ever have a serious thought anymore?"

He blinked fast, giving her his best doe-eyed look.

Her lips twitched and he knew it was taking a lot of effort for her not to laugh.

"Define serious, Little Bird. I'm serious as hell over you and the pumpkin." He pulled her up and moved his arm around her waist, pulling her flush against him. "Beyond that ... I can't seem to get too upset about anything since the day you married me—I mean, there's rough stuff and all. Like you scaring me to death with the early labor, and now Donny being sick, life..." He kissed her cheeks and forehead and chin. "But you and that baby girl are the two very best things I've ever done. Every single time I see you, my heart short-circuits and I feel a rush to my heart, my brain ... my *other* brain..." He moved her hand down to the front of his pants and pushed against her, grinning. "I don't think I'll ever stop being in awe of the fact that you married me, Sparrow Kate Sterling."

Journey made gurgling noises from her spot on the floor. She was on her back now, both feet in her mouth.

Ian shook his head, laughing at the baby, while he leaned in for one more kiss from his bride.

"I love you, Ian," Sparrow said against his lips. She leaned back and suddenly turned serious. "I'm so happy it terrifies me."

He frowned and put his hands on either side of her face. "Why? What do you mean?"

"Life is so up and down, I think I ... I just can't imagine us getting away with being this happy forever."

He leaned his forehead against hers. "We've already gone through hell, baby. It's time for us to enjoy this heaven." His fingers traced down her neck, to the especially outstanding cleavage she had since having the baby. He pressed a kiss there, between her breasts and wanted to stay there forever.

"I am definitely enjoying this heaven," she said, her voice breathy.

"Woman, you can't do that sexy voice and then stop me from making love to my wife," Ian said, his own voice raspy. "God, my need for you never stops..." He reluctantly lifted his head and looked at her through a lust haze. She stared at him with the same craving. He twitched in her hands, and she gripped him harder, making him crazy.

He looked at the baby, still happy with her feet, and shifted Sparrow to the wall in the hallway, just out of Journey's eyesight.

"Shhh," he whispered, putting a finger to Sparrow's lips. She nodded.

He had his jeans open and her underwear shifted to the side in a blink, not wasting a second this time before pushing all the way inside. They'd learned to steal their moments when they could. He knew she was beyond ready, by the way she was breathing. She wrapped her legs around him and rolled her hips, her urgency letting him know she didn't want to go slow either. Their eyes stayed focused on each other, as his hands gripped her thighs and he slammed into her again and again and again, until he felt lightheaded. He didn't let up. Her eyes were glazed in that way they got before she lost her mind. He fucking loved it when she lost her mind on him. She began whimpering when she was close and it was his undoing. His tongue dove into her mouth, claiming her moans. He pumped everything he had into her and she cried out into his mouth as she pulsed around him.

"Dadadada," Journey sang in the living room.

He let out a shuddering breath and kissed Sparrow's forehead.

"I'll be right there, Pumpkin," he rasped. "I'm in your mom right now. One sec." He lowered Sparrow to the ground.

Sparrow swatted him on the shoulder, hard.

"Ow! Baby! What?" He slowly pulled out of her and pulled her skirt down before tucking himself back in his pants.

"Behave!"

Her eyes were fiery, but he knew she was far from mad. This was how his girl looked when she was satisfied.

He eyed at her smugly. "Really? Pretty sure you'd be disappointed if I ever behaved…"

Sparrow mentioned she'd already made the lemon caper sauce for his favorite chicken dish, so he went with plan B. He'd wanted to take her out to eat and then show her the surprise he'd been hiding for too long now, but that's the trouble with surprises—they're hard to pull off when you're working alone. He put Journey on his shoulders and set the table while Sparrow finished making dinner.

Sparrow looked so tired while they ate. She seemed happy and content, looking after him and Journey in a way that always made him fall even harder for her. He didn't know if it was this way for everyone, but she could do something as simple as touching his cheek when he complimented her cooking, and he'd think, *I could die right now, complete. Life can't get any better than this.*

"I'm sorry—I can tell you're worn out, but I don't think I can wait another day," he said. "I'm a little nervous to show you, not gonna lie."

"I'm so curious now, I don't think I can sleep until I know whatever it is," she said, nuzzling his nose.

"I realized last night that *I* won't sleep until you know what it is." He laughed.

"So that's what has had you tossing for weeks!" She shook her head and leaned forward to squeeze his chin.

He watched as her hair fell forward and got lost in the valley of her chest. She was smiling when his eyes finally lifted to hers. God, he loved her.

Journey was on her hip as they walked to the car. Sparrow placed her in the carseat, and he buckled her in, while Sparrow got in the front.

After Ian won Best Album, they gutted their tour bus to accommodate the baby and bought another bus for the band. In place of the bunks, they had a crib and cabinets built in, complete with a changing table. It was finished weeks before Journey was born, and she'd spent more time there than their place in L.A.

He hoped Sparrow wouldn't kill him for making this new 'celebrity-sized' purchase without her.

They drove for about thirty minutes, the customary length of time it took to get anywhere, so she had no clue what they were doing. Soon they were in Malibu, driving along the coastline. Sparrow pointed out one massive mansion after the next, wondering who lived in these houses. They turned a corner and the sunset was out of this world. He couldn't have timed it more perfectly if he'd tried. He turned into a lot that was thick with trees and stopped the car.

She looked at him in question and he hopped out of the car and ran around to open her door. He took her hand and pulled her next to him, then leaned in for a quick kiss and opened the back door to get Journey. Once he had her out of her carseat, he turned to Sparrow, glad there was still enough light to see everything, but knowing they needed to hurry before the sun set.

"This way," he said, taking her hand.

They walked through the trees until there was a clearing. Just ahead was plush sand, and beyond that, the ocean.

He stopped while they were in the clearing, the area opening up into a vast space overlooking the water.

"I thought our house could be here," he said. "What do you think?"

Sparrow's eyes were huge. She swallowed and looked at him in shock. "This is ours?"

"All ours, Little Bird." He tugged her closer and kissed her forehead, and then Journey's. "Think we can make a home here?"

"I can make a home with you anywhere, but yeah, this looks ... like a dream," she said, turning around and moving toward the ocean. "I can't imagine being able to see this view all the time!"

He watched her turn around, laughing and squealing with excitement. He tried to swallow around the huge lump that formed in his throat and hid his face in Journey's soft waves while he blinked back the emotion.

Yeah, life can't get any better than this.

The rehearsals became more intensive and Roxie loved every second. She felt challenged, and yet, fully capable of everything Anthony threw at her. They were only on their fifth rehearsal, but already they were becoming more of a cohesive team. It felt really good to work off all her frustration and passion when she got out on the dance floor.

Leo was adjusting really well too. She had gone home for lunch the past two days and each night they went out exploring when she got home from work. Chloe took that time to either get a break or sometimes she hung out with them. Roxie thought Chloe seemed lighter with each day away from Alex. The move had been good for all of them.

Working through one of the fast songs that had more of the pop/lock moves that Beckham was known for in his shows reminded Roxie of the dance-offs she'd done back home, only Anthony took them to the next level. As soon as the song was over, he turned on the slower song "Shadows" where Brooke and Vanessa mirrored each other's movements and Roxie danced just outside of them. *Leo would totally be making fun of me right now if he saw this.* A smile crept up on her face as she thought about it. She usually danced like this when she was pretending to be the sleep fairy in his room. Anthony told her to freestyle around the girls for now, but that she would be trailing Beckham later.

Midway through the song, Beckham walked in the room. Her skin felt hot when his eyes landed on her. They scorched through her like a glassblowing torch, melting her into something she didn't recognize. She tried to tune him out and keep her movements fluid. There was no way she could react to him like she had the other day. If she was going to do this tour, she needed to be professional ... not act like a snotty bitch. Better yet, she just needed to stay off of Beckham's radar altogether. She had absolutely no time for his type, whether he was her boss or not.

The song ended and Roxie walked toward the stack of clean hand towels. Beckham beat her there and lifted one up to her.

"Need this?"

"Thanks," she said and turned around to grab a water bottle.

Anthony walked over to them and said, "I'm glad you're here together. I wanted to talk about this song and a couple of the other slower ones. We'll need to have extra time to work on these. I'm thinking let's get after it tomorrow. What do you think?"

Beckham looked startled and then stretched his hands up over his head and left them in his hair. "Uh ... whatever you think. It's Saturday, though. Did you have plans, Roxie?"

"Well, kinda ... but..."

Anthony studied her. "I told you I'd be owning your time," he said. "So, I suggest you clear your plans. Unless you want me to hand all your solo parts over to Vanessa ... Beckham? Is that what you wanted anyway?"

Beckham's feet shifted and he glared at Anthony. "We have time. And it's up to Roxie, whether she's up for the extra work or not."

Roxie put her hands on her hips. "Please stop talking like I'm not right here!" *Shit, I have to start controlling my mouth. Dammit, dammit, dammit.*

Both guys stared at her, stunned.

She backpedaled quickly. "Sorry, I'm not trying to be ... uh, I will try to clear my schedule. Is there any way we can meet early in the morning? And how much time do we need?"

Anthony looked at her, half-awed and half-ticked. "Okay then, little miss. Let's meet from 6-12 tomorrow and Sunday morning." He took a step toward her and leaned close to her face. "And get your attitude on straight. There's only room for one prima donna around here." He looked over at Beckham and pointed at himself. "And that's me."

They laughed, while Roxie felt sick to her stomach.

"I really am sorry. I'm not normally ... it's not ... I'll be there."

"That's more like it!" Anthony smiled as he walked away.

Beckham groaned. He looked at Roxie with what seemed to be an apologetic grin. "Thanks. Listen, Roxie. I think we got off on the wrong foot."

"You got that right," she muttered.

He looked at her incredulously. They stared at each other for what seemed like forever, until Roxie couldn't look at him anymore.

Finally, Beckham leaned in closer to her. "Whatever I've done to piss you off, I'm sorry. I'd like to start over, if that's okay with you. We're gonna be working together closely, and if you're not good with me ... it will show."

Again, the silence.

She stood on her tiptoes and whispered in his ear.

"I'll *never* be good with you." She tried not to inhale his scent as she got closer. His breath smelled like cinnamon and his skin smelled like something she wouldn't mind sinking her whole face in. "But I will fake it and no one will ever know the difference."

She stepped back and gave him a smile that was as bright as the California sun. She reached out her hand and he shook it, troubled by her words but lured in just the same. When their skin touched, an electric current zinged through and shocked them both, causing them to jump back at once.

"Ow!" he said.

She just smiled bigger.

He walked away from her, certain she had a voodoo doll of him at home.

Beckham stayed for rehearsal and he and Roxie were paired together several times. The whole group was part of the practice, but she was always the one selected to shadow Beckham. It was his first time to work with them and he seemed to have already learned every dance long before they got there. Roxie had always been impressed with the way he moved. All through high school, she studied every single music video he made and never failed to record every live performance. Dancing with him now was surreal. She could feel the energy radiating off of him, almost knew his move before he made it. It was easier than it had been dancing without him there. Everyone worked harder, did better. He made everything Anthony choreographed come to life.

This was what she'd trained for ... forever. This was what she'd given up when she got pregnant with Leo. It was all worth it. She stumbled, getting distracted in her thoughts. *Don't blow it, Roxie.* Beckham grabbed her arm and pulled her into him, doing the salsa and staring into her eyes like he owned her. The way he looked at her when they danced—like she was a delicacy he was scared to touch but also wanted to devour—she could almost feel her defenses begin to fall. But no, she hated him. She *needed* to hate him. No matter what. There was no way she could let him in. Not again.

She'd Googled his eye color before. She was embarrassed thinking about it now, but as she looked into them again, she remembered that she'd done it more than once. His eyes were such an unusual grey blue. Constantly changing. *Chameleon eyes, just, like him,* she thought. Never trust a guy that doesn't even have a distinguishable eye color.

He laughed. She'd also studied videos of his laugh. It was the best laugh. If she didn't hate it so much, she'd love it. It was not contained. He always laughed with everything and almost sounded like a geek when he did.

"What?" she snapped.

"*What* is going through that head of yours, Roxie Taylor?" He stretched her out and pulled her back along the front of his body. Her eyes widened when she felt a little too much of him. "Your hair is amazing, by the way. I've never seen it down."

"Don't try to distract me," she said through clenched teeth.

He laughed again as the song ended. She yanked her hand away from his and before Anthony could start the song from the top again, Beckham said, all humor gone, "Why do you hate me so much?"

The music picked up again and they went through every move, not tearing their eyes away from the other. The tension was excruciating, but neither could look away.

When he pulled her tight to him this time, he said softly, "I asked you a question."

Before she was swung out into a twirl, she replied, "It would take too long to tell you all the reasons."

A flicker of hurt crossed his eyes and then he laughed the full-on laugh that had never failed to charm her.

"Are you joking? Am I being pranked? If so you are cracking me up!" His laughter faded away as he looked carefully at her. "Are you always this hateful?"

Roxie ignored him and concentrated on the rest of the song. He was gonna bust her vibe if he didn't shut up already. She thought ignoring him would make him mad, but it seemed like he just got more and more amused by her. He turned up the sex about ten more decibels and when he pulled her in for the last cross-body hold, she gasped when she felt him against her back.

Hard and substantial, just like she remembered.

6 DOME

Beckham's alarm went off at a very crucial part in his dream. Roxie was naked under him and she was looking up at him smiling. Like she adored him. Her long legs were wrapped around him and...

He hit snooze and willed himself to go back to the dream.

He ran his fingers through her hair and gave it a little tug. It was so short, it made her neck scream to be kissed. Her eyes closed as his tongue trailed down that pale neck and teased her breasts...

Shit! He hit the snooze again.

This time he was awake and Roxie's true features came into focus. She wasn't skewed like she'd been in the dream. Now her hair splayed out on the pillow as he imagined her grinning up at him while he drove into her.

Her eyes didn't look at him nearly as adoringly as they had in his dream. He squeezed his eyes shut to try and change them from scorn to adoration.

Sick bastard, he thought later as he went into the bathroom, feeling much better. *You need a woman. Bad.*

At least now maybe he wouldn't alarm her with his traitor dick every time she got near him. He'd managed to hide it from everyone but Roxie the day before.

Just add one more huge notch to his growing list of embarrassments where she was concerned.

She looked away, as if the thought of even seeing him made her want to cease living. He couldn't take his eyes off her. And he couldn't wait to touch her again. Although he'd have to start chanting "Grandmother, grandmother, grandmother!" to avoid embarrassing himself with her again. This morning's dream only made him more aware of her.

It wasn't like she was the most beautiful girl he'd ever seen. He'd been with many more beautiful, but he couldn't for the life of him remember who. She had such an expressive face. Thick eyebrows, wide-set, eyes— sometimes green, sometimes blue—that pulled you in and spat you out, thick blonde hair so long it made you want to get lost in it, and pale, smooth skin; she didn't fit the typical model mold he'd dated. He couldn't remember ever being so interested in a face, though. Those lips. And then the way she moved so gracefully. Her body was made to be a dancer, lean and sculpted. Her breasts were perfect, not too big, not too little. His gut clenched and he groaned inside. One shoulder was exposed, showing her hot pink sports bra. Her nipples poked through the shirt like there was nothing that would hold them back. She turned around to put her bag down and he saw her ass in yoga pants for the very first time. The baggie sweats had been nice the day before, but fuck him, these were like a second skin.

Sweet almighty Mary and Joseph! He was desperate. *Mother Teresa's great-grandmother!*

It was like a work of art, the Michelangelo of booty. *Tight and juicy.*

Yeah, he was already coming up with a melody. Her ass was what songs were made of ... the songs he'd written in middle school. He'd never claimed to be the most mature person out there anyway.

She turned around and his cheeks lit on fire. He knew for a fact no woman had ever made him blush, whether he was being an asshole or not. Back in his heyday of women, not so long ago, he'd actually been quite smooth. So there had to be some sort of spell she'd weaved on him.

He pulled the coffee he'd bought for her out from behind his back and it was the brightest her eyes had gotten so far. *Ah—Miss Taylor has a weakness!* He made note to bring her coffee for every early morning rehearsal they had together.

She snatched it out of his hands. Greedy.

He raised an eyebrow at her aggressiveness.

"Thanks," she said with her raspy voice. It was always husky, but sounded especially so that early in the morning.

He smiled and her eyes softened. Just a touch, but enough to make him breathe easier. "Thanks for coming out so early. I know you didn't really commit to giving up your weekends, at least not this early in rehearsals. You're a quick learner, we'll have it in no time, I promise."

"It's fine," she said softly. "Thanks for this opportunity."

He paused, not expecting that. Maybe she was warming up to him...

"Just keep your weapon away from me," she added, with a raised eyebrow.

No, she hadn't warmed up.

Anthony walked in, looking like he hadn't slept in a week. He probably hadn't. David apparently hadn't taken the breakup well.

"You all right?" Beckham asked.

Anthony lowered his fedora. "Ugh, don't ask. When I get home from work every day, David starts calling every ten minutes. I finally picked up last night at midnight, just to tell him to never call again. We ended up talking until three. He said he never meant to hurt me ... that he was just having a mini what-am-I-doing-with-my-life crisis and acting out." He said it all so matter-of-fact, as if it were nothing, but his lower lip trembled a little.

Roxie put her hand on his arm. "Men suck. I'm sorry."

Anthony smiled at her. "Don't they? Thank you, hon. Come on, let's get to work."

If the day before had been a disaster where Beckham's focus was concerned, this rehearsal was a thousand times worse. Beckham and Anthony had worked out the choreography weeks before; Beckham knew the material inside and out. But he kept getting distracted by Roxie. The song was all about seduction and the way she looked at him as they moved—he could have sworn she was seducing him.

He closed his eyes to shake it off and imagined her with short hair again. So weird. When he opened them, her long hair was whipping around in her ponytail. He squinted his eyes. Those lips, her beautiful neck, blue-green eyes staring up at him. She twisted gracefully around him and then he grabbed her waist and held her close, as their hips rocked in time with the slow, but driving tempo.

"Have I met you before, Roxie?" He stared at her, curious.

She went completely still. Her face went white, and she turned around quickly, but he'd already seen the look. She stalked over to her water bottle and kept her back to him. He walked behind her and put a hand on her back. She jumped.

"Everything okay? Need a break?" Anthony asked from across the room.

Roxie nodded and this time she did run out of the room.

What the hell? This girl was all kinds of unpredictable. He shrugged at Anthony and paced the stage as they waited for her to come back.

When ten minutes went by and she still hadn't returned, Beckham told Anthony he'd go look for her. He looked everywhere. There was no sign of her. Finally, he went outside and saw her sitting in her car. He knocked on her window. She jumped again.

"Sorry!" he yelled. He opened her door and squatted down so he could see her better. "What's going on, Rox?"

She turned to face him and he froze when he saw she was crying.

"What's wrong?"

"I made a mistake coming here. I-I can't ... I can't do it," she whispered.

"Roxie, you're the best dancer we have. You can totally do this." He grabbed her hand and squeezed it hard, trying to convince her he meant it. He meant it with a force that surprised him. The thought of her leaving had him panicked.

"I really can't." She shook her head and then leaned her forehead on the steering wheel. She was still for a couple of minutes and when she lifted her head, she looked determined. "I am so sorry to do this, but I need to get out of the tour. I-I'm so grateful you gave me a chance, but I made a huge mistake. Please, *please* let me out of the contract. I know it's a huge inconvenience, but it's still early enough ... there are so many dancers that would jump at this opportunity."

"I want *you*," he said sincerely. "Roxie, look at me." She didn't, so he kept talking. "We need you—you're the one who makes it all come alive out there. You've gotta know that with that attitude you must be a brilliant dancer to still be here." He grinned, but it dropped when he saw another tear falling down her cheek. "We can't lose you." He felt like he was talking to a board. "What's going on here? Why do you want to leave? I would send everyone *else* home before you!"

Roxie narrowed her eyes. "My, how things have changed..." she said, her tone caustic now.

"What do you mean?" He was beginning to get nervous. She didn't answer. He looked at her for a long time. "Wait—was it because I asked if we'd met before? *Have* we?"

She pulled her head back and leaned it against the headrest. "Oh, this is so fucking rich. I can't believe you. Either you're fucking stupid or the biggest fucking jerk that ever lived."

Beckham stood up, angry now. She was swinging his emotions around like a game of tetherball.

"I don't know what you're talking about, but I would be glad to listen if you'll explain it to me."

"Look, I can take a lot of things, but don't make me out for the fool. If you recognized me, you should have just said so from the beginning." She looked at him then and he nearly staggered to his knees from the daggers.

"I didn't recognize you!" he said quietly. "I was drawn to you the moment I saw you, but I didn't know we'd met before. I still don't know w-"

She practically choked on a laugh and a sob. "I don't know why I ever thought I could make this work. It was a stupid, *stupid* idea." She started up the car. "I've gotta go."

He grabbed the door before she could shut it.

"Please stay. I'm sorry—I don't know what I did to make you so angry, but I promise I'll make it up to you. I need you on this tour."

She wiped her face and nodded once. He backed away from the car and she slammed the door. Her tires squealed as she drove out of the parking lot.

Chloe and Leo were outside when Roxie pulled up, and they both came running when they saw her crying.

"Why you cryin', Mommy?" Leo wrapped his arms around her leg and looked up at her with the sweetest eyes.

"I'm just tired and frustrated," she told him. "And I needed to see my boy."

FADE TO
Red

Leo hugged her harder. "Here I am."

"Here you are." She hugged him tighter.

Chloe studied her and finally came over to hug her too. "Well, we're glad to see you. We were gonna go to the beach as soon as you got home. Want to head out soon?"

Roxie nodded. "Sounds good."

Leo reached up for Roxie to pick him up. He put his hands on either side of her face and peered at her carefully. "You feelin' better?"

"I am now."

"Good. Wanna hear a joke?"

"Of course."

"'K ... what did the cat ask the zombie?" He bit his bottom lip to keep from yelling out the punchline.

"Hmm ... I don't know. What?"

"*Meow's life?*" He'd started laughing before he got it all the way out.

"Meow's life?" Roxie pulled back, looking in Leo's eyes.

He stopped laughing but couldn't stop grinning. "Yeah, you know, like ... how's life? Meow's life ... 'cept zombies are already *dead*." His lisp was extra heavy when he got excited.

"Wow, that's actually a pretty good one, Leo."

The beach calmed Roxie more than she'd thought possible. When she left Beckham, she was strung so tight, every muscle felt jittery. Now, just looking out at the endless waves and feeling so incredibly small—it made her anger slowly fade away into the tide. She would get back to hating Beckham again tomorrow, but for now, she welcomed the peace.

They found a spot to lay their blanket and stretched out. Leo barely ran in the water and quickly hightailed it back to their towel, teeth chattering. The cold water always shocked him, but he kept going back in for more.

67

"So what happened?" Chloe asked.

"I don't wanna talk about it," Roxie groaned.

"Oh no, you're not getting out of it." Chloe poked Roxie in the side.

"He asked if we'd met before," Roxie whispered.

"Shit!"

Of course that's when Leo surprised them by running back to get warm.

"What'd you say, Auntie?" Leo's head whipped around faster than lightning.

"I said, 'Sit!' Come on, sit by me and I'll warm you up!" She looked at Roxie guiltily.

"Hmm, yeah," Leo said, but he went and sat by her anyway.

Roxie flicked Chloe in the arm. Leo sat for all of a minute and then ran back to the water.

"What did you say back?" Chloe stared at Roxie, who was watching Leo jump up and down in an inch of water.

"I got out of there … after I basically got stuck on the f-word and told him all the ways he was fucking stupid."

"*No!* What did he do?"

"He apologized for whatever he'd done to make me angry and asked me not to leave the tour."

"Wait—you're thinking of leaving? No, Rox. You have to do this." She grabbed Roxie's arm and forced her to look at her. "I know this is so hard, but you've done the hardest part—seeing him again. Now that you've gotten past that initial shock, you have to go all the way. We'll finally get ahead a little bit. You've worked so hard, for so long. There's no other way you can make money like this—not any time soon, anyway. And this is the safest I've felt since I met Alex. I didn't even realize until being away from him this long, how much I was still fearful that he was around every corner…"

Roxie put her arm around Chloe. "I'm so relieved you got away from him. You seem more like yourself than you have in a really long time."

Chloe leaned her head on Roxie's shoulder. "I feel more like myself," she admitted. "I let him control me far too long. I mean, I get why it was easy for him to control me when we first started dating—I was 14. Remind me one day not to let my daughter date that early." Her laugh choked in her throat and sounded painful. She sat up and looked at Roxie. "I'm embarrassed, Rox. I wasted so much time with an abusive boyfriend. I never thought I'd let someone ... hurt me. I'm the baby of the family—you guys have loved me my whole life. Why would I put up with that trash?"

"He lied to you, made you think he loved you one minute, and then turned on you after you trusted him," Roxie said softly. "It happens all the time, Chlo-bo. Just be so grateful that you got out. You took control."

"So can you, Rox. You're controlling this situation for your son and his future. You can do this. It's a really *huge* deal that you got in to begin with ... you can't give up now."

"He just ... Beckham's very..." Roxie couldn't get out a complete thought, so she gave up trying. "We'd be okay without the money. We've gotten by before this."

"Barely. And do you really want to live in your tiny apartment the rest of your life?" Chloe snapped.

"Well, no, but ... being around Beckham was a lot harder than I expected, too. And I'm paired up with him, Chloe! I never expected that when I tried out. I thought I'd be in a big group of other dancers and that I might not even have to deal with him! And I'm being awful—I should have been fired a couple of times already. It's mortifying, really, how awful I become when I'm around him!"

Leo came back then and they stopped talking about it. They enjoyed the rest of their day at the beach and Roxie tried to put Beckham out of her mind completely. When they got back home, she checked her voicemail and there was a message from Anthony. He told her he expected her there the next morning for the full rehearsal with Beckham.

At the end of the message, he said, "Beckham said it was his fault you left this morning, so I'll let you off the hook. *This* time. But there better not be a next time. If you have an issue, come to me directly and we'll work it out."

The next morning on the way to rehearsal she made up her mind to stick it out. No matter how intense things got with Beckham, no matter how much she cringed every time she saw him, no matter how her insides liquified every time he touched her. She was doing this for Leo. He deserved so much more than she'd been able to give him.

It physically hurt her to walk in that morning; her pride was sweating through her pores, but she held her head high. She was a few minutes early, but Beckham and Anthony were already there. She looked them both in the eye and nodded at Anthony.

"I shouldn't have left without telling you. It won't happen again."

"Okay. We'll forget about it and move forward. You ready to work? Thousands of girls would kill to be in your spot," he reminded her.

"I'm ready."

Beckham handed her a coffee and she mumbled her thanks. She took as many gulps as she could before they got started and then popped some gum in her mouth. She might hate him, but she still wanted to smell decent when she was grinding up against him.

She barely looked at Beckham, but as soon as the music started and they began to move together, the magic began. Their chemistry was undeniable.

Beckham began showing up at all the rehearsals. And she'd thought he might stay to himself a little, but he was always in the center of everything. He had an easy way with everyone else. In the middle of lunch one day, he started doing imitations from *Harry Potter* and had it down perfectly.

He was in the middle of going back and forth between Dumbledore and Snape:

"He has her eyes..."

(A gasp from Snape.)

"If you truly loved her..."

"No one can ever *know*..."

He nailed it and Roxie started laughing along with everyone else. He noticed her laughing and cut off in mid-sentence, his cheeks suddenly tinging with pink. She quickly stopped and the hurt that briefly crossed his eyes made Roxie's stomach clench with guilt. The rest of the week she went home for lunch.

Anthony had asked her to meet every weekend so far and each time she agreed without any argument. When she walked in, Beckham's eyes burned on her like they had every day for weeks now. He tentatively gave her the coffee he'd continued to bring and she quietly thanked him. This time, though, his hand brushed against hers when he handed it to her. She looked up quickly and almost dropped the coffee.

"When am I gonna win you over, Roxie Taylor?" he asked quietly.

"Never," she replied.

He laughed nervously. "Well, at least you're honest. I'd like to talk to you after the rehearsal today. You run out of here so fast every day, I can't seem to get to the bottom of what I've done to make you despise me."

She studied him.

"What are you thinking?" he asked.

"I'm thinking that you're not used to someone not falling all over themselves just because they're near you."

He blinked and bit his lip, a grin just under the surface. "You're right. I'm not. Can I be honest now?" He raised his eyebrows and leaned in when she didn't answer. "It gets annoying."

She rolled her eyes just as Anthony started the music. Today she was dancing on her own. It was a song where Beckham was supposed to stand like stone while she tried to 'win back his affection' with her dance. Anthony talked over what he wanted from her, showing her specifically in some sections, but then letting her take it from there. It was all about the emotion. She put every ounce of heartache and loss she'd felt, every bit of anger and also the longing…

When the song ended, the room was silent. Roxie tried to discreetly wipe the tear that had fallen toward the end. She'd gotten too caught up in it.

"Wow," Anthony finally spoke. "Do you think you can do that every night? That was flawless."

They wrapped it up quickly and Roxie was on the way to her car when Beckham stepped beside her. When they reached her car, he moved in front of her car door.

"Remember I wanted to talk?"

"I never agreed to that." She crossed her arms over her chest.

"I'm just getting tired of this … animosity you seem to have toward me. What have I done?"

"If you don't remember, I'm not going to remind you!" she snapped.

"I just need to know." His chest rose while he stared at her. "Did we … sleep together?" he asked, cringing.

She tightened her ponytail and put her hands on her hips. "Why does it matter?" she finally said.

"So we did," he groaned.

To her horror, tears welled up in her eyes. Oh God, she was making such a fool out of herself.

"Let me go, Beckham. I'm tired. I just wanna go home."

FADE TO
Red

He moved, but touched her shoulder. "Roxie. I-just ...
I'm sorry."

She held her hand up for him to back off and he did.
And once again, he watched her car squeal out of the
parking lot.

7 FLIGHT

Ian took his band with him the next time he went to the warehouse. The guys were pumped about the new tour development. Beckham had some of the country's best musicians—players Ian and his guys couldn't wait to mesh with on the road. This collaboration felt like a huge step up in each one of their careers. Donny was happiest of all. During Ian's last two visits, he'd taken credit for what he liked to call the 'best collaboration of the decade' and Ian gladly let him. He was glad to distract Donny with something besides chemo.

"Who needs groupies when there's all this eye candy?" Chris said when they walked inside.

Aaron was quick to agree. Charlie had a girlfriend, but his eyes were still wide as he took in the dancers and singers rehearsing.

"You didn't tell us, man," Chris nudged Ian.

He shrugged. Honestly, he hadn't thought much more beyond the fact that they danced well, especially the girl Beckham was dancing with—Ian couldn't remember her name. He grinned when he saw the way Beck looked at her. The guy wasn't kidding—he had it bad.

"I knew you were whipped, but have you become *blind?* Jeez, Ian, look how flexible they are..." Aaron groaned.

He thought about Sparrow doing yoga and wished he was home. She'd been working on it for a year and a half and had actually gotten damn good. It had been comical at first, although he'd tried hard as hell not to laugh. She nearly gave up, due to how hard it was, being a bit physically challenged in the balance/tripping on nothing department. She stayed with it, though, and it had helped her immensely—she rarely got bruises now from bumping into everything, and she hadn't fallen in over a year. It became their challenge to see if she could hold her pose while he teased her body in every way possible. He knew all about flexible.

The guys teased Ian all the time about being Sparrow-whipped. He knew it was true and he owned it with pride. There was no other woman for him, period. He didn't believe in the saying, 'Once a cheater, always a cheater', because the very core of his heart had changed. The broken parts that made him who he was had been welded back together. The scars were there to make him appreciate what he had, but new skin had grown in its place. He didn't view women the way he used to. They still came on to him all the time—it was part of the business—but he had no emptiness to fill, nothing to prove. That made all the difference. *Sparrow* made all the difference. You didn't lose the love of your life and then get her back and not learn something from it.

The song ended and Beckham slowly backed away from the girl, like he hated to do it. He turned toward Ian, but it took a minute before his eyes focused. Ian's laugh seemed to shake him out of the fog.

"Ian, come meet everyone," Beckham said, motioning them forward. He walked toward them too, holding out his hand to Ian and pounding his back. "Sexiest Man Alive right here, people!" he yelled, laughing.

FADE TO
Red

Ian gave his hair a yank and made a face. "So how does it work—do you suddenly stop being sexiest when someone else is selected? Am I gonna need therapy when that happens?"

"It's why I've won so many times," Beckham teased. "They see how down I get about losing the title and slap it on me again."

Ian introduced Beck to the guys, who were sufficiently awed, and then Beck took them to meet the crew. He met the band leader, Hollis, first. Great guy. Everyone was friendly, some seemed especially star-struck, which cracked up both Beck and Ian. Beck's sister, Sierra, shook when she met him. Ian elbowed Beck when he teased her about it. There was a dancer, Brooke, who seemed like trouble. She did a thing with her tongue when they were introduced, which Ian thought might be some sort of tick or something, but then she did a weird stroke with her finger down the middle of his palm when they shook hands. He dropped her hand like it burned and moved on. Eventually, Beck reached Roxie. He touched her shoulder and she stiffened, moving away from him and closer to Ian.

Shit. Ian watched Beck's face drop and tried to lighten the situation. He shook her hand and then motioned between the two of them.

"The two of you make it look easy up there. Wish I had your moves, man." He nodded at Beckham. "It's a good thing I have my guitar to hide behind. Saves everyone the pain."

"We'll have to work on that, get you out of your comfort zone." Beckham grinned. "Anthony's a great teacher, aren't you, Anthony?"

Anthony shot Beckham a look and then smiled at Ian, gripping his hand. "I would be honored to work with you. I love all your music. I listen to your album all the time!" He realized he was still shaking Ian's hand and stopped, but didn't let go.

"Thank you so much," Ian said. "And I'd be honored if you'd help me up my game—I need to take Sparrow dancing more."

"She is beautiful, just beautiful," Anthony gushed. Finally, he let go of Ian's hand.

"Inside and out," Ian said. "She is it for me."

He looked at the girl Brooke when he said this. She'd inched closer and closer to him, until her shoulder pressed into his. He backed up and the motion made her weave ever so slightly. She put her hand on her hip and steadied, not sure what to make of him. Good. He'd probably have to spell it out for her at some point, but hopefully not today. He wanted to at least get through this first introduction with everyone.

"You'll meet the rest of the crew in later rehearsals. By the time we go on the road, we'll have double this."

"Wow, this already seems like a lot of people," Chris said.

"Yeah, large crew." Beckham wiped a hand over his face and cracked his neck. He gave them a tired smile. "We were just getting ready to break for lunch. You got here just in time." He put an arm over Ian's shoulders. "I'd like to go over some of our ideas with Hollis and Anthony … your guys should sit with us too. I know you and I have talked it to death, but I'd like both bands to hear from you how you see them fitting into your sets, and vice versa."

Ian reached over and pulled at one of Beck's waves that had shaped into a curl.

"Great hair, man. Don't let Sparrow get ahold of this. I'll be out of a wife." The guys around them laughed and Ian talked on, oblivious. "You are inspiring me already, Beck. Organization is *not* my strong suit. I can talk music all day, though, so let's get to it."

Anthony had taken Ian seriously about the dancing and scheduled him to come to some of the choreography rehearsals. He still didn't feel very comfortable dancing with these professionals, but Anthony insisted he looked 'fabulous' and that no one would ever know he was nervous. Once Ian got more comfortable, Anthony scheduled one-on-one rehearsals for a couple of Ian's songs. He'd come to Ian all excited after the last rehearsal.

"I have an idea for your song, 'True Love Story'," he said, talking a mile a minute.

"Lay it on me," Ian said.

"I think Sparrow should come out and dance with you on this," Anthony pressed his lips together and then put his fist to his mouth, his eyebrows creased together in what appeared to be bliss or pain. "Can you imagine? The audience. Will. Lose. It."

"Oh, I don't know. She's … not one for big crowds, kinda shy…"

"Just let me talk to her about it," Anthony pleaded. "I have the vision. I can already see what she needs to wear…"

"She'll want to wear a turtleneck to cover her splotches." Ian chuckled.

"What?"

"Sure, ask her. I'll see if she'll come sometime this week."

Sparrow and the pumpkin were going with him to rehearsal that morning, their first time to meet everyone. He was excited to show them off. Sparrow needed the lift—they'd gotten everything moved into storage and were now living in their bus. They'd parked it on their new land. Ian had tried to convince her that they should at least find a furnished condo until they went on the road, but she wanted to put all their income toward the new house. She swore she was fine, but he knew she hadn't been writing as much, wasn't sleeping great, and she might not want to admit it, but he could tell she was a little overwhelmed being on the bus with a baby full-time.

"It'll be good practice for the next year," she'd said.

"It means we'll be on the bus *longer* than a year…"

"Which will make us all the more grateful when we finally move into our new house."

He couldn't argue with that logic, but he wanted to make sure she got out more. The paparazzi made her nervous—rightfully so—and she didn't venture out much on her own. She FaceTimed Tessa and her parents a lot, but that wasn't the same as having friends nearby to hang out with … especially as a new mom.

They pulled into the parking lot and he patted her hand. "They love you already," he told her.

She gave him a nervous smile and tugged on her black short shorts.

"You look sexy as hell," he whispered, leaning over to kiss her.

"There's that baby girl!" Vanessa squealed.

Everyone crowded around when they saw the girls were with him. He'd been showing them pictures of Journey for weeks now. He introduced everyone to Sparrow. Beckham gave her a quick hug and Journey a kiss. She reached out and tugged on his hair, getting such a laugh from everyone, she jumped and her face crinkled into a cry. She buried her face in Sparrow's neck and peeked back out at all the faces. Beckham played peekaboo with her until she was laughing again and pretty soon when he reached out to hold her she went to him.

He held her close and lifted his eyes to the ceiling. "Oh, this girl can have whatever she wants." He put his nose to her dark wavy hair and sniffed. "And she smells so good."

Ian smiled. "Nothing like it, man."

Anthony stood in front of Sparrow and took both hands.

"You are even more breathtaking in person," he said. He backed away, still holding her hands and looked her up and down. "That is one hot outfit. All creamy, demure lace on top and chiffon black shorts up to there." He lifted one eyebrow and nodded.

Her cheeks turned rosy as she thanked him and he looked at Ian like his every fantasy had come true.

"She's perfect for you!" he said.

"You've got that right," Ian agreed.

Roxie had stayed back and when she finally came forward she had a little bag in her hand. Ian had told Sparrow about Roxie and how he thought Beck liked her. She was a cool girl—funny and nice … well, to everyone *but* Beck. The way they danced together canceled out all that animosity though.

Roxie introduced herself and held up the bag. "Ian's been showing us her pictures, telling us all the new things she's doing. I hope you don't mind—I've been working on this during my breaks…"

Sparrow opened the bag and stared at Roxie. "Oh my goodness! That's so sweet. Thank you!" She leaned over and hugged Roxie, which seemed to catch Roxie off guard.

Inside was a beautiful yellow sweater. Ian reached out and touched it.

"So soft," he said, smiling at Roxie.

Sparrow held it up. "I love it—it's beautiful! Thank you so much. I can't believe you did that before even meeting us."

Roxie smiled. "Ian talks about you guys so much, I feel like I know you."

The dreams didn't stop. Beckham dreamed about Roxie almost every night. They were either dancing or he was exploring her body like a man starved. He didn't know if his dreams of her were memories or just the desire he'd had for her from the moment he saw her. Knowing how he'd wanted her from that first day, he couldn't understand how he could ever forget her, but there was a stretch of time before he'd gone in rehab that he'd never even admitted to himself how bad off he'd really been. There were significant chunks of time that were completely lost—he couldn't remember anything with clarity. The shame of that lingered before he ever saw Roxie, but knowing she had also been involved, and obviously hurt, ate away at him.

A few weeks before they were supposed to go on the road, he'd had another dream and showed up at rehearsal looking haggard. He kept his distance from her now when they weren't dancing, watching her laugh and talk with the others. She seemed a little older than the rest, more mature. Everyone, including Anthony, was crazy about her. When her guard was down, which was miles high with *only* him, she was charming and funny. And caring— nurturing even. During any down time, she pulled out her knitting needles and made it look incredibly cool. Even Shelton, who was the snarky one out of the bunch, wore the scarf she made for him every day.

She'd won Sparrow over within the first three minutes of their meeting. Now Sparrow came in frequently, and she and Roxie always chatted away like they'd been friends forever. He was glad they'd hit it off so well.

But he wanted in. It was more than making it up to her. It was more than sex, although that's all he could think about, at first. But every day he was around her, he wanted to know her. *Really* know her.

Lately she stuck around for lunch, disappearing less and less, and making him hope that she was finally getting more comfortable around him. But today, when they took their lunch break, she gave a wave and took off. On a whim, he followed her, telling himself it wasn't creepy at all that he tried to make sure she didn't see him.

He didn't have to follow her for long. She pulled up to a Taco Bell and hopped out of the car. She waved at someone, but he couldn't see who. Taking a deep breath, he put on a cap, parked, and got out of the car.

Roxie laughed her throaty laugh, looking toward the window of the restaurant. Beckham stepped beside Roxie and started walking in with her like it was no big deal. When she noticed him, she stopped walking in the middle of the parking lot.

"Beckham? What are you doing here?" Roxie said sharply.

"I ... followed you. Sorry." He tried to judge how mad he'd made her this time. "I wanted to know where you go when you disappear, maybe surprise you." He tried to smile, but it came out lopsided and guilty. "Now I realize what a bad move this was. I just-I want us to get along, Roxie ... I thought maybe away from everyone else, you'd talk to me? Maybe tell me what I can do to make it better?"

"I've made it a point not to tell you anything," she said, but without her usual anger.

The words stung, but she looked so distraught he couldn't be too upset with her. He put his hand on her arm.

"Please, hear me out. I know you hate me. I want to know everything that happened, everything that I screwed up before with you. But first, can you ... try to get to know the person I am now? Trust me, I don't follow every dancer home from rehearsal," he said with a laugh. When she didn't laugh, he wiped the smile off his face. "I don't want all this tension between us. It'll show when we're dancing. We need to find a way to work past this."

"I think we're working together just fine. Do you not think I'm doing a good job?"

"You're doing an amazing job," he conceded. "But imagine how much better it would be if you didn't despise me." He laughed lightly and when she still didn't, he looked at her helplessly. "Help me make it right," he pleaded.

"You can't make it right," she whispered.

A few cars drove around them. One honked and Beckham took her elbow and guided her to the sidewalk.

"What did I *do* to you?" He turned around and put his hands against the brick. Before turning around again, he said: "Roxie, you have to tell me what happened."

"I can't." She held her lips together to keep from crying.

"Then why did you come? Why did you agree to do this tour with me?" His stare pinned her to one spot.

"You and Anthony—you're the best there is. I didn't think I would make it! And then when Anthony called and I saw how much I'd make ... I couldn't turn that down! My sister had this obsessive, abusive, jerk boyfriend. She was with him for years and needed to get away from him, and ... we've both struggled for a long time. I just ... I should have, but I couldn't say no."

He turned and put his hands on her arms. "I'm glad you couldn't. So your sister is staying in town too?"

She nodded.

"I'd love to meet her. She's welcome to come hang at the warehouse anytime." He took a deep breath and then went for it. "Can we call a truce? I'm not so bad..." His voice trailed off and he lost his thought. Her lips looked so perfect. If he could just get a little closer to her mouth...

He nearly stumbled when she took a step back. *Such* an idiot. Holding up both hands, he took his own step back and shook his head. He put his hands on his head and left them there.

"I don't know what my problem is. I'm sorry. I can't stop blowing it with you. Look, I will stick to keeping this professional ... even though I feel something with you that I don't want to … ignore," Beckham paused, but when Roxie still didn't speak, he continued. "I won't cross the line with you anymore, Roxie. No more following-you stunts…"

"That would be good, thank you." She gave a small smile to counter some of her sarcasm.

Her smile fell before he could blink. Dammit, she was so hard to read.

She took a deep breath and blew it out of her mouth. "Professional, you said." Her voice shook at first, but grew stronger. "Yes, that's the only way." She nodded and avoided looking him in the eye. "We have to keep it professional. Deal?" She held her hand out.

He shook it and tried to ignore the heat he felt in her touch as they stared each other down. He should have been disappointed by what she'd said, but he saw warmth in her eyes that hadn't been there before. It almost made him … hopeful.

Beckham lifted Roxie's hand to his lips and planted a soft kiss on it.

There was the tiniest flicker of a smile before she scowled and pulled her hand away. "We made a deal!"

He raised his eyebrows and couldn't stop the smile that covered his face. "What?"

Her hands were on her hips and her forehead was all scrunched up.

"*What?*" he repeated, laughing.

She waved her hand in the air, dismissing him. "Go home already. Use your Beckham Woods charm on someone else."

"There's the Roxie I know." He laughed. "See you tomorrow, Rox. Wait—so you think I'm charming?"

She narrowed her eyes at him. "Lose the hat, never get such a short haircut again, and you might improve on the charm factor."

"You don't like my new haircut?"

She just continued to stare.

"So basically how I was before I got this new haircut, minus the hat?"

He took the hat off and threw it in the garbage can, then made a slight bow in front of her. When he stood back up, he raised his eyebrows and she rolled her eyes. "Right. I'll get started on growing the hair. Got any good tips for that?" He backed away, still smiling and unable to look away from her.

She looked so cute angry.

Almost as good as she'd look in his bed.

Shit. Hopeless.

8 DWINDLE

There had been additions to the wall. Several, in fact. She learned quickly that Beckham's manager was worthless in providing any information; he was more of an annoyance. Beckham's bodyguard, Howie, looked like a block but had ruined her plans more than once. Chloe, the airheaded brat who was just *always there*. The girl needed to get a life and do something irresponsible once in a while. Like, look away, or better yet, walk away, so trouble had a chance. And it angered her every time she looked at her masterpiece dart wall and saw the little boy. She had a larger picture of him and he was covered with tacks.

She'd known to be cautious of that bitch, Roxie. Having a cute little boy like Leo was even more of a draw than a puppy, although she hadn't seen Roxie utilize that yet. To add salt to the wound, she'd seen Beckham and Roxie at the show the night before. They were like pure sex together. She'd been so angry by how turned on she got just watching them. Beckham was *hers*, and she didn't share.

Roxie had some secrets. It was a good thing she was the only one who seemed to know them. She just needed to make sure it stayed that way.

The goody bird bitch Sparrow was always around Roxie now too. It was starting to seriously piss her off. One more person interfering with her target. If it became too big of a problem, Sparrow might have to get hurt just enough to go home. Ian deserved a little fun on the tour anyway. He was way too much man for that twit.

It was all a matter of spacing it out ... one hit at a time.

She picked up her bow and shot a dart in the center of Roxie's heart. It would feel good getting her out of the way.

But, first things first...

Leo.

She just had to bide her time.

9 HALF-MOON

The week before they left for three days at Christmastime, Anthony stepped everything up about a dozen notches. He worked them non-stop. They were *ready* for the tour. He gave them a list of instructions of what they could and couldn't do while they were gone. Roxie was surprised they were even allowed to go home at all. Anthony made them swear they wouldn't gain an ounce and to dance at least four hours every day to maintain their strength.

Being paired with Beckham so much isolated her from the rest of the group at times. It hadn't been a problem— she got along fine with everyone, just had to work a little harder to keep it that way. She'd danced her whole life and was used to the competitiveness that drove the profession, so she wasn't too worried about it. The only one who hadn't warmed up to her at all was Brooke, but Roxie assumed that was just because Brooke wanted Beckham so badly she couldn't see straight. Or Ian. Roxie wasn't sure which man Brooke wanted the most.

She tried to not take it personally when Brooke was rude to her, which was often, but Brooke didn't really like *anyone* but Beckham, Ian, and Anthony. The tour would be interesting when the six dancers were all crammed together in a bus—without anyone to soften the blow.

She'd gotten fairly close to Sparrow in a short amount of time. Sparrow was quiet at first, but once she was comfortable, the girl was hilarious. Roxie had never had so much fun with any girl, besides Chloe. They'd gone Christmas shopping a few times and hung out whenever Sparrow came to rehearsals, which was frequently once she met Roxie and Beckham's sister, Sierra. Roxie really liked Sierra too—the three of them just clicked. Vanessa was okay, too, but it was hard to have much of a conversation with her. So Roxie was glad Sparrow and Sierra would be on the tour—friends would make the separation from Leo and Chloe a little easier.

Roxie had managed to maintain a friendly distance from Beckham, even though their bodies were in close contact all day long. He'd grown his hair out, like he said he would, and the thought that he would do that for her secretly thrilled her. She didn't say a word about it, of course. He also *mostly* did what he promised, keeping everything professional, but in reality, every time he touched her it did things to her insides that got her all tangled up like old Christmas lights. Each day they were together was a steady buildup, until it was all Roxie could do to not wrap her legs around him and never let go.

The minute she would think a thought like that, she became stiff as a board and Anthony would yell at her to loosen up. She knew Beckham felt her weirdness, but he didn't show it. It seemed as if he became even nicer and more fun to be around. He gave her space during the breaks, he was unfailingly kind and attentive, but no more so than he was with everyone. It was only when they danced that she thought he might still feel that … electricity. Everything else faded and it was just the two of them in their own little world.

The way he was being so kind to her despite her coldness made her feel like such a bitch. She'd *never* treated anyone the way she'd treated him. *Ever.* She'd be ashamed of herself if she didn't know he deserved every bit of it.

FADE TO
Red

Still, it was hard when he was acting so nice. That was just it, he was probably acting. She'd never wanted to see him again, and here she was, behaving like someone she didn't recognize. It was vital—she had to protect her heart from ever cracking even a tiny bit to Beckham Woods.

"Make it look like you want him more than life!" Anthony yelled at her.

Beckham smirked at her as she stared into his eyes.

"Do you, Roxie? Do you want me more than life?" he whispered.

He looked too serious for how playful his voice sounded. Roxie rolled her eyes at him and he gripped her tighter. Her head fell back and her mouth parted, as his hands skimmed the sides of her body, touching just the edges of where she really wanted him to touch her.

"Yes! Yes!" Anthony purred.

Of course, they were playing a part. But it took every ounce of willpower to not get caught up in the way her body reacted to his. It felt entirely too real.

She missed the beauty of San Diego. L.A. felt like a different world at times. She needed the trip home. Time to breathe. But the time away was just a tease. It went by so fast. Roxie, Leo, and Chloe spent every second with Joey, watching movies, going to the beach, and catching up on all the time they'd missed with him. Her parents walked around with pleased peacock posture, so happy to have all the littles back in the roost. Roxie ate whatever she wanted and besides going on one early morning jog, she barely moved. Anthony was going to kill her. On the drive back to L.A., she knew she'd have hell to pay the next morning. It was worth it. When they got home, she stretched out on the bed with Leo cuddled up to her, and they took a long nap together.

Roxie and Chloe brought more clothes from home this time, so it took longer to unpack than it had to pack. Leo played a video game while Roxie started a load of laundry.

The phone rang when she walked into the kitchen. She jumped and Leo, practically on her heels, jumped too. He'd had undivided attention from every adult for days and was feeling the letdown of getting back to normal.

She gave him a kiss on the forehead and answered the phone.

"Hello?"

"Hey, Rox. How was your trip? It's Beckham…"

He had never called her before, but sounded so nonchalant, she tried to sound the same.

"Hi! Um, great. Did you go home too? Or, where did-?"

"Sierra and I went to my mom's. Anthony came over too … and David. The Sterlings came over for dessert. My mom wants to steal Journey."

"I bet!" Roxie laughed and then wasn't sure what to say next.

The clock ticked loudly in the kitchen as the silence stretched out between them.

"I missed you," he said quietly.

"What?"

"You heard me."

"You missed being abused?" she asked.

He laughed. "I guess I must have," he admitted.

"*Professional*," she reminded him.

"I missed *professionally* feeling your body next to mine."

She could hear the smile in his voice—the voice that dripped with seduction, reminding her of why he made millions. She cringed at how excited it made her to hear him saying those things to her. Hated knowing that she'd missed him too.

"I'm hanging up now." Roxie tried to sound angry, but knew she wasn't pulling it off very well.

Rehearsals were about as hard as Roxie had imagined they would be, but Anthony seemed to be extra forgiving. His reconciliation with David must have helped because, as hard as he tried, he just couldn't seem to get agitated at any of them. It was a huge contrast to the week before Christmas.

When Roxie took off her sweatshirt to start rehearsals, Brooke lifted her eyes and pointed to Roxie's behind. "Looks like you grew another ass while you were gone, Roxie."

Roxie nodded. "Nice one, Brooke. Thanks." She gave an extra little booty jiggle in Brooke's direction and walked to where everyone else was gathered. No one else ever seemed to hear when Brooke decided to pounce, so it was a waste of time to do anything other than ignore her.

The money she was making was all that pushed Roxie. And being able to dance. Every day after rehearsal, it didn't matter how exhausted and sore she was, she practically sailed home, so content to be doing exactly what she'd dreamed of her whole life. She knew she had already improved a thousand times since they began rehearsals, which was hugely gratifying. The only thing that could make this any better was if it weren't with Beckham. But she had a feeling he was also what made it so good...

On New Year's Eve, Beckham threw a huge party for everyone involved in the tour, including their significant others. When he invited everyone, he said he'd considered giving everyone a break from each other, but they were becoming a cohesive group and ringing in the year together would solidify that even more. Beckham had rented out a club that Roxie had seen once in *People* magazine. She didn't know if she'd ever get used this craziness.

Chloe talked Roxie into going. She wanted to stay home with Leo, but Chloe argued with her, saying Leo would be asleep by 8:30 anyway. Like clockwork, he was out, so Roxie went to the party.

A waiter went by with a tray of drinks. Roxie grabbed one and downed it. She didn't know why she felt on edge, but she wanted to shake it, and fast. She grabbed another drink and took her time with this one, watching everyone dance.

Brooke and Beckham caught her attention. He was holding her hand and twirling her out and she came back in with a vengeance, grinding up against him. He stepped back, putting space between them, and it made Roxie smile. He usually looked for every opportunity to be as close as he possibly could when they danced together.

"He *never* looks like he wants to get away from you," Sparrow whispered in her ear.

Roxie looked over and smiled at Sparrow, then shook her head. "He's good at what he does," she said.

Sparrow's eyes gleamed as she smiled bigger. "You're beautiful, Roxie. And nice, smart, sexy … trust me, he notices."

"Hey, you're not playing matchmaker, are you? Nuh-uh, don't get any ideas. Not interested." Roxie took another gulp of her drink. "Where's Ian?"

Sparrow made a face. "He's changing Journey and himself. She had a blow-out and managed to ruin both of their outfits. Thankfully, Anthony found a shirt for him to borrow."

Roxie pressed her lips together, but still busted up. "I can't believe I missed that!"

Just then Ian walked toward them wearing a tight, short-sleeve denim cowboy shirt. Roxie and Sparrow lost it all over again. Roxie wiped her eyes as Ian reached them. He held Journey facing out, so she could see everything. Her feet kicked happily.

"Well howdy, Partner." Sparrow could hardly get the words out.

Ian eyed the two of them and his lip quirked up to one side. He shook his head and looked down at Journey.

"You're all happy now, aren't you, pumpkin?" She looked up at him and gave him a dimpled grin. "Yeah," he cooed at her. "I'd feel good too if I'd gotten rid of more than double my body weight in POO."

Journey giggled and bounced up and down. When she saw her mom and Roxie laughing, she laughed and bounced harder.

Anthony asked Sparrow to dance, and Ian and Roxie chatted for a few minutes while she finished her drink. She moved toward the dance floor, unable to stay away for too long, ever. Justin and Vanessa were slow dancing and oblivious to everyone else. They were up and down, their lust and disgust for each other seesawing back and forth every day. Today appeared to be up for them. Brad and Shelton seemed to only have eyes for each other too.

Great. The tour is gonna be one huge hook-up, she thought. She wondered if Brooke and Beckham might be a possibility … if they'd ever had any of the intense moments she'd had with him. It didn't matter; in fact, it might even help her to get past these confusing thoughts she kept having about him if he'd focus on someone else. Shoving Beckham out of her mind, she closed her eyes and began to move.

She didn't even open her eyes when she felt his hand in hers. He brought her body flush with his and they moved without any thought. She felt his lips brush against her neck and then by her ear.

He whispered, "I don't want to dance with anyone but you."

She didn't say a word, just allowed her movements to say all that needed to be said.

Just a few days after the New Year, the buses rolled out of the warehouse parking lot long before the sun came up. Headed to northern California, they were officially on the road.

"Think you can live with me on this bus the whole tour?" Beckham asked Sierra.

"Ugh. I don't know," Sierra groaned. "It's a long time."

Beckham threw a pillow at her. "C'mon. You love me."

She smiled. "I *am* glad to not be cramped with people I don't know. Thank you for that." She looked around. "And this is a pretty sweet bus." She propped her feet up on the couch. "You've done really well for yourself, little brother."

He sat down across from her and waited for a jibe to come.

It didn't.

"You sure you're ready to give all this up?" she whispered.

He'd told her to be careful of what she said, with the bus driver in close range. It wasn't that he didn't trust him exactly, but he'd learned the hard way that people could be bought fairly easily for a story. Just one more thing he was tired of … never knowing which one of his 'friends' would spill their guts to a gossip magazine.

"I … yeah. I think so."

There was something about this tour that already seemed different, though. He felt more grounded, less anxious. He didn't know if it was being around the most laid-back man he'd ever been around—Ian—or if it was the way the songs had all become new again. Roxie made him feel…

He searched for the word in his mind—what did she make him feel?—and realized it was simply that she made him feel at all. After years of numbing his feelings, his emotions were waking up, and it was as if he was trying to walk on feet that had fallen asleep. He was a prickly, stumbling mess, but it still felt better than being dead.

He turned the conversation to non-threatening topics and they chatted all the way to San Jose. It was always a little rough the first few days of the tour, getting into the swing of things, but he'd worked with the same crew the last three tours, so he had no worries. They were scheduled to eat a late lunch and then everyone would do a quick soundcheck. By next week, someone else would do the soundcheck for him and he would mostly be free during the day.

Roxie was the first one Beckham saw when he went to eat.

"Come sit with me," he said before he could stop himself.

"Yeah, but you're ... Beckham Woods." She put a shaking hand to her mouth and looked at him with awed eyes.

Beckham leaned in closer and gave her a cocky smile. "Did you just now notice that?"

"Maybe." Roxie smirked.

She looked at the tables filling up around them. It was a large room to fit the camera crew, lights crew, stagehands, dancers, backup singers...

"Do you even know who all these people are?" she whispered. "Some I've never even seen before today!"

"Of course I do!"

"Are they gonna think it's weird that we're sitting together? Am I taking someone's seat? It is kinda weird, right? Why *are* you being so nice to me?" She rambled and then clamped her hand over her mouth and turned those piercing eyes on him until he squirmed.

"I like you, okay?"

"You *like* me?" Roxie's nose crinkled up.

"Yes. I do." He tried to look in her eyes, but couldn't stop looking at her mouth.

"You don't know me, and I've been a bit spiteful to you," she said.

"Oh, I got that. You're a kitten with claws," he teased softly. "But I think it's an act." He held up his hand when she started to argue. "Sparrow loves you, and I've come to think she's a very wise person."

"Sparrow loves everyone," Roxie said, smiling fondly.

"No ... she ... wouldn't if you were ... cruel," he stuttered. "I see you with everyone else and even though you're sassy, you're one of the nicest people here. I like *all* of what I know so far."

She played with her ear lobe and looked almost shy. "How can you say I'm nice after the way I've treated you?" She shook her head. "An act, huh? Interesting."

"Exactly," he laughed, "you're a mystery that I want to solve."

"What fun would that be? A mystery is only fun because of the unknown. Once you figure it out, you'll be on to other mysteries."

He nodded. "I can see where you'd think that. But here's the deal, Roxie," he leaned in closer to her, "and let's just stop talking 'hypothetically' about mysteries here ... I want to know *you*. Period. The fact that you're *mysterious* doesn't make me want to know you more or less; in fact, it's just getting in my way at the moment."

She blinked fast and looked away. Her mouth curved just slightly, like she was holding back a grin.

"I hope you'll like me a little better this time around," he said.

And just like that, all the progress Beckham thought he was making fell apart, as her face clouded over and her eyes grew hard.

She stood up from the table and leaned over to whisper into Beckham's ear.

"I work for you. You don't know me. I don't know you. We don't *need* to know each other. Got it?"

She stood up straight and was about to walk away when Beckham put his hand on her arm.

"Roxie? You might say that now, but we're just getting started onstage together. You tell me all I need to know when you dance with me. It's a different beast with the

FADE TO
Red

energy of a crowd out there. You'll be addicted to what that pulls out of you. *Every. Single. Night.*"

He grinned as her eyes got huge and laughed as she walked away. He couldn't wait to get on that stage with her in just a few short hours.

The first show was a huge success, receiving acclaim from the critics:

'Kept the audience hypnotized...'
'Woods exuded an effortless charisma that Sterling matched perfectly. The two of them together are sizzling magic.'
'Hearing the fusion of these two superstars is the ultimate experience...'

Beckham didn't see Roxie the next day. He had an interview set up at the bus with *Rolling Stone*. He didn't want to talk about his addictions anymore and it always went back to that or whoever he might be dating. He let his bodyguard, Howie, know exactly how much time he intended to spend with the journalist and when Howie should intervene.

After lunch, there was a knock and Howie walked in.

"Mirielle Wethers from *Rolling Stone* to see you?" Howie said.

"Send her in."

A gorgeous redhead walked in wearing tight jeans and a T-shirt. Her cleavage was the first red flag. The determination in her eyes was the second. It should have been the other way around, but he knew her type. The two usually went hand-in-hand when the woman led with her breasts. He had it right the first time.

"Beckham Woods?" she purred. "Mirielle Wethers. Thank you for meeting me."

"You're new," he said with an edge.

"Are you gonna hold it against me?" She sat down on the couch next to him, leaning forward.

Beckham groaned. "Tell Matt I'm holding this against *him*. The bastard." Beckham knew Matt, his favorite journalist at the magazine, was trying to bait him with an overly eager sexpot who was willing to do whatever necessary to boost her career off of this interview.

Mirielle stuck her candy red lips out in a pout, pretending to be wounded. "Aw, come on. Let's not get off on the wrong foot. There are much better ways to get off…" She licked her lips slowly.

Beckham moved to the other couch. "Shall we start the interview?"

After twenty minutes of trying to steer Mirielle's line of questioning to something other than his rehab stint and the actresses he'd last been seen with, he stood up.

"If we can't talk about the music, I'm done here."

She stood up and touched his arm. "I need this interview, *please* give me something…"

"If you can't find anything worth writing about in the music, either I'm doing something wrong or you're not meant to do this."

The fire lit in her eyes and she stepped back like she'd been hit.

"Tell Matt I missed him. You can see your way out." Beckham pointed to the door, just as there was a knock.

Howie walked in and nodded at them both. "Your next appointment is here," he said.

"Look, Mr. Woods, I just need a little more of your time, please. Can you … please give me a few more minutes?" She gave Howie a dismissive wave.

"I'm all out of minutes," Beckham said. "Howie? Can you escort Miss Wethers out?"

Mirielle stood there for a few seconds, fuming. She looked at Beckham and then decided to change her tactics.

"Thank you for your time." She leaned over, her chest rubbing against his as she kissed his cheek.

His breath caught and he stepped back. Mirielle smiled, at least part of her mission complete as she left the tour bus.

Going backstage after sound check, he went searching for the green room. He had junk food on the brain and needed to hunt some down. Opening the door, he realized he was in the wrong room right away, but then noticed movement in the corner. The room was sparse; a few speakers and cases were on the floor, and a couple of poles that went into the rafters of the exposed ceiling. Roxie was circling one and Beckham lost all rational thought when she jumped on it, landing high, and did the splits before winding her legs back around the pole and going upside down. She dropped and he jumped forward to help her, but she hadn't fallen, she was just working her way back up the pole without ever touching the ground. Faster and faster and faster she turned, her legs flying and flawless. She moved until he was dizzy. Time leaped into fast forward motion and her movements spoke to him from somewhere cavernous. She slowed and her head faced the floor and her legs reached up to the ceiling ... and then she was right side up again.

Oh please, don't let it end. Beckham blinked and she was standing by the pole, circling it the way she had been when he came in.

He'd never seen anything so erotic and he'd seen plenty try. Nothing had ever come close to watching her.

She turned; her face radiant. Her mouth dropped when she saw him. He closed his mouth when hers opened.

She started to say something then stopped.

He stepped forward. "Roxie. That was ... *unbelievable*."

"Favorite class I've ever taken—pole dancing," she said, blushing.

"You can't be embarrassed. You were born to do that." He pointed like an imbecile. She'd rendered him stupid. "Everyone deserves to see you on a pole," he said, eyes twinkling.

"Not gonna happen," she said.

"Just me then…" He let his eyes wander down her body again and nodded in appreciation. "Yeah, I'd prefer that too."

She groaned, but he caught her smile right before she turned and left the room.

10 EVACUATE

Anthony was right. The crowd went insane when Sparrow came onstage. They didn't dance—it was all Ian could do to get her to come out in front of the crowd, but she let him serenade her. It had been a hit every night thus far and was something Ian looked forward to now in the show. He saw her standing to the side, waiting for her cue, and winked. She started out nervous each night but relaxed once she moved toward him. It was a song he'd written for her when they'd been broken up, not his usual gritty blues-filled soul, but his heart pouring out. It was no secret she'd brought out the sap in him. He smirked to himself ... yeah, so much of a sap that it was a struggle for him to keep it together every night to sing the song.

The strings and guitar played the opening notes and Ian began to sing.

I remember once upon a time
When your heart and mine became entwined
A world of wonder testified that we were meant to be

It was this moment that Sparrow made her entrance, and the applause was deafening...

It was like a fairytale romance
Two enchanted lovers holding hands
We vowed that time and circumstance would never come
between…
And now we've learned it's not as easy as it seems
And real life can steal the magic from our dreams
But I believe true love was made for times like these

Sparrow's eyes filled each time he got to the chorus. She gave him a shaky smile and he leaned over to give her a quick kiss, earning another roar from the crowd. Her skin was hot from being flushed and nervous.

And I believe in happy-ever-after
You and me and love will find an answer
Darlin', this is not the final chapter of our true love story

I remember warm December nights
Starry skies and snow-white mountain heights
Eyes that danced like candlelight to an ageless song
Snapshot memories of moments past
Come back like forgotten photographs
The love we made was made to last for a lifetime long
It's true that life can do its damage to our dreams
And love is not always as easy as it seems
But I believe true love was made for times like these

And I believe in happy-ever-after
You and me and love will find an answer
Darlin', this is not the final chapter of our true love story

I may not be your knight in shining armor anymore
But I believe that we are still worth fighting for
If you'll only kiss me and say that you'll forgive me
I know we can get that magic feeling back once more

Before the last chorus, the music cut back and he stopped and held her against him as he sang it one more time. When the final notes rang out, he put his hands on her face and kissed her. He didn't care if thousands of people were cheering or not. He lived to love this woman.

"You and me and love," she whispered before walking away.

He felt that tug he always felt when she walked away—like he wanted nothing more than to run after her.

"I love you, baby!" He yelled in the microphone.

She laughed and flushed as everyone stomped and screamed.

Normally when he was done for the night, Sparrow and Journey were somewhere backstage, either hanging out in one of the green rooms or talking to Roxie and Sierra. Tonight, Sierra found him first and told him to hurry to the bus.

"Sparrow fell right after she walked off the stage. She says she's fine, but her foot is bruised and huge." She winced when she saw his face. "Anthony and a paramedic are with her now."

He rushed through the parked buses until he reached theirs. He nearly ran over Anthony in his hurry. He was trying to console Journey, who stopped fussing when she saw Ian, reaching out for him to take her. She smiled at Anthony once she was in Ian's arms, the little rascal. Anthony chuckled and rolled his eyes.

Ian moved past him and hurried to Sparrow. He kissed her cheek and assessed her eyes before he looked at her foot. He knew she hated crying in front of people, even him, but he couldn't believe she wasn't bawling. It was bad.

"Oh baby. It looks awful. You think it's broken?"

She made a face. "I'm okay." Her breath hitched when the paramedic put an ice pack on her foot. "It hurts, but it's not terrible." She swallowed hard.

"Yeah, not buying that," he said.

"This is Tyler." She motioned to the paramedic. "He's pretty sure it's just a bad sprain, and I think so too…"

"Rest, ice, compression, and elevate." Tyler's voice was very low and fast, and he didn't smile or blink. "She needs to rest it for at least 3 days. Do the ice in 15-20 minute intervals, with 40 minutes between intervals to prevent frostbite. I've compressed it, as you can see. Make sure when you wrap it again, it's not too tight. And keep your feet elevated to at least your heart level, Sparrow." He took a quick breath and kept going. "You can take both acetaminophen and ibuprofen. If it's not feeling better in a few days, you'll need to get an X-ray."

"I'll be fine," Sparrow insisted. "Thank you, Tyler. I'm glad you were here."

When Tyler left, Anthony and Sierra sat on the couch across from Sparrow.

"He was intense," Sierra said.

Sparrow giggled. "Rest, ice, compression, and elevate," she said, as low as her voice would go.

Someone knocked on the door.

"It's Roxie," she called.

Sierra opened the door and Roxie came in, looking worried.

"Are you okay? Did you tell Ian what happened?"

Sparrow stared at Roxie and shook her head. "I'm not even sure anymore," she said softly.

"Sure of what?" Ian asked, frowning.

"It all happened so quickly, and I'm not positive—you know what a klutz I am!" Her arms flailed. "I just don't know…"

"Would you please just tell me what happened?"

"I think I was tripped." She bit her lip and looked down. "I'm not positive, so I hate to even accuse anyone, but Roxie thought she saw it too, before I even said anything."

"Who?" Ian scowled. "You mean on *purpose?*"

She nodded. "Maybe she didn't mean for me to get hurt, just wanted me to ... look dumb, or something."

"Who?" he repeated.

"Brooke."

Ian gritted his teeth. "You've gotta be kidding me. I knew she was trouble," he muttered.

"Really?"

"Yeah, she keeps trying to be all up in my space, and I keep making it obvious I want no part of it." He put his hand on Sparrow's cheek and leaned in. "You know that, right?"

Sparrow smiled. "I do know," she said softly. "I've seen her, and," she motioned to the girls, "we've had a few discussions about her."

"She didn't like that one of the dancers wasn't given a part on that song—she's been saying that on the bus," Roxie added. "I'm not sure what her game is ... she's all over Beckham too."

"I'll talk to Beckham, and I'm also gonna have a chat with Brooke." Ian's face was tight.

"No, she'll just deny it! I'm not even positive myself!" Sparrow moved the pillows behind her, so she could sit up taller on the couch. "I'd rather stay out of her way, and if she so much as blinks at me wrong, I'll take care of it."

Ian snorted. "If you think I'm letting this go, you're crazy."

Sparrow glared at him.

Roxie cleared her throat. "We're just a text away if you need us." She motioned to Sierra and smiled at Sparrow. "For what it's worth, I think you should listen to Ian."

They left quickly and Ian turned back to Sparrow. "You really want to fight about this?"

"You really want to tell me I'm crazy in front of our friends?"

"I didn't mean it like that and you know it."

She lifted an eyebrow. "Pretty sure you did."

He shook his head and Journey mimicked him, shaking her head too. He stopped and she stopped, then looked at him to see what they were doing next.

When he looked at Sparrow again, she was smiling at the two of them. He bent down to kiss her. Journey patted Sparrow's back and got loose from Ian while they were kissing. She laid her head on her mama's chest and put her thumb in her mouth.

"God, I love my girls," Ian said, taking in the picture they made. He moved to the couch across from them and sat down. "If you want to confront Brooke, I'll back off and let you do your thing, but promise me that someone is with you when you do. I don't trust that girl. We can decide what to tell Beckham after that."

"Maybe she was just trying to be silly and didn't expect me to get so hurt…"

His blue eyes darkened as he just stared at her. Finally: "I'm not even gonna respond to that."

Sparrow shot him a look of her own and pressed her lips on the top of Journey's head. Journey's eyes were drooping and within seconds, she was out.

A loud knock on the door made Journey jump, and her eyes popped open. Ian felt the frustration he'd never known until becoming a father—he wanted to strangle anyone who woke up his child.

"We need to put a sign up in the window when she's sleeping," he grumbled.

Sparrow smirked. "Okay, Grumpa."

"You're so lippy tonight," he said before opening the door. "If your foot wasn't so hurt, I'd take you over my knee."

"I'd like to see you try, Mr.-" Her words were cut off when she saw who he'd let inside the bus.

Beckham and Brooke.

"So sorry you got hurt tonight, Sparrow. Is it broken?" Beckham asked.

"Tyler thinks it's a bad sprain."

"Still hurts like a mother-" Beckham paused when he saw Journey smiling up at him.

Brooke cleared her throat. "I told Beckham I wanted to come with him to talk to you—I feel terrible about what happened."

"Do you?" Sparrow asked, not sounding very convinced.

"Well, yes. I think the whole thing was my fault." Her words came stumbling out. "I was rushing backstage and tripped on something, and I think it's what made you fall." She stepped closer to Sparrow, but kept glancing at Ian and Beckham. "And then it was chaotic back there. When I knew they were going to get help for you, I thought I better hurry onstage for the next song. I felt so bad not knowing for sure what happened."

Sparrow's eyes narrowed, but she gave a slight nod.

"I'm so glad it's not broken." Brooke flashed a toothy smile.

"Yeah, me too," Sparrow said.

"You look exhausted. We better let her rest, Beckham," Brooke said, stepping toward Beckham and putting her hand on his arm. "Please let me know if there is *anything* I can do."

"Me too," Beckham added. "I can make sure there's unlimited ice cream delivered while you're recovering…"

"Not necessary!" Sparrow smiled.

Ian gave Sparrow a look, trying to gauge whether she wanted to say anything else. She shook her head slightly, and he reluctantly let it go. He didn't trust Brooke, but maybe she hadn't set out to purposely hurt Sparrow. He'd just have to keep an eye on her.

Beckham was taunting her … and winning. Roxie ignored him every time she saw him, but onstage every night, he was right. She couldn't hide the fact that she was putty in his hands. Her body trembled when he touched her. It was the only time she looked at him honestly, so she took full advantage, not taking her eyes off his. She lived to have her hands on him.

They'd been on the road eleven days and they were both getting more daring each night. During the Vegas show the night before, she'd been sure he was going to kiss her right there, but he teased her by coming as close as possible before pulling away. The audience had gone wild, screaming and cheering. She'd been disappointed he hadn't kissed her and knew she had it bad.

She made a cup of coffee and looked at the time. Leo usually called her or Skyped when he woke up every day, but she hadn't heard from him yet this morning. She missed him terribly, even though Chloe and Leo had already met up with her quite a bit in the past week and a half. They'd driven to the closer places and had flown once. Five days out of eleven wasn't too bad, she told herself. No, it was *awful*—she hated being away from him for any length of time. After each paycheck, she planned to deposit two thousand in savings and then go online to hunt down the best deals for plane tickets and hotels.

She stretched out on the couch and took sips of coffee, while her thoughts sluggishly wandered back to Beckham. She was making herself sick thinking about him so much. She knew she was sending conflicting messages, not only to him, but to herself. He might seem harmless right now, but she knew full well the effect he had on her. He was deadly. She wouldn't let him destroy her life. Once was enough.

They were spending a couple of days in Vegas, one more concert there, and a couple of TV spots. Then they'd be making the long haul to St. Paul and then Chicago.

Roxie's stomach growled so loud it should have woken up the entire bus. No one made a peep, so Roxie quietly left the bus, the sunshine nearly knocking her over with its brightness.

Beckham was just walking out of his. She hadn't even realized their buses were parked next to each other. He was wearing a fedora and sunglasses. She would have recognized him instantly by his relaxed stride alone.

"What are you doin'?" Beckham asked.

"Looking for a massive buffet," she said softly.

"That's what I wanna do!" Beckham whisper-yelled back. He looked at her with his eyebrows raised. "You okay if I join?"

She gave a little shrug and he lifted both arms in the sky.

"Roxie Taylor sorta said yes! Woohoo!"

She raised her eyebrow back. "Is that how you read that?" But she couldn't help the grin that was covering her face.

"It's exactly how I read that. Breakfast date with Roxie," Beckham teased under his breath. "Want the best breakfast or the really good and fastest?"

"The best."

"I knew there was a reason I liked you."

"I've never eaten so much in my life," Roxie groaned.

"There's more. You have some work to do."

Beckham had ordered one of everything. They polished most of it off, but there was still a plate with heaping pineapple French toast. Roxie hit her limit with the omelet, potatoes, fruit, and beignets.

They had snuck into the Wynn the back way, avoiding any screaming fans. Beckham kept his head down the few times they came into close contact with people. She was shocked that he managed to stay undetected … until he took his hat and glasses off in the restaurant.

The conversation was easy and light, even though people suddenly started coming by the droves to ask Beckham for his autograph. He was kind to everyone and posed for a few pictures. Roxie was impressed that he didn't seem bugged at all by his meal getting continuously interrupted. The manager eventually came to their table and said he could take them to a private dining room. They hurried down the hall, into the much smaller room, and what was left of their food sat at an elegant table. Roxie picked at the French toast.

"Do you get sick of all the attention?" Roxie asked.

"You know ... I recognize the fact that the fans are the ones who got me here, but ... yes. I do get sick of it. It isn't that I'm not grateful. I am. It does get grueling, though. I know it sounds cliché, but I'd rather just be about the music. That starts to become only a small part. I miss the days when I could sing in a small club and not get mobbed everywhere I go. I know it's a mixed bag. I should be happy for the success, period, but I'm not cut out for this. Especially not sober." Beckham leaned back in his chair and stretched.

Roxie nodded. "I can only imagine. It's exhausting seeing you deal with it during this one meal. It's constant, isn't it? I mean, the crowd outside each arena when we pull into every town is enough to send me running for cover."

Beckham laughed. "You should do a meet and greet with me sometime. It's great and sometimes very, very frightening."

"No, thank you." She smiled as she said it.

He leaned forward, taking her hand in his and lacing his fingers through hers. "Please?"

She grew very still but didn't take her hand away. "What are you asking for exactly?" she whispered.

"Everything. I'm asking for everything."

He studied her eyes as she tried to keep the alarm out of them. His other hand stroked the inside of her wrist.

Without taking his eyes off her, he lifted her wrist to his lips and kissed it, so soft that she shivered.

"You have me right here," he said, kissing the palm of her hand.

"Why me?" she whispered. "Why now? I don't know what you could possibly like about me at this point..."

"I like that I can barely touch you like this and yet it feels like my skin is going to explode from it. I like the love we're making onstage every night. It's driving me insane, you know." She started to protest and he shook his head. "Don't pretend it isn't true. It's totally what we're doing." He leaned in closer, until his head was an inch from hers. "I like the way you make everyone laugh and the way you've made everyone (but me, by the way) a scarf. I like that you ate all this food with me. I like everything about you except for the fact that you sometimes act like you want nothing to do with me." His voice got lower and lower. "I like the heat in your eyes when I make you angry. I like the way your lips curl up when you try to hide a smile from me. I like that I want to be around you all the time. I like the way you look in everything you wear. I like imagining you out of everything you wear."

She took her hand away from his. "*Sometimes* want nothing to do with you?" She tried to laugh, but it was weak. "I think that's exactly it right there. I'm the only girl who doesn't want you."

"That's all you heard of what I just said?" He laughed. "And not true," he said, taking her hand back in his. "That's *not* why I like you, it's what I *dislike* about you, and ... are you *sure* you don't want me?" He leaned over until his forehead touched hers. "Tell me you're sure and I'll stop."

"I'm sure I *shouldn't* want you," Roxie said.

"Two very different things. I'll take it," he said.

He put his hands on either side of her face and kissed her. Soft and gentle, but completely turning her world upside down. Her heart lifted like dandelion dust flying toward the sun.

"I knew I would like that about you too." He touched her lips with his finger and then followed with his tongue, teasing her, while he looked into her eyes.

Roxie's heart drummed through her chest. He was torturing her by taking his time, and he knew it. He smiled against her lips, as his tongue ventured inside, taunting her with his restraint. His fingers brushed against her cheek, leaving fiery sparks underneath her skin, until she felt consumed. She put her hands in his curly hair and pulled him closer, deepening the kiss.

His composure went out the window.

He moaned and gripped her hair in both fists as he explored her mouth.

A feverish dance; it was an extension of the way they moved together on the stage. She'd never felt anything more perfect. It was as if she were floating, and yet, grounded at the same time. Nothing existed but the two of them.

Until the fog broke and the commotion nearby was suddenly loud enough to penetrate their bubble. They slowly broke the kiss, but Beckham didn't let go. Their server walked in, apologizing for the disturbance. Roxie jumped and collided into Beckham. He backed away, holding his nose.

Their moment was lost.

11 YIELD

She didn't look at Beckham once as they walked back to the bus. But fuck it all ... kissing her had been worth it. He wanted to ask if he'd really blown it with her, but the thought of how she'd felt in his arms was too right. It couldn't be a mistake. She wanted him too, no question. It clarified everything for him.

When they reached the buses, Roxie said, "That can't happen again, Beckham."

"Why not?" he asked, his heart deflating.

"I know you might remember me differently—if you ever start to remember me at all—but I'm not just some groupie, Beckham. I can't just ... have meaningless flings whenever I get a whim. I'm a responsible adult who has to make responsible decisions and you are *not* a responsible decision." She turned around to walk away.

It was like a sharp kick in the gut. He felt sick.

"Roxie, wait. Please. Don't shut me out again. It was just a *kiss*."

She glared at him.

"I know," his voice rushed out, while he held onto her arm, "it was so much more than that, wasn't it? I felt it too."

He looked at her and wished she could see into his mind and heart, how he felt about her.

"I'm not proud of my past. Not at all." He looked up at the sky and took a breath. "Please hear me. I don't need another meaningless fling, Roxie. I want *you*. We're not there yet, but ... I'm dying for you to give me a chance. And I *don't mean sex*," he said, through his teeth. "I mean, me. Please give *me* a chance."

Her face softened for a second. He really thought she might say yes.

"I've gotta go," she whispered.

He nodded, backed up a step, and let her go.

Beckham and Ian had to be at the TV station that afternoon. Anthony had gone to check the size of the studio the day before and said it was too small for everyone. Roxie would be the only dancer. She seemed fine with Ian and the guys in the band, cracking jokes about the billboards they passed on the way, but she didn't look at Beckham the whole ride.

Right before he and Ian were supposed to go chat up the host, Rrrrrandy Reynolds, Beckham's cell buzzed and it was his manager. Nate knew he was due to go on air. Beckham pushed the silencer and seconds later, Anthony called.

Crap, what's going on?

He put his phone in his pocket and walked out to meet the smiley, tan guy. He didn't know why he'd agreed to do this show. The guy had jackass written all over him.

Once they had him all hooked up and did the preliminary greetings, they did the countdown to live. 5, 4, 3, 2, 1, cheesy music played.

"Beckham Woods and Ian Sterling! Welcome. The two of you have taken the entertainment industry by storm with this combined tour, playing sold-out shows every night. That has to be the best feeling in the world. What made you decide to tour together?" He looked at Beckham.

"It's been great. When we saw an opportunity to work together, we both jumped at the chance," Beckham said. "Being onstage with Ian every night—most fun I've ever had."

The host and camera crew let out a loud 'Awwww' and Beckham and Ian both laughed.

"I'm the lucky one," Ian added.

"We've got a bromance going on, folks," Randy Reynolds said, facing the camera. "Lots of romance on this tour, it seems. Your wife is on the tour with you, right, Ian?"

"Yes." Ian smiled.

"You two have been heating it up onstage too." He pointed behind them and a clip played of Ian and Sparrow kissing after their song.

Ian laughed. "Keepin' the love alive," he said.

"You're not the only one!" Randy pointed to the screen behind Beckham.

Beckham watched, stunned, as two pictures of him with Roxie flashed in slow succession. Both pictures showed them locked in a passionate kiss, but one was especially explicit. All he saw was tongues. Roxie would kill him. He turned and tried to see her reaction, but the lights were too bright.

"Bastard!" came out of Beckham's mouth before he could stop it. He wanted to first wring the restaurant manager's neck for basically handing the photographer a perfect shot and then have a go at the guy in front of him. "What kind of show is this?"

Randy laughed at Beckham, as if they were in on a joke together. His smile dimmed somewhat when he saw the look in Beckham's eyes, and he started talking quickly to cover the awkward pause that filled the air.

"What happens in Vegas doesn't *always* stay in Vegas," he said with a nervous chuckle. "It's great to see you dating again. There's been a long lull, hasn't there? You haven't really been linked with anyone since … your rehab stint. Who's the lucky lady?"

"I'm here to talk about the show tonight. 8 p.m. at MGM Grand. Hope to see you there," he said to the camera, paused a moment, and then pulled off his lapel mic.

Randy frantically motioned for the cameraman to cut. His expression was panicked until the camera turned to Ian. Randy's face suddenly brightened with his phony smile.

"So how does your wife handle all the groupies? I know they must come out in the droves with both you *and* Beckham."

Ian sat back in his seat, crossed his arms, and stared down the host. He didn't say a word. The man began fidgeting. Sweat beaded on his forehead and upper lip.

"So the music…" he started.

"There we go," Ian leaned forward, "that's the direction you take in interviewing a musician. What do you want to know?"

"I-uh, what have you learned musically from Beckham and what do you think he's learned from you?"

"I've learned that I suck as a dancer, unlike Beckham. And musically, playing with someone as talented as Beckham makes anyone better. Pushes me to work harder." He shrugged. "You'd have to ask him what he's learned from me." He gave the host a shit-eating grin that was not returned.

"Thanks for your time today. Ian Sterling, everyone. Make sure you come out to see Ian and Beckham Woods tonight. After the commercial, we'll…"

The producer rushed as far forward as he could without being in the shot. He was shaking his head and sliding a hand across his throat.

"We'll b-be back," Randy stuttered. His shoulders drooped when the commercial started. "I thought they were singing," he said to the producer and waved an arm toward Ian.

Ian was already taking off his microphone. "Doesn't look like we'll be singing today," he said. "Jerky thing to do, man, bringing up rehab and then pictures of an obviously private moment? Not cool."

Randy sneered, nothing close to a smile, phony or otherwise.

Ian shook his head, gave him the bird, and stalked off.

The band and Roxie were on the sidelines, watching everything. Beckham was pacing the hall by the exit. No one said a word. They filed out behind him and crawled back into the limo. Somehow Beckham ended up by Roxie.

"Shit, I coulda slept longer," Taz joked.

T.J. bopped him on the head. "Shut up, Taz."

They all looked at Beckham and Roxie. She flushed and looked out the window.

"I'm really sorry, Roxie," Beckham said softly.

She looked at him and barely nodded. "I know you didn't mean for that to happen."

He leaned his head back on the seat and pulled out his cell phone. He had a few voicemails and texts waiting. He texted Howie, even though Howie was in the limo with him.

We need more security. 24 hrs. Extra on Roxie.

Howie checked his phone then looked at Beckham and gave a subtle nod.

As soon as they got back, he went straight to his bus. There was a room booked for him at MGM, but he'd given it to Sierra. He went and stretched out on his bed and called Nate.

"Hey, there you are. Was trying to catch you before you went on the show."

"Pictures of me with Roxie—are they everywhere?"

"Yep."

He let out a string of curses as he got up and paced the bus.

"I like this girl, Nate. I don't want to scare her off. She's not even sure she likes me most days."

"Well, that's a twist," Nate said. "Maybe we'll keep her."

"Shut up."

He laughed. "So … I've gotta ask. I'm assuming Roxie is the one you called about before the tour—is that right?"

Beckham was quiet. "I forgot about that," he finally said.

"I'll take that as a yes. Listen, there are a few ways to play this. You can either wait for it to die down, which means don't get caught with her again. Or, you can just enjoy your tour and not worry about it. Get your picture with some hot fans—or better yet, I heard Taylor Swift will be at tomorrow night's show. We'll get a picture and let that circulate a bit."

"No way am I gonna get messed up in that. She'll be writing a song about me," Beckham scoffed.

"That wouldn't be all bad," Nate mused. "You know she's always been hot for you."

"Piss off, man," he muttered. He pulled the phone away from his ear when Nate's laugh got too loud. "Dude, really."

Nate took a deep breath, but the laugh was still in his voice. "There's always the last option, which I wouldn't mind seeing…"

"What's that?"

"Date Roxie and be out with it. You need a girlfriend, Beck. You've paid penance long enough."

"I kissed her this *morning*, and believe me, it was not her idea."

"Okay, just tell me how you want to spin this and I'll get it started-" Nate paused.

"She's got me all wrapped up…"

"You've got it bad."

"Fuck me, I know it."

Beckham looked for Roxie at dinner, but she wasn't there. He saw Sierra grabbing three desserts and jogged over to her.

"Hey. Have you seen Roxie?"

"She's in the bus. Hiding." Sierra grinned.

"Is she mad at me?"

"Oh yeah, probably," she said.

"*Probably?*"

"From what I've seen, she seems to stay mad at you." She took a bite of cheesecake and pointed her fork at him. "I like this girl so much. And that was even before I knew just how tightly she had your balls in a vise."

"Oh, you know what?" he groaned. "Don't start, Sierra."

She laughed.

"Just tell me … how do I get her out of the angry?"

"How much do you like her, Beck?" Sierra's expression turned serious. "You know you've had enough notches on your bedpost…"

Beckham stared at her. "You too?" He ran his hands through his hair and glared at her. "Okay, I deserved that. But … seriously … *mean.*"

She shrugged and sampled the chocolate cake.

He shook his head. "She's different. I want to get under her skin and know what makes her angry heart tick."

She paused mid-bite.

"God, I know this is wrong to say because you're my brother, but … that was kinda hot," she finally said.

"Is everyone talking about it?" Roxie asked the minute she let Sierra on the bus.

Everyone was at dinner so she had the bus to herself.

"I might have heard a little buzz about it. Honestly, I think everyone thought you might be dating a while ago."

Roxie tried to tackle her as she walked by and Sierra went sprawling on the bus floor.

"Ow! Dammit, Roxie!" Sierra yelled. "You don't know me well enough for that yet!"

"I'm so sorry! I can't even believe I did that, after what happened with Sparrow! I didn't think you'd go down!" Roxie cried. "Are you okay?"

"I'm fine," Sierra said with a smirk. "Gonna start calling you Brooke."

Roxie clamped her hand over her mouth and started laughing hysterically.

Sierra pulled her down and hit her over the head with a pillow. "Quit being so bitchy! Go get laid by my hot rock star brother. He wants you bad." As soon as she said it, she shuddered and mumbled under her breath, "Things I never thought I'd say…"

Roxie stopped laughing. "What did he say?"

"He wants to get in your skin and know what makes your angry heart tick," Sierra quoted. "If that isn't sexy, I don't know what is."

"This is so weird," Roxie snapped back.

"*Go get laid and get it over with!*" Sierra repeated, louder.

"Shush! Someone might hear you."

"I thought everyone was gone," Sierra whispered.

"They are, but … someone could have heard … outside."

Sierra rolled her eyes. "Oh lord."

"Seriously, what am I gonna do?"

They sat up and leaned their backs against the couch.

"I've never seen him like this, Roxie. He's never fought for anyone."

Roxie's forehead crunched into a tiny V.

"He's made a lot of changes, especially the last year, and ... I think you can trust him."

"I don't know if he's changed or not. I do know that I should have never risked coming on this tour. It was stupid. Stupid, stupid, *stupid*. I have to just keep my space. Do my job, get paid, and that's it. No more, no less."

Sierra looked at Roxie. "He's one of the good ones, Rox. He really is." She looked like she was going to say more but stopped.

"What?" Roxie pressed.

"You have the potential to hurt him, really hurt him. That, in itself, is a huge shift."

"No more than he's already hurt me, I guarantee that," Roxie whispered.

"What do you mean?" Sierra leaned up and faced Roxie. "What has he done?"

"I—forget I said that. I'm just frustrated by this day. I need to get ready for tonight."

"Okay, but tell me if I need to go beat him up." She lifted an eyebrow and smiled. "I can totally take him."

"I'm sure you can." Roxie got up and put the pillows back on the couch.

"All right, well, don't hide for much longer. You'll appear *guilty*." And with that, Sierra made her way to her bus. "And watch your back. I owe you a good tackle."

"You totally do, but please, don't you dare!" Roxie laughed. "I have to protect my bones for the next year at least."

"I can't hear you!" Sierra yelled as she shut the door.

Sparrow texted a few minutes later.

Sparrow: You've been withholding, girl! Spill!

Roxie: I'm too busy hiding. Sorry I haven't been over today. It's been ... eventful.

Sparrow: You're only safe from me because Ian's hovering worse than a new mother. And when he can't, Bodyguard Will is.

Roxie: I've noticed a lot of guards too! Have they always been around?

Sparrow: Will hasn't. If it doesn't work out with Beck, you need to have a look at Will. :) But from what I saw of you and Beck kissing, I'm thinking it will ALL work out. And then some. DANG, girl!

Roxie put her head in her hands and groaned.

By the time the show was over that night, pictures of Beckham and Roxie looking like they were ready to rip each other's clothes off onstage, along with the pictures of them kissing, were all over the news and Internet. Chloe left six messages. Her parents and brother called at different times throughout the day, wanting to know why she hadn't told them about her relationship. She was mortified and scared. *Terrified* would better describe it … her resistance to Beckham was barely hanging by a thread.

Roxie spent the next day hiding with Sparrow. Ian kept bringing them food, so they wouldn't have to leave the bus, except during the show. She dreaded going back on her bus that night, but sucked it up. The next couple of days they made the long drive to St. Paul. They hadn't been there long when Beckham knocked on the door to see if she would come play in the snow. He looked so adorable standing out there, cheeks rosy from the cold, and his eyes bright and beseeching. Roxie said no and then felt horrible when she saw the flicker of hurt on his face. Guilt spread through her body like a weed.

He walked away, and Brooke moved past her and threw a snowball at him. Roxie stepped away so she couldn't hear their laughter mocking her. Jealousy quickly replaced all guilt.

A few hours before the show that night, he came to the door again. Vanessa let him in.

He gave everyone a quick wave and looked at Roxie.

"I need to talk to you," he said.

Roxie looked around. All eyes were on them. "Okay."

"Alone. Can we go in the back? Or would you come over to mine?"

"I'll come with you," she said quietly.

They didn't speak as they walked to his bus.

"Have a seat," he said formally.

"I can't stay long." She kept standing.

"Have you noticed your bodyguard, Johnny?" he asked. "And Al? Although you probably don't see Al most of the time."

"*My* bodyguard? I thought they were for everyone. They're both kinda hard to miss."

"I should've let you know I was doing that. With those pictures getting out—just can't be too careful." He looked away. "Roxie, I'm going crazy here. Please…" He rubbed the stubble on his chin and then put his hand on her arm. "We have these moments when I think we're getting somewhere, and then … you pull back, say it can't happen, avoid me … but the way you look at me is a completely different story."

She didn't say anything, just noticed the way his eyelashes curled up at the ends. Leo's did the same thing. She was envious of those lashes.

"I've had dreams about you with really short hair," he said so quietly she barely heard him.

She jumped when he ran his fingers softly down her neck.

"I've had dreams about kissing this neck." His eyes looked like stormy waters. "I don't know what's real and what isn't. Tell me. Tell me what's real, Roxie."

She swallowed hard.

"I've tried to forget," she whispered.

He put his hand on her cheek and whispered, "If you won't help me remember, will you at least let me help you forget?"

"I can't."

"Why not? I'm not really that bad, am I?"

She wouldn't look at him, even though he tried to make her by lifting her chin.

"Roxie," he said softly.

When he said her name with such conviction, it broke something inside of her. She ached to believe in him. She wanted more than anything to know that what Sierra had said about him was true, and that she could put aside her responsible, analytical self for a moment and just *feel*. She caved and finally looked at him, and her heart plummeted even further.

Without overthinking it, she kissed him. He sucked in a sharp breath and kissed her back with the same fury. She held onto his hair and walked into him until the back of his calves hit the couch. She nudged him and he sat down, pulling her with him. Her thighs wound around him as tight as they could go, straddling him, and still he pulled her tighter and groaned into her mouth.

The door banged shut and Sierra said, "Ahh, sorry!"

Roxie jumped off of Beckham, turning bright red. She couldn't look at either one of them. Beckham took her hand and stood up beside her.

"Great timing," he muttered with a scowl.

Sierra laughed. "I'm really sorry." She looked at Roxie and lifted her eyebrows. "I'm glad you listened to me."

Roxie groaned. "This is so messed up." She let go of Beckham's hand and walked toward the door. "I'll see you later."

"Wait, Roxie, don't go. Come on … hang out with us."

"I'm out of here," Sierra said at the same time.

"I'll go get ready. It's later than I thought…" Roxie made a quick excuse and ran.

12 EBB

Every picture of Roxie was charred. The girl's blonde, sunshiny looks didn't look so sunshiny *scorched*.

Their kiss was playing over and over again in the edges of her mind. *No. No.* Her body trembled.

No.

She envisioned her sharp dagger hanging out of the girl's throat. She'd had a feeling about Roxie from the beginning and should have offed her as soon as she saw them onstage together.

The frame she held of Beckham slipped out of her hands. Shards of glass scattered across the floor. She got on her hands and knees, ignoring the glass as she grabbed his picture. Her palms were prickled and now bleeding, but his picture was still perfect.

No harm done.

She brushed her thumb against his smiling face. She'd do anything for him. It had been that way since the first time she'd seen him. She'd been his ever since.

She'd come so close, so many times now. At one of his shows, he'd looked at her, devouring her with his eyes.

The guard wouldn't let her go backstage that night. But revenge was sweet. She made sure his blood trickled out slowly.

She was too close now. Just a slight change of plans.
Roxie.

Roxie would have to go first. Security was tighter and she'd have to be more careful, but she'd always loved a challenge.

She twitched and on shaky legs stood up and made her way across the room. She grabbed her pills and tossed one back. The twitching stopped a few minutes later. Blood continued to slowly trickle down her arms and onto the counter, but she didn't notice.

There wasn't time to make any mistakes. It would take discipline and the cunning of a fox.

She smiled. Within a few days, Roxie would be dead.

13 PASSAGE

"I like that Beckham Woods." Ellen smiled. "He is a *hunk*."

Ian snorted at his mom then twisted around when he heard Sparrow laughing.

"My wife agrees," he grumbled.

Her lips lifted on one side, along with an eyebrow. "You don't?"

He took a long drink of water. "Yeah, yeah, he's pretty hot." He rolled his eyes and winked at his mom.

"He doesn't even come close to your hotness, Orville," Sparrow said. "Except when he dances ... and ... sings."

He lowered his head but didn't take his eyes off her, giving her a look that made her shift in her seat. "You want me to dance and sing, baby?" he asked softly. He leaned across the table and settled right in front of her face. His nose touched hers. "Seems like I remember some good times in this house doing just that," he whispered. His lips moved to her ear. "Maybe we can go upstairs in a little bit and reminisce."

He moved back slowly and sat down.

"Dang," Sparrow said shakily.

"You *do* remember," he said, smiling.

Sparrow glanced nervously at Ellen, but she was focused on Journey. She hadn't set her down since they'd pulled in the driveway that morning.

"Do your parents always act like this?" Ellen asked Journey.

Journey let out a long string of gibberish, and when they cracked up, she did too.

And then Ellen repeated what she'd been asking since they got there: "Are you *sure* you can't stay longer?"

"I wish we could, Mom. I really do. I'll have to fly you out when we've got a few days off."

They stayed around the house visiting, until it was time to go to the venue. On the drive, Ian caught Sparrow laughing to herself and smiled, wondering if she was thinking about when he'd carried her upstairs. He'd completely shocked her with his moves in the little striptease reenactment. And she'd shocked him more by taking his hand and showing him how instantly turned on it made her. He freaking loved *married* Little Bird; she was all kinds of bold.

"*Dang girl, dang girl, dang girl, dang girl, dang girl, dang,*" he sang softly.

Sparrow lost it then. She shook her head and wiped her eyes as she tried to catch her breath. "You are such a nut."

He kissed her hand. "Your hot nut, you mean."

"Ew."

"Yeah, that didn't work, did it?"

"No." She took another deep breath and looked at him. "Seriously, though, *Magic Mike*. Where have *you* been this whole marriage?"

He smirked. "Gotta spread some things out, little at a time, to keep the love alive."

"Our love is alive," she said, waving off his words and then pointing at him. "I'm gonna need to see that again, *tonight*, the minute you're off that stage."

"Yes, ma'am."

Beckham took the last picture with a fan and then he couldn't get out of there fast enough. Howie stepped into place beside him as he walked out the door.

"Johnny said it took some convincing, but she agreed to wait in your bus until you got there," Howie said.

Beckham grinned. "Tell Johnny he's getting a raise."

She was drifting off when he walked in. His eyes drifted down the length of her body, stretched out on the couch, and he couldn't stop smiling. Someone yelled outside and Roxie jumped up, dazed. He steadied her.

"Hey, thanks for waiting for me," he said, pulling her in for a hug.

"I'm so tired. I better get going."

"No—really?" he asked, unable to hide his disappointment. "Stay. We can sleep."

She laughed. "Seriously?"

"Well, I'm kinda tired, too. It was a great show though. I'm always a little wired after one like that, even though I'm exhausted."

"Yeah, I know what you mean. I get like that too. Tonight everything was just working. You sounded amazing."

He opened his mouth to say something and then stopped. "You really think so?"

"I wouldn't say it if I didn't mean it."

"I wasn't sure you liked what I do."

"Are you kidding? I love your music."

"You *do*?"

She nodded.

"I'm shocked. This day has been so enlightening."

She frowned then choked back a laugh, all in a matter of seconds—her face a clear window of warring emotions.

"Can I get you anything to drink?" he asked.

"Water sounds good."

"Are you always this easy?" He smirked.

She turned her head to the side. "I think you know the answer to that."

He laughed, grabbed a water out of the fridge, and handed it to her. "I do like this new, improved side I'm seeing," he teased.

All of a sudden, the bus lurched and they began moving. She held onto the counter and looked around.

"What are we doing? What about Sierra?"

"I hope you don't mind. She said she'd hang out with the people on the other bus tonight."

"*What?*"

"Come on, it'll be fun. We can sleep. Or we can talk all night, if you want. Or whatever..."

"That was awfully presumptuous of you," she yelled.

He pulled her to him and took her hand. "Don't be mad. I'd like some time with you. We can watch movies ... anything you want. Please? If it's really that bad in here with me, I'll stop the bus and you can get on yours. Deal?"

"You should have asked me." She bit the inside of her lip.

He stroked the inside of her wrist; it felt like satin. She stilled and watched his fingers.

"Would you have said yes?"

"No."

"Thought so."

She huffed. "You're not my type, Beckham. Let's just get that clear right now."

"Really? Didn't seem that way earlier..." He grinned mischievously. "I'm not your type, huh?"

She waved an arm over his body and said, *"This* is not what I'm talking about..."

He winced and then forced a smile. "So I have a 50-50 chance, is what you're saying."

She gave him a small shove.

"Look, we can argue all my flaws another time. Will you stay?"

FADE TO
Red

She nodded.

He exhaled. "Woohoo," he muttered under his breath. "I hated the way we ended things this afternoon when…"

"Not gonna happen," Roxie interrupted.

"Right. No. I didn't mean that we'd-…" He pressed the palm of his hand on his eye and looked at her with the other. "Let's watch a movie—here or the bigger TV in the back?"

"Well, your bus is incredible, by the way," she said. "I don't think I told you that earlier. I'd like to see the back, even if we don't stay there."

He turned around and led the way. On one side a twin bed fit into an alcove tucked behind curtains, and on the other wall was a bathroom and long vanity.

"Sierra's space," he said.

"It's great. Looks like a fun, little hideaway."

"Yeah, I've tried to give her my room, but she swears she loves this more."

He opened the door to his room and Roxie gasped. She wouldn't have believed a room like this existed on a bus. Cabinets and a flat screen TV were built-in on the left side. On the right side, a king-sized bed seemed to float out of the wall, with windows above the headboard. A section of glass ceiling over the bed gave a full view of the sky. There was still plenty of room to walk around on both sides of the bed. Another bathroom was to the right of the bed, at the end of the bus.

"What do you think? Back here?"

"No question!" She stared at the night sky moving above them. "I've never seen anything like this."

"Get comfortable," he said. "The bed is really the only place to sit back here, but it's roomy and I'll keep my hands to myself."

She sat with her back against the headboard, tucking her legs under the covers. He did the same, making sure to keep some space between them, and flipped through the channels. Once she realized he wasn't going to maul her,

135

she relaxed and didn't jerk away when his shoulder brushed hers.

"If you see something you wanna watch, tell me," he said.

She surprised him by scooting closer and laying her head on his shoulder. He didn't want to breathe, for fear of messing up the moment. But a few minutes later, he heard her breathing change and realized she'd fallen asleep. His heart kicked up a few beats with the thought that maybe she did trust him. He waited a few moments and then kissed her hair before closing his eyes too. She smelled like heaven.

An hour later he woke up with Roxie in his arms. They were completely under the covers now, both lying down, with Roxie's leg wrapped over his. He brushed her hair back and kissed her head again. He'd never felt anything better than this. Whatever it took, he wanted to win the heart of *this* Roxie—the one whose body and eyes told him something very different than her words.

He was having the best dream when Roxie squeaked next to him. He forced his eyes open and she sat up. She turned and stared down at him, mouth gaping open.

"Hi," he whispered, smiling.

She rubbed her hands down her face and muttered some nonsense back to him.

"Are you sleeping okay?" He pushed a strand of hair out of her eyes. She looked so adorable. "It's still the middle of the night. You should go back to sleep."

She didn't say anything for a long time and finally nodded. "I feel like I slept a long time."

"Me too."

Her voice sounded raspy and made everything inside him clench when she spoke.

"Sorry, I didn't mean to fall asleep so early."

"I love your voice." He lightly tickled her back.

Her wide eyes didn't blink. He was afraid he might have forced her silent with that comment.

"I slept better than I can ever remember sleeping," he admitted.

"Me too."

To his surprise, she laid down and nestled back into his shoulder. He thought she might have fallen back to sleep when she said, "I do think you've changed, Beckham."

He swallowed hard and waited to see if she'd say anything else. When she didn't, he said, "It means a lot to hear you say that. Thank you."

They were quiet for a few minutes and then Roxie got up and left the room. He heard her shut the bathroom door and while she was in there, he went to his bathroom, brushed his teeth, and tried to calm his hair a little. He was wasting his time with that.

When she came back in the room, she sat on the end of the bed. "Wanna go back to sleep?"

"Not really. You?"

She shook her head.

"Roxie? Can we talk?"

She looked away. "You can't make it right, Beckham. Okay?" She pulled on the sleeves of her shirt. "Can't we leave it at this sort-of-a-friendship thing we've finally got going? Isn't that enough?"

"I hope we're friends. I know I'm pushing it when we're ... getting along," he studied her reaction, "but I can't help but think it won't really be a friendship until I know our past."

"I've never met a man who wanted to talk so much." She scowled.

"I've had some therapy." He tilted his head and made a crazy face.

She laughed and it took everything in him to not kiss her.

"Can we have coffee first?" She bit her lip and peeked through the shade. "Where are we?"

"Close to Chicago, I think. But yes, to coffee. It'll make this day last longer. Are you hungry yet? I'll feed you breakfast, lunch, and/or dinner, if you'd like."

Her eyes glowed, but he couldn't tell what she was thinking. He wondered if he'd ever be able to.

"I like breakfast anytime."

"Good answer."

He went into the kitchen and started the coffee. He pulled out the eggs and bread and asked how she liked everything. The mood was light between them as they both worked to get breakfast on the table. As soon as it was ready, they sat down and ate quietly.

Her nerves picked up when she finished eating. He took her hand and waited.

She took a deep breath, and he reached out with his other hand and traced her jawline.

"Whatever you have to tell me, I'll listen. You don't need to be nervous with me. Okay?"

She began the free fall.

"I was—am—a huge fan of your music. Like, posters on my wall during high school kind of fan."

Her cheeks tinged pink when she said it. She started tearing pieces of her napkin onto her plate and wouldn't look at him.

"I was quiet, didn't have many friends, didn't really date at all ... I spent all my free time dancing. I saved up my money for your show—made my sister so mad because our parents wouldn't let her go. She's four years younger than me," she paused, her eyes skirting toward his. "I didn't want anyone to go with me because I was on a mission. I was going to meet you." She leaned back in her chair. "I got there and worked my way up to the front. It felt like you were singing to me the whole night. We were this close." She held up her hands to show him. "When the show was over, your guard let a few of us backstage and we went with you and the band to a club. We started talking there and then we danced together." She barely blinked. "It was good then too."

Her lip trembled and he wanted to pull her in his arms and kiss her, not hear what she had to say. He'd thought he wanted to know, but he was afraid he really, really did not.

"It was an incredible rush to not only meet you, but to actually dance with you, to have your attention ... I thought there was an instant tug between us so strong that even you felt it."

Her eyes flickered to his and looked as blue as he'd ever seen them. His heart had started to pound back at 'it was good then too' and wasn't slowing.

"I was naive. I thought magic was happening between us. When you kissed me, I imagined you felt it too. I thought every dream I'd ever had was coming true. We danced until the club closed. You did have more alcohol than anyone I'd ever seen, but like I said, I was naive and you didn't seem drunk to me. You asked me to go to your hotel with you, and I didn't even second guess my decision for one instant. I'd wished to be with you since I'd gotten hormones. Of course, I was going to lose my virginity with you, and hopefully be with you for the rest of my life too..."

Beckham dropped her hand and felt desolate instantly. He put his head in his hands. "Oh God..." Now he was the one who couldn't look at her.

"I'd say my first time was probably better than most. The second time I felt like I'd gone to heaven and didn't want to come back to earth."

He glanced up and she gave him a small smile, but there were tears running down her cheeks now. He reached up to wipe them and she turned her face.

"We fell asleep then and a few hours later, a huge man came in the room, not Howie, someone else. He woke me up and told me I had to go. You were completely out of it, never woke up. There were tons of pill bottles on the nightstand, and I did wonder if you were okay, because I made a lot of noise while I got dressed, hoping you'd wake up and tell me to stay, but you never did. Your bodyguard or whoever he was didn't give me any choice, he escorted me to a cab and sent me on my way. I knew you couldn't possibly want that, so I followed you to the next show I could make a week later and spent every dime I had getting another ticket. I did the same thing as before, worked my way up to the front, dancing. But you were fixated on someone else that night. I just thought you didn't see me and once you did, you'd be with me, so when I saw them doing the same thing as before, I ran back with the group going backstage. You had your arm around the petite brunette you'd watched during the show and I walked straight up to you. I said, 'Hey, I didn't get to tell you goodbye!' You said 'hey' but looked confused. You started walking away and I ran after you, saying, 'You don't remember me? How can you not remember me? It was just a week ago!' You pulled the girl tighter to you and said, 'Sorry, babe … I meet a lot of people…'"

Roxie stood up and walked to the kitchen counter.

"It gutted me. I left that night and drove the three hours home in a fog, devastated. My sister found me crying in my bedroom. I told her we'd kissed the week before, but then you didn't remember me. She couldn't get past the fact that we'd kissed at all, she was so proud of me. I didn't bother telling her the rest. I didn't want her to know what a fool I'd been."

Beckham came behind her. "Roxie."

She stiffened and he stepped back. The silence grew until Beckham felt like he would explode.

"Roxie," he said again and his voice broke. "I don't even know what to say." He took a staggered breath. "I can't tell you how sorry I am," he said. "About every single part of that." He rubbed his eyes and her face slowly came into focus. "You've treated me much better than I deserve. I can't believe you didn't kill me when you saw me again."

He bit the inside of his cheek. "This doesn't make it any better, but just know that I had to be high out of my mind to ever forget you. It doesn't seem possible. The moment I saw you dancing on that stage in San Diego was like a high beam turning on in my chest. I've lived each moment since then wanting to be with you." He reached his hand out to touch her cheek, but stopped and let it drop. "I despise who I was and I pray every day that I don't get even *close* to being like that again."

He closed his eyes and when he opened them and looked at her, the tears were falling down her face again. It killed him to see her pain.

"I have to believe I never really forgot," he said quietly. "And that's why I haven't been able to let you go."

14 SUBMIT

Roxie and Beckham sat on the couch. They'd stopped to fuel up and she'd nearly gotten off then, but he'd begged her to stay. She didn't know what to say to him. It had all been said. Well, not all. There was always more to say, but, for now, she was done. Something close to relief was surfacing.

"Can I touch you?" he asked softly. "Hold your hand?"

The look on his face since she'd told him was already haunting her. She'd thought about this conversation many times over the years, imagined telling him off and inflicting him with some of the hurt she'd felt. But now that she'd told him, the bitterness she'd carried felt more like the sorrow that it really was. Being around him the last couple of months and seeing that he was more decent than she ever knew—it made a big difference. Maybe the hurt would ease now that she'd confronted it.

She let him take her hand. They sat quietly, but it wasn't uncomfortable.

"Can I ask you something?"

She nodded.

"How old were you?"

"18."

He looked slightly relieved. "How old are you now?"
"23."

He looked at their hands and squeezed. "I don't know if you even can, but I hope one day you can forgive me, Roxie," he finally spoke. "I'm so sorry I hurt you." He lifted her hand to his cheek and held it there. He looked at her, his eyes unwavering, and she believed him.

"Thank you. I think ... it's time I move on. Worse things have happened than all this." She shrugged. "We were both a lot younger and both made mistakes," she said. "I've acted like a child this whole tour. I'm sorry I've been so difficult. I'd hoped I wouldn't even have to deal with you, you know, get lost in the group." She gave a small smile. "Once I realized it wasn't going to be that way, I should have left instead of being so awful to you."

"I'm glad I talked you into staying. You're the only one I've been able to see, Roxie." The grey in his eyes seemed lit from behind. "And you have nothing to be sorry about." He lowered their hands to his thigh and played with her fingers. "I know it's too soon to ask, but ... do I have any chance in hell with you?"

This time the silence was painful. It dragged on and on until he stood up and looked down at her. She stared up at him and was unable to look away. She tried to speak a few times, but couldn't.

He pulled her up and they stood inches apart. They'd stood this way so many times before. Every night they'd touched more than this onstage, but now it was more intimate than it had ever been. She reached up and touched his hair, his ear, his cheek. His breath caught and he leaned into her hand. Her eyes closed as she traced his nose and his lips.

"I think maybe you've always had a chance with me," she whispered.

Her eyes were still closed when he kissed her. Their lips had barely locked when her stomach dropped out. Her tongue touched his bottom lip, making him squeeze her tighter against him. Slow and deliberate, he teased just under her top lip until she gripped the back of his head and drew him in deeper.

Nothing felt close enough. She couldn't tell if he was trembling or if it was just her. He fisted her hair, pulling her back to look at him, and when she did, he stalked forward and pinned her against the wall. His eyes looked wild, the color undefined, but the intensity made her whole body feel like lead. He lifted her up and wrapped her legs around him, his hands squeezing her thighs, but not going past that point.

The restraint was making her crazy. He kissed along her jaw and down her neck. She arched her back and he pulled away again, cursing under his breath. His eyes searched hers.

"I've had the hardest time reading your signals," he said in a raspy voice.

"I won't play games if you won't, Beckham," she whispered. She felt reckless and couldn't bother caring at the moment. "What do you want?"

"I haven't been playing games. I want *you*. Remember? I said I want *everything*."

They stared at each other for a moment before crashing into each other again, holding nothing back.

A faint knock on the bus door got louder and louder.

"I'm not answering it," he whispered. "Let's pretend we aren't here." He carried her toward the back room. His hands gripped her bottom as he lifted her higher and he squeezed. "Ahhh. Fuck me. I've been dying to do this for months." He squeezed her cheeks harder. "You have the best a-"

The knocking got louder.

"Ignore it," he whispered.

"You should see who it is."

He growled and set her down, bending to level with her eyes. "I'm busy."

She crinkled her nose and laughed, backing up. He advanced, intent and steady, ready to pounce.

When she reached the door to his bedroom and stepped in, he put his hands on her shoulders and turned her around, her back to his chest. A mirror faced them and he looked at her in the mirror before moving her shirt aside and kissing down her neck and shoulder. He glanced up and saw her watching him and smiled, his tongue softly tracing where his lips had been.

Her eyes closed and she leaned her head back onto his chest. His hands went under her shirt, igniting her skin.

"Roxie," he whispered, his fingers tickling her stomach.

She opened her eyes and he was still watching her in the mirror. He unbuttoned a button on her shirt, and another, and all of them until her breath was sucked dry. With a flick of his hand, her shirt was on the floor and her chest fell with each exhale.

"I've been waiting a lifetime for you, Roxie Taylor," he said softly.

She reached up and unclasped her bra and turned around.

"You can't possibly know how beautiful you are." His voice was hoarse.

He picked her up again, burying his face in her breasts, and kicked the door shut behind him. She leaned up on both elbows when he laid her on the bed. He stood over her.

"I can't move," he said. "You're too much to take in, lying there on my bed."

"Don't make me wait," she whispered.

He jumped into action, tossing his clothes on the floor while her eyes grew round.

"You sure about that?" He pointed down, half-embarrassed and half-brazen. "You called it my weapon before—but seeing you naked makes me more than a little dangerous."

She gulped. "Please."

He was over her in no time, bracing his hands on either side of her shoulders. As he was about to slowly sink into her, she wrapped her legs around him and pulled him all the way in. He closed his eyes and stayed completely still.

"You're full of surprises, Roxie Taylor," he finally said.

"I'm an all or nothin' kind of a girl," she said between jagged breaths.

She swiveled her hips and he groaned.

He pulled out and plunged into her. And again, deeper. She trembled and gasped when he went even deeper. Her eyes closed and she shook her head back and forth on the pillow. When she opened her eyes, his eyes were still on her as he drove into her again and again. Faster.

"Give it to me, Rox. I want it all."

He put her legs on his shoulder to go even deeper and she felt it in every part of her body when they both dove headlong over the edge.

Hours later, he was apologizing for how small the shower in the bus was.

"Well, it's not built for two," Roxie teased.

"Come here then, I'll just crawl back inside you and we'll have more room."

She splashed him with water and laughed. "I need time to recover. You wore me out that last time."

He kissed the tip of her nose, looking at her with what she could only perceive as devotion. *I must be dreaming.*

"My poor girl. Let me get you to bed."

She got out of the shower and turned to see if he was getting out. He was right behind her, his mouth hanging open, staring at her backside.

"Sorry, it's going to take forever for me to get used to seeing you naked. You are exquisite, Rox—hey! Don't cover up that work of art." He scowled at her and pulled the towel back down. His smile took over his face again. "There..."

She snatched the towel back and lifted an eyebrow. "I'm cold."

"I have just the thing for that ... it'll take care of the ache I left inside you. You won't even have to move," he whispered. "Come here."

He pulled her back to the bedroom and worshipped her body with his mouth and tongue and fingers until she was crying his name again and again and finally begging for him to stop.

Her eyes were still closed when his hands ran lightly over her hip. She looked at him over her shoulder and smiled.

"I thought I was dreaming," he said.

"I think we both were."

"This feels awfully real." He turned her over to face him and leaned over her. He sank into her, an inch at a time. She closed her eyes and arched into him.

"It does," she agreed.

There was a knock on the bus door. It sounded distant at first and then turned into pounding.

"Shit."

"They're serious this time," Roxie said.

"I guess I can't ignore them forever."

She shook her head. He pushed into her one more time and kissed her. Then he pulled out.

"I'm bloody murdering whoever this is," he muttered. "Don't forget where we were."

She nodded, wide-eyed, unable to tear her eyes from him. His body was so beautiful. She didn't know another word for it. She wanted time to just stare at him. He threw on his clothes and closed the bedroom door behind him. She sat on the bed, trying to catch her breath.

Anthony's voice carried through the bus, but she couldn't tell what he was saying. He didn't sound happy, but it was hard to tell with him sometimes. He acted way more aggravated than he ever was. Beckham's voice rose too, and she heard her name. Roxie stood up and walked to the door to see if she could hear anything else. She was about to go out there and caught a glimpse of herself in the mirror. She looked like she'd been thoroughly sexed up.

Exactly, she thought, and giggled. She heard her name again, this time closer. She threw her clothes on and sat on the bed, putting her head in her hands. This couldn't be good.

There was a quick rap on the door and Beckham opened it. "Can you come out here? I want you to hear this."

He took her hand and walked her out to the couches. Anthony stood with his hands on his hips and glared at both of them.

Beckham motioned to Anthony. "He doesn't think this looks good—you staying on the bus with me—and doesn't want tension with the other dancers. No 'preferential treatment' allowed on his clock. And I want you both to know … I don't give a shit whether anyone cares or not." He kissed her hand and his grin was mischievous and cocky and made her heart tumble over itself. "I *do* prefer you over anyone else I've ever met in my life and I don't care who knows it. If I had my way, you'd be on the bus with me the rest of the tour and move in with me afterward."

Roxie's mouth dropped and Anthony squealed. She looked at Anthony and he was pressing his lips together, trying to look mad and not too excited at the same time.

Beckham wasn't finished.

"In fact, *would* you please stay? We can work it out with everyone. They'll understand. I need time with you,

Roxie." He leaned down and kissed her neck and she jumped.

She took a deep breath and a step back from Beckham, dropping her hand from his. "I-I should go ... Anthony's right. I don't want to make anyone u-"

His smile fell. "Think about it? Sierra can be on here with us too. Please. No games, right?" He leaned in and put his hands on her face, looking in her eyes. "I'm afraid if you go out that door, I'll lose you again ... I don't want any more barriers." He backed up and put his hands on his head. "God, I sound like a frickin' wuss. But I *don't care*! We finally got somewhere!" he yelled. Quieter, he said in her ear, "I've never used the words 'made love' in my life, before *you*, but that's exactly what I did with you."

Roxie's heart hummed, but she glanced at Anthony who looked about ready to burst into dance right there on the bus. She took a step away from Beckham.

"I'm not going anywhere—well, except back to my bus, but ... that's not what I meant. Uh," she laughed awkwardly, "let me get used to the idea of not hating you." She gave a wobbly smile. "We should try taking things a little slower. We seem to have the sex figured out." Her face grew warm, but she ignored it and went to stand by Anthony.

Beckham pressed his lips together and looked down. "If that's what you want, okay, but ... we don't need to go slow for me, Roxie. Just so we're clear. I know what I want."

Anthony clapped his hands together. "Well, this was really fun. AND informative. I think you're making the right call, Rox." He winked at her. "But let me just be the first to say," he clasped both of their arms, "you guys will make the prettiest babies."

"Oh my God!" Roxie groaned. "You're both crazy."

Beckham just raised an eyebrow and smiled.

The whole clan was hanging out when Roxie got on the bus. Justin did a cat call and Vanessa laughed, hitting him in the arm.

"Someone had a good night," Brad said wistfully.

"So did you," Shelton muttered.

"Totally," Brad answered. "But look at her. She's all sparkly."

Brooke's arms were folded and she didn't say a word.

"Hi!" Roxie gave a general wave.

"Details!" Vanessa demanded.

"We talked." Roxie shrugged. "Had some things to clear up…"

"Oh please. You can't tell us you only talked!" Shelton yelled. "Take a look in the mirror, honey!"

The guys laughed and Vanessa shushed them. "Let her talk."

"That's all…" Roxie said. "What did I miss?"

Brad looked like he wanted to kill her for not spilling more dirt. Vanessa just looked determined.

Roxie walked back to her bunk before anyone else could say anything. She crawled in the dark and felt something all over her mattress. Flipping the little light switch on, she looked around. Little strips of material were everywhere. She opened the curtain so she could see better. Her blanket from home had been cut into tiny strips. It was the blanket she and Leo always cuddled under to watch movies together. The books that she kept by her pillow were shredded.

Just like that, her mood tipped upside down. Tears filled her eyes and she hit the wall with her fist. She grabbed a handful of material and paper and walked back to where they were still discussing whether she'd slept with Beckham or not.

"Who did this?" she demanded.

All eyes turned in her direction.

"What are you talking about?" Shelton asked.

"Who destroyed my blanket and books?" Roxie shouted.

Vanessa stood up. "Show me. What happened?"

Everyone walked back to the bunk and gasped when they saw it.

"Did you do this, Brooke?" Roxie got in Brooke's face. "You did, didn't you!"

"No! Get out of my face. Why would I do that?"

"You're the only one who has it out for me!" Roxie yelled.

Brad took her arm. "Let's get Anthony and Beckham and figure this out. Come on."

"I don't want to waste Anthony and Beckham's time if you're not going to tell the truth," Roxie said quietly to Brooke.

"There's no way you can think I did any of that," Brooke whispered, her lip trembling and then settling into a sneer. "And certainly no way you can prove it."

Everyone looked at Brooke then and it was silent for a beat.

"Shit," Shelton muttered.

Roxie moved so fast, Brad couldn't stop her. She shoved Brooke against the wall and said, "You leave me and my things alone. Got it?"

"I. Didn't. Do. It," Brooke said. And then louder, "But *someone* sure does hate you..." She started smiling and then laughed until tears were running down her face.

Roxie's whole body shook. She let Brooke go and walked off the bus. Johnny was standing outside, guarding her door.

"Let's go find a good deli, Johnny. I need to be around someone normal."

"Sounds good to me."

Hanging out with Johnny helped. He was a nice guy, nothing too intense or deep, but very pleasant. Exactly what she needed after experiencing every emotion possible in the last 24 hours. After they ate, she sat outside and

Skyped Leo and they talked for a couple of hours. She didn't know what she'd do if she couldn't see him every day like this, even though it sucked that it was through a screen a lot of the time. His visits helped more, but Skyping helped them get by. So far they hadn't gone more than a week without seeing each other. Even though it was expensive with all the plane tickets, it was completely worth it.

When she got to hair and makeup, her normal girl, Suzanne, seemed to realize she needed a boost and did a cute braid in her up-do. Roxie loved it. Tracy, the makeup artist that usually did Roxie's makeup, was out sick, so the new girl, Coco, took over. She was a little heavy handed, but when she was done, Roxie had to admit that the crimson lipstick totally matched the mood she was in.

Beckham was pacing the bus when Sierra got on.

"I don't know whether the pacing is a good sign or not," she said.

"Well, she left, so, obviously not a great sign, but," he bit his lip and beamed at her, "we did have a great night."

Sierra made a gagging noise. "TMI, little brother, TMI!"

"No, not what I meant! Well, that too, but it was so much more than that. I feel better than I have ... ever. We talked. A lot. I know why she's been so angry all this time. I deserved every ounce of it, but ... it was a perfect night."

"When did you become such a girl?" Sierra laughed.

He stood still. "I know. I'm making myself nauseated, but I don't even give a fuck." He looked at her and laughed. "I think I could love her, Sierra."

She dropped her bag on the floor. "Really? Isn't it a bit soon for that? You've had one good night with her and *love?*"

"Maybe. Maybe not. I don't know. It doesn't feel sudden. She's invaded my brain for nearly four months now. I've never felt this, that's all I know."

Sierra wrapped her arms around him. "I'm so happy for you, Beck. I really am."

"I want to have Mom fly in—maybe when we're in Atlanta or New Orleans—so she can meet her."

"You've never had Mom meet a girlfriend. Wait—*is* she your girlfriend?"

He hit her over the head with a folded up magazine.

"Oh yeah, maybe you *are* finally growing up," Sierra snorted.

He rolled his eyes at her. "I know. Let's not get ahead of ourselves."

"You're the one who's all 'I could love her' and blah-de-blah!" Sierra laughed. "Prepare Mom, so she doesn't pass out from the shock…"

He bopped her over the head with a banana.

"Ow! Why do I keep getting hurt over this relationship? Use a pillow next time, dammit!"

He resisted texting Roxie all afternoon. He was afraid he might have already scared her off. He'd lost his mind since the moment he met her. Well—oh God, he couldn't believe how he'd treated her before. Just further proof that getting clean was the best thing he'd ever done. He'd been a complete asshole. The fact that she was even considering giving him another chance was unbelievable. He had so much to make up for and couldn't wait to start.

He talked to his mom but didn't tell her about Roxie. He'd wait and surprise her, despite what Sierra said. He bought a ticket for her to meet them in Atlanta in a few days. He showered and did vocal exercises while he shaved. Maybe Roxie would stay with him at least part of the drive tonight. They had a long trek to Tampa and she didn't have to stay the whole night if that made her uncomfortable.

It only took one touch, and her stiff posture let him know they'd lost ground. Before last night, she'd begun to melt into his touch. There was no melting tonight. When her eyes met his, it was confirmed. His voice faltered and he missed a beat. Scrambling for control, he held his mic out to the crowd and let them sing a few bars of his song while he looked at Roxie. She wouldn't look at him.

He wanted to throw her over his shoulder and kiss some sense into her, but he threw his frustration into the music instead. She matched his aggression, and it was hot as hell.

As soon as they'd done their final encore, he whispered in her ear. "I'm not giving up. You're coming with me tonight."

"No, I'm not," she whispered back to him.

And then she surprised him. "Anthony was right," she said over her shoulder as she walked away.

What the hell did you mean by that?
He texted her in the middle of the night, unable to stop thinking about her. He was startled when she answered right away.

I need to keep the peace on the bus. And it was all going so fast anyway.

And a minute later: **I'm still not sure about you, Beckham.**

He cursed and continued tossing and turning all night long.

The next day was torturous. They drove all day and didn't arrive in Tampa until late that evening. He ran along the beach at midnight and got up with the sunrise, running until the stitch in his side wouldn't let up. He was so distracted he ran into another jogger and nearly knocked her over. She never even said a word when he apologized. Hopefully she wouldn't show up later in the media, looking for money to exploit his absentmindedness.

He hadn't texted Roxie again. He didn't know what to say. He was snappy with Sierra that afternoon and she told him to go run again. He would have if it hadn't been time for dinner.

Nate called as he was leaving to eat.

"Have you seen the latest pictures?" he asked.

"No—where?"

"I emailed them to you. Hang on, I'll text it real quick."

When Beckham's phone buzzed, he pulled back and opened the picture. It was a little blurry, but it looked like him dancing … a long time ago.

"What is this?"

"Recognize the girl you're with?"

He looked at the picture again and to the left of him, her eyes staring up at him, was Roxie.

"Shit."

"Yeah."

"Is this news to you?" Nate asked.

"No, she told me about it the other night … I didn't remember her."

"These are the things you're supposed to tell me, Beckham, so I can do damage control. The press is running with this. I hope you really like this girl, because the media will either have you married in about two minutes or they will demolish her."

"I do," Beckham said. "I really like her."

156

"Okay, well, I'm gonna have another talk with Johnny and Al to make sure they're on top of her—you know not everyone will be excited about this."

"I know. Thanks, Nate."

Beckham heard him before he saw him. That little voice sounded so familiar. He rounded the corner of his bus, rushing to get inside the auditorium on time.

"Beckham!" the little boy called. He dropped the hand of the girl he was with and ran over to Beckham.

The girl waved shyly at Beckham but stayed back.

"Mavid!"

Leo's head fell back and he laughed. "You're so funny."

That lisp. It slayed Beckham. "So great to see you, little dude. What are you doing here?" He bent down and gave him a fist bump.

"Visiting my mom."

"Awesome. I haven't seen your mom since tryouts! Where has she been hiding? Are you having fun?"

"Yeah, just got here, but we went to the beach once already."

"Well, that's great."

"And you see my mom every-"

Howie put his hand on Beckham's shoulder and cleared his throat. "Sorry to interrupt, but it's time." A golf cart rolled up to Beckham.

"Sorry, buddy, I gotta get to the show. You watchin' tonight?"

"Whatever she says." He pointed a thumb behind his shoulder and grinned.

"Gotcha. Well, I'd love to see you again before you go. You should come visit me on the bus..."

"Yethhh!" Leo shook his fist up and down and ran off, yelling, "Bye, Beck!"

Beckham smiled all the way to the back entrance. He jumped off the cart and ran inside, waving to the fans who were screaming on the sidelines.

Suzanne hurriedly put product in his hair and tamed the waves. Someone new powdered his nose. She grinned at him and got to work.

"Who are you?" he asked.

"Coco—Tracy took a few days off."

He glanced down and tried to hold still and not sneeze while she passed the makeup brush over his face. She had on a pair of cowboy boots that were an unusual shade of blue.

"Cool boots." He held still but his eyes studied her. "You remind me of someone..."

She smiled and shrugged. "I hear Zooey Deschanel sometimes."

He laughed. "That's it—you really do look like her! It's a compliment. She's a nice girl."

Anthony came through, clapping his hands. "Move it, Beck. They're gonna be bitter pretty soon if you don't get out there."

"Thanks, girls. I'm gonna trust that you made me look good in less than five minutes." He made a face and ran toward the stage.

Roxie was smiling tonight. Not at him necessarily, but it was apparent she was happier than the last time he'd seen her. He'd take it. Either way, whether she wanted him or not, they were scorching together onstage. He never wanted to look away. She turned him inside out. It was all he could do to focus on the words of the songs. He lived for every moment he could touch her again.

Backstage, he bypassed the VIPs and ran to catch up with her before she went to her bus.

"Tonight, Roxie. Come with me. Let's have dinner ... or walk on the beach? We have a short drive, so I don't think we'll be leaving until later."

"I have family here ... I think we're gonna drive on to Miami and stay in a hotel tonight."

"I'd love to meet your family..."

She nodded. "Yeah, you will. I still need to tell you all about them." She looked over his shoulder and cringed. "You better go though—a riot's starting back there with beautiful, impatient women..."

He leaned over and kissed her quickly on the cheek and then the top of her hand before he went to autograph CDs and cleavage and shirts. He drew the line at underwear. Never again.

15 VACATE

Ian borrowed a car that morning, so they could go swim in
Roxie's hotel pool. It felt like summer in Miami—January
be damned—and he wanted to take advantage of it.
Donny called right before they left. They usually spoke at
least once a week, with Ian wanting to hear everything the
doctors were saying, and Donny only wanting to talk about
the tour. But this morning he sounded happier than he had
in a long time. He was done with chemo, and his doctors
couldn't believe he was doing so well. Donny said he had a
whole new outlook on life, and that it was worth it to be
sick, to feel this grateful for life now.

   After they hung up, the conversation kept playing
back in Ian's mind. He loved Donny and hoped he had a
lot of years left. But he didn't ever want to get so detached
from living that it took nearly dying to see what he had.
The thought seemed foreign now—he knew how great his
life was and didn't think the gratefulness would ever fade,
but … it happened all the time. Even people who seemed
to have it all struggled with complacency, boredom …
discontentment. What kept passion alive?

   Water splashed in his face and he was glad for the
distraction. He didn't need to get all emo on their morning
off. He'd keep thinking about it though and maybe a song

would come out of it, maybe some answers. He looked down at his little girl and thought his love for her would explode right out of his chest. She loved the water. He held her back against his chest and her little feet went crazy, kicking. Leo jumped in the pool and swam up to him, smiling at Journey. The little boy was such a nice kid, and he was gentle with Journey, so that made Ian like him even more.

Sparrow jumped into the pool and wrapped her arms around his back.

"You okay?" she asked. "You're so quiet today."

"Just thinking. Talking to Donny got my mind going about some things."

He turned around to face her and pulled her close. Her legs still fit around his waist with Journey between them.

"Do I tell you enough how this life with you is the best gift I've ever been given?" he asked, reaching out to touch her face.

"Every day."

Sparrow stretched out on a lounger next to Chloe. Roxie and Leo played in the pool for a while and then went to get a snack at the vending machine. When they came back, Leo got back in the pool and Roxie stayed by Sparrow and Chloe. They were talking in hushed voices and laughing a lot, which made Ian suspect they were discussing sex. Sparrow claimed he thought everything was about sex, though. Not necessarily true ...not *everything*. He'd done a lot of reflecting today without sex being in the forefront of his mind. Granted, keeping passion alive did involve sex too, but ... okay, maybe everything did go back to sex. But, really, what was so wrong with that?

Leo did a huge jump in the pool and Ian called out: "Solid 7!" Journey laughed so hard she got the hiccups. "Journey thinks that should've been an 8."

Leo wanted to make her laugh again, so the game began. Ian and Journey were the judges; Ian with a score between one and ten, and Journey with how loud she cackled. She thought Leo was the funniest human she'd ever seen.

They'd met Chloe and Leo once before, but Roxie usually didn't come around when he was in town. Ian didn't blame her. He'd want his family all to himself too. Sparrow always spent extra time with Roxie when Leo went back home. She was lost without her boy.

The girls sat up and Roxie jumped off the lounger. He and Leo paused the game to see what was going on.

"I forgot my outfit for tonight!" she yelled. "I'll run over there now, so I'll have plenty of time to eat and get ready. Wanna ride with me, Leo, or stay in the pool?"

"Stay in the pool!"

"Of course." She smiled and blew him a kiss. "I won't be long!"

She hadn't been gone five minutes when a redhead walked into the pool area and asked Sparrow if Roxie was still there. She stopped in mid-sentence when she saw Ian and he regretted not going underwater when he saw her come in the gate. She looked like a vulture ready to strike. She stepped closer to the pool and looked down at him.

"Ian Sterling? How did I get so lucky?" She flashed teeth and put a hand on her hip. "Roxie Taylor sure gets around."

"Not sure what you're implying. I'm here with my family," he said.

Leo popped up beside him.

"Hey, Leo, would you please sit with the girls for a minute?" Ian asked.

"And then I can get back in the pool?"

"Of course."

Leo swam to the ledge and climbed out.

"And you are?" Ian looked at the girl.

"Mirielle Wethers, with *Rolling Stone*. I've been leaving messages for you for weeks. Looks like I just needed to find Roxie to find *you*." She smirked and stepped into the shade.

"Ah, Mirielle, you need to stop with the Roxie innuendos. Beckham told me about you and if I'd wished to speak to you, I would've called you back. That's how that works." He looked over his shoulder to Sparrow. "Hey, baby, could you come here, please?"

Sparrow shifted her long legs off the lounger. He got out of the pool and enjoyed watching her walk toward him.

He looked at Mirielle, who wasn't bothering to hide her annoyance. "This is my wife, Sparrow. If you say anything about me, it should be that I love my wife. We're having a little time off before the show tonight, and I'm asking you to leave. Now."

Her eyes flashed and she stepped closer. "I just want-"

"No." He handed Journey to Sparrow. "Call Will," he said under his breath.

Sparrow walked away with the baby and called Will. He'd taken a break right before Mirielle came, but Ian knew he wasn't far. In moments, Will was walking toward them.

"Quit giving *Rolling Stone* a bad name—we know you don't work for them anymore." Ian turned and said over his shoulder: "This is Will—he'll make sure you get to your car safely."

He put a towel around his neck and waited until Mirielle was gone before getting back into the pool.

Roxie pounded on Beckham's door.

"Hey! Come in!" He was smiling until he got a good look at her face. "What's going on?"

He took her hand and led her up the steps. She was clutching something in one hand, but held onto him with the other.

"Hey, you're shaking. What happened?"

"I went to wardrobe just now—I meant to grab my first dress last night, so I could hang out at the hotel as long as possible, and-" She held up her dress.

It looked like a blowtorch had been taken to it. Completely charred. Beckham barely touched it and material crackled to the ground.

"What the hell?" His eyes were huge.

"All of my outfits are like this. Only mine. After the other night, when I stayed with you ... my blanket and all my books were cut up into little pieces. I didn't-"

"*What?* Why didn't you tell me?" he demanded.

"I didn't want to bring you into it. I hoped it was just a pointless stunt and nothing serious." A tear fell down her cheek and she angrily swiped it away.

"Hey, come here." He hugged her close then pulled back just enough to study her face. "This involves me, whatever happens with you. I care about you and want to make sure you're always safe. I can't do that if you keep me in the dark. Don't shut me out. Okay?"

She nodded.

"What's going on here?"

"Well, I was mad, but now I'm scared, too. I confronted Brooke and-"

"Wait a minute—Brooke? You think she did this?"

"She's the only one I've had any issues with and she seemed to think it was funny the other day. She said I couldn't prove that she did it."

Beckham shook his head. "Brooke? I know she's not the nicest person, but I've never thought she'd do anything this awful. You really think it's her?"

"I trust everyone but her. As crazy as it sounds, I still think she purposely tripped Sparrow, hoping she'd get that song with Ian. And I don't know how anyone else would get on the bus."

"Okay, let me get my phone. I'll need to talk to Nate and security, and eventually Brooke too."

Anthony knocked before Beckham had called anyone. Nate stood beside him, mumbling something under his breath.

"You look like the grim reapers, coming to carry us off to our death. I guess you've heard about it already?" Beckham asked, stepping aside to let them in.

They stopped short when they saw Roxie.

Nate cleared his throat. "I wanted to wait until after the show but didn't want you blindsided by any reporters. There's a pile of reporters out there, ready to pounce on this story."

"How would the reporters know about any of this?"

Nate and Anthony looked at Beckham like he'd lost it.

"What do you mean? They're the ones who came out with the story," Nate said.

"How did they find out about Roxie's things?"

They looked at Roxie then and back to Beckham. Nate shook his head. "No, I don't know anything about that..."

"The story just came out about the two of you having a son," Anthony jumped in.

"What? What are you talking about?" Beckham stuttered.

They all looked at Roxie and she turned completely white. Her mouth opened, but no words came out.

"*What?*" Beckham said, turning to Roxie.

She knew her eyes looked wild and she shook her head, but still couldn't say anything. Tears fell, but she didn't know if the tears were new or from all she'd just told him.

"I didn't believe it was true, but now I'm not so sure," Anthony said, staring at Roxie. "We came over here to do damage control with the press, but it looks like the joke might be on us. Is Leo Beckham's son, Roxie?"

"Are you kidding me? *Leo?*" Beckham looked at everyone in the room, as if the facts were striking him like bullets, one right after the other.

Her stomach fell. She realized how this might look. She'd been distant and angry from the beginning, trying to do everything she could to keep him at a distance. Instead of using it to her advantage, she'd been shaken that the press had taken their pictures. Most dancers would have killed for any press, but she'd been the opposite of what he'd expected every time.

And he'd taken her virginity and forgotten about her. She had every reason to be bitter.

She knew it didn't look good, but she couldn't seem to stop shaking long enough to defend herself. This day—it was one too many slivers of insane.

Beckham walked within a foot of Roxie, all earlier softness gone. He stopped in front of her and put both hands on the wall, on either side of her face. He leaned down until they were about an inch apart.

"Who is Leo, Roxie?"

"My son," she whispered.

"You have a—that little boy is *yours?*" He shook his head, but his eyes still didn't seem focused. "Why didn't you tell me you have a son? Is he *mine?*" His voice was quiet but harsh.

She shoved him away from her. She felt like she was looking at a stranger.

"*No*, he isn't yours! What the hell are you thinking?"

"Let me see a picture of him." He pointed to Nate and grabbed the paper out of his hands. A picture of Leo and Roxie was blown up. He sucked in a breath and sat down, staring at the picture.

When he looked up at Roxie, his eyes were tortured. "I know Leo. I met him. At the audition, I met him. I saw him again yesterday. Mavid," he whispered. He shook his head. "He's ... a great kid." He looked at the ceiling and stood back up, walking close to her. "Here's what the hell I'm thinking: *he looks like me*! I'm thinking, how the hell did I not see it the very first time we met? I'm thinking, you've been hating me since you got here and I haven't fully made sense of it. Until now..." He ran his hands through his curly hair and pointed at it and then the picture of Leo. "His hair is just like mine. His eyes are the same weird color as mine ... the way we-" His voice broke and he hit the wall next to him.

Roxie jumped. She was terrified and ready to bolt. "I *told* you why I hated you. And Leo looks like his *dad*."

"I didn't realize how *much* you really hated me. Now I know. I just ... I can't even believe this. I want to get to know him." He took a jagged breath. "*Fuck*, Roxie. How could you keep this from me?"

"He is *not* yours," she hissed.

He studied her face. "Look at me and show me the truth. Right now I only see lies. You've been lying to me all along. Why didn't you tell me you had a son?" He laughed, but it sounded hollow. "We slept together. Don't you think you should have told me that little fact about yourself?"

Pain zigzagged through her heart and she staggered back against the wall. "I've just tried to do a good job. And yes, I've gotten carried away with you. I've ... lost my mind ... about you. Again." A sob escaped and she clamped her hand over her mouth, the tears pooling into her hand. "I've missed Leo so much, I cry every time I talk to him. I've never been away from him like this. He's come to see me throughout the tour, and I figured you'd meet him when the time was right. I just needed to get through the tour. I didn't expect..."

"I'd like to get a paternity test," he said. As if she hadn't spoken a word. "If you won't willingly do it, I'll get a court order to make it happen."

She gulped and looked everywhere but at him. "I only came here to dance and to provide for Leo. It's obviously not working. I need to leave-" She stopped when he grabbed her arm.

"You're not making sense. We have more than *worked*, we've had something between us from the very beginning ... or at least, the beginning that I can remember. But that has nothing to do with this. Or maybe everything to do with it. I just want to know the truth! Why aren't you telling me the truth?" he asked desperately.

"You're not listening. I am *telling* you the truth! I have raised him and loved him and he is just fine without someone who is a drunk, drug-addicted, woman-chasing dick of a father. He's *mine*. Now, let go of my arm."

"You conveniently left out the time frame of when we slept together. How long ago was that? And what happened? Did we not use a condom?"

Roxie swallowed but didn't answer.

Anger washed over him like a red haze. He had tunnel vision for Roxie and she had to grip the wall to keep from crumbling to the floor.

"You fuckin' answer me, dammit. You don't get to go silent on me anymore," he whispered in her ear. "I've been drowning in those eyes from day one. I just didn't realize they were going to be the death of me."

The infatuation and lust unraveled around her, dropping instantly. The genuine affection she'd recently felt for him shriveled up. She'd thought they might actually be falling for each other, something real this time, but could see that was gone nearly as quickly as it came. They say there's a fine line between love and hate, but since it wasn't really love yet, it was so easy to dive right back into hate.

When Nate spoke, Beckham jumped back. For a moment, Roxie had forgotten anyone else was in the room.

"You can settle this easily, Roxie. Please don't make it complicated. I'm sorry we bombarded you today—we didn't even know you'd be with Beckham—but it looks like you have some explaining to do. Beckham deserves to know the truth. If this drags out in court, it will be a huge spectacle and cause an untold amount of grief for all of you. Reporters are already all over it. If we settle it quietly, it will become old news fast."

Roxie looked at Beckham, not even trying to hide the terror in her eyes. She touched his arm and her hand was shaking.

"Please, believe me." Her lips trembled. "He's *not yours*."

Beckham moved back until his legs hit the couch. He sat down and stared at Roxie, his eyes lifeless.

He looked at Nate and Anthony. "Can you find out how to get a paternity test done quickly? I want to be absolutely positive one way or the other."

"It will be easy if you are both agreeable to it," Nate said. "We can get someone to come test all of you—I don't think it takes very long to get the results. Roxie, you won't resist a DNA test, will you?"

She shook her head. "No. But it's a waste of time."

"Find someone who is reliable and can keep their mouth shut," Beckham said, ignoring her.

Nate nodded and immediately started dialing his cell. "I'll be right back." He held his finger up and left the bus.

"I'll just give you two a moment." Anthony backed out of the bus.

She could feel Beckham's eyes on her. She avoided looking at him.

"Why won't you tell me when it happened?" he asked.

"I feel just as sucker-punched as you, Beckham. The three of you all staring me down with hungry eyes when we're discussing *my son*. I can see now why you might wonder if he's yours, but it never crossed my mind that you would since he *isn't*. I met his father right after you and went out with him because, silly me, he looked a little bit like *you*."

"I'm sick of your smart-ass mouth," he muttered.

"Well, you've been all about it before now. Make up your damn mind."

He glared at her.

"Let me know when you want to do the test and I'll come back. In the meantime, I'm getting out of here."

"Don't even think about trying to get out of this, Roxie."

She leaned over him and got in his face.

"You can quit with the threats right about now. I might be bitchy, but I'm *not* a liar. I told you what happened between us and I don't owe you jack shit. And so help me, if my little boy is hurt in ANY way whatsoever because of this, you will pay."

He waved his hand dismissively, looking like he might hit the wall again. "Go," he hissed at her, "get out of here."

Roxie went back to the hotel and straight to her room, immediately looking up 'paternity tests' online. She was terrified there would be some loophole that would give Beckham doubt and he would try to take Leo away from her. She hoped he wasn't that vindictive, but she'd seen a side of him today she hadn't seen before and it scared her. When she saw that tests were 99% effective, she fell back on the bed and tried not to hyperventilate.

Johnny had gone back and forth with her from the bus to the hotel. When she walked to the pool to get Leo, the Sterlings had just left. Al was there guarding Leo and Chloe. Johnny told her Al would most likely start watching Leo full-time. Two additional guards would cover the other shifts. She didn't have time to have a freak out that she now had a life that involved needing constant security, but she was positive that would catch up with her later. Leo was splashing around the kiddie pool and Chloe had her feet in the water.

"Hi, loves!" She put on a cheerful face.

"Get in, Mom!" Leo sang.

"I need to talk to Chloe for a minute and then I will," she said.

"What's going on? You have the death grin on your face right now," Chloe said softly.

"You're not going to believe what just happened. I'm going to have to say it in code."

Chloe nodded and leaned in. "I have something to tell you too."

"Oh. You go first."

"A reporter came looking for you. Ian put her in her place and his bodyguard, Will, made sure she left. Will is *hot*." She laughed. "Okay, your turn."

"News is saying Woods is-" Roxie mouthed the rest. "*Leo's dad.*"

"Where in the world did they get that?"

"I have no idea."

"Well, what did you tell Bec-Woods?" Chloe looked at Leo, but he was on the other side of the pool, swimming toward them.

"That he's not, of course!" Roxie said it through her teeth and smiled at Leo as he got closer.

"So he's really not?" Chloe asked softly.

"Really not what?" Roxie's forehead went into tiny creases.

"Really not Beckham's?" she asked incredulously.

"I can't believe this." Roxie shook her head. "*No*, he's not. Why? You thought he was?"

"Well, yeah, I kinda did," Chloe admitted. "You've never told me everything that happened that night with Beckham. He even looks like him, Rox! I've thought it

FADE TO
Red

more than ever with you being on this tour—you've been
so weird with him."

"Look, Mama, I can hold my breath underwater!
Count!" Leo went under.

Roxie started whispering fast and snippy. "I lost my
virginity to him, Chloe, and then he had no idea who I was
the very next week. I've been carrying around that little
grudge with me for the last 5 years or so."

"Oh," Chloe looked at Leo who popped up, "I hoped
he was."

"How many seconds was that? Twelve?"

"Maybe thirteen," Roxie told Leo.

"I'm gonna do fifteen this time!" And back under.

"So he really is Kenneth's?"

"Yes! I told you he was Kenneth's back then!"

Chloe sighed.

"Why does everyone think I'm such a liar?"

Silence.

"And stop being so disappointed!" Roxie snapped.
"Just because Beckham looks all shiny bright with his
cleaned up self doesn't mean he is."

Leo popped up between their legs. "Was that fifteen?"

"Fourteen," Roxie said.

Back under.

"It's just sad because I bet Beckham actually wants
him to be his. And no one is a bigger loser than Kenneth,"
Chloe trailed off until the last words were barely said out
loud.

Roxie started to say something and then stopped. It
was true. Beckham had seemed almost disappointed when
she'd said he wasn't Leo's father. She had a moment of
sadness that Leo didn't have that.

She'd barely dated Kenneth, quickly losing interest
when he had nothing behind his good looks. They were
over weeks before she found out she was pregnant and he
wanted nothing to do with the baby. That was fine with
her. She wanted nothing to do with Kenneth. Back then

173

she'd wished it *was* Beckham's baby. She went through stretches of romanticizing the whole situation, making Beckham the father, but the more trouble he got into, the further she got from that fantasy.

"It doesn't do any good to wish. It's just not true."

"Well, damn."

"What did you say, Auntie?" Leo's head came out of the water and he was grinning.

"I said dammit," she sighed.

16 WANE

She paced the floor and studied her makeshift collages. She wished she was back in her apartment where she could think clearly. Everything had gone to hell. There was no way that was Beckham's son. No *way*. *She* was supposed to have his son.

She snatched the remote from the counter and turned off the TV. This changed everything. If Leo was Beckham's son, she'd have to ... accept him. She didn't want to upset Beckham. If he lost his son, he'd have a hard time getting over that and it would take longer for him to love her. She'd just have to get Leo to like her.

She'd need a few more days than she thought to deal with this news. It was going to take a little more work. The heightened security had been a bitch to deal with—it was driving her insane.

She removed the tacks from the latest picture of Leo she'd just put up by her bed. One by one she dropped tacks in her hand until there were so many, she barely felt it when one pricked her and she began bleeding all over the linoleum. She fixed the small holes in the picture, trying to piece them back together with her fingernail. In some places, you could barely see there was a hole there, but in others, it gaped even wider. His eyes, in particular, looked weird with all the holes.

The longer she looked at it, the worse she felt. Tears ran down her face when she looked at Beckham's son. She put a towel over his head and went and printed a new picture. When it popped out of the printer, she wiped her nose on her arm and pinned up his new picture.

There, that was better.

She would love him too. She'd always wanted to be a mother.

17 ROUND

Everyone just needed to stay the hell away and let Beckham process everything he'd heard in the last two hours.

Nate called him an hour before he was supposed to go onstage. "I'm bringing someone to do the testing during intermission. It'll take a few days to get the results back, but we can get started on finding out the truth."

"Thanks, Nate. In the meantime, what do I do about Roxie?"

"She's a huge part of your show. I can't imagine someone filling that role at this point. Can you two do your job, no matter the outcome of the test?"

"I can't imagine pulling that off. At the moment, I regret ever meeting her." He let out a big breath, not believing what he was saying. "I don't know if I can move on, Nate. I'm beyond pissed. Why didn't she tell me she had a little boy? She's had plenty of time to tell me. It just doesn't add up."

"I don't know, Beck. Think about it, though, she could be telling the truth. Why wouldn't she tell you if he was yours? She talked about providing for him. She could have gotten millions out of you by now, if that's what she was after."

Beckham squeezed his eyes shut. "You're right. If he's not mine, I'll owe her a big ass apology. But if he is, I'm gonna have a hard time ever seeing her face again. I'll just have to so I can see my son."

The words 'my son' echoed around his brain, staggering him with their weight.

He thought of his conversation with Leo and how much he'd liked the kid in such a short amount of time. His heart raced at the thought of Leo being his little boy.

"Sounds like she's gonna be around a while, either way." Nate brought his attention back to the present. "Time to step up those acting skills."

Anthony showed up before he left the bus.

"Roxie says she's not dancing tonight," he said, wringing his hands.

"Like hell she's not. If I have to fake it, so does she."

"Beckham, she's shaken up. You need to talk to her. She told me about her burned clothes."

Beckham lifted his eyes to the ceiling. In all the excitement, he'd forgotten about that. He felt bad for a moment, but then caught himself. What if this was just another stunt she was pulling? That didn't make sense ... why would she ruin all her clothes? He was losing it. Fuck it, he needed a drink more than life.

"Are you listening to me?" Anthony gave him a little shake. "We had to send someone out to buy her something to wear tonight. And then this with her ... son. I don't know—maybe it's not a good idea."

"Roxie thinks it's Brooke messing with her things, which we need to deal with, but I can't even think about that right now. We have security on Roxie. Howie set up security for Leo. And the press isn't gonna hurt Roxie, they just want a story. She'll be fine. Tell her if she wants her paycheck she needs to get out there."

Anthony's stare leveled him. "Beck, I know you're angry, and I don't know what to make of all this, but Roxie is not a bad person." He put his hand on Beckham's shoulder. "And I've never seen you happier than you were the other day, with her."

Beckham shrugged. "I don't know what to think anymore."

"I'll see if I can get her out there."

Before Anthony was all the way out the door, Beckham called him back in.

"Hey, where did all this come from anyway? Who leaked this story?"

"That trampy journalist was on a gossip show earlier, pretty sure it was her." Anthony pursed his lips. "Mariette? Miriam? Mi-something Wethers."

"Well, fuck me. Mirielle Wethers. I don't know whether to thank her or bury her. Maybe both, if I'm lucky."

Ian stepped beside him as they walked through the back halls of the auditorium.

"I've heard about the mess with Roxie and Leo," Ian said. "We were at their hotel today swimming and Mirielle stopped by. That woman is a snake, Beck. I wouldn't trust anything she says."

"How long have you known about Leo?" Beckham asked.

"I met him the last time he visited Roxie."

"Funny. She has sex with me but doesn't trust me enough to tell me she has a child?" Beckham rubbed his eyes and squinted at Ian.

Ian held his hands up. "I don't get why she didn't tell you about him. Makes no sense to me. She's so proud of him, I'm shocked she hasn't talked about him non-stop on this tour, but she hasn't. She told Sparrow that we're the only ones who know about Leo because of Journey—she's wanted to remain professional, but knew we'd understand how much she misses him." He studied Beckham and gave his hair a tug. "It's weird, I've never thought about Leo

179

looking a thing like you, but I do see similarities. That being said," he pointed at Beckham, "Roxie is decent, and if she says he's not, he's not."

Beckham stopped walking and glared at Ian. "Nice to know where you stand."

Ian shook his head. "I'm standing right here beside you, and I'll also continue standing by Roxie. I haven't known either of you a helluva long time, but I know you've both become good friends to Sparrow and me. If I have to be the one to talk sense into either one of you, I will." He put his hand on Beckham's shoulder and gave it a shake.

Beckham returned the favor, shaking Ian a little harder than necessary, until he felt better.

"How are you so laid-back all the time?" Beckham asked.

"Lots and lots of sex with my beautiful wife," Ian said. "If you and Roxie can get on the same page as each other pretty soon, maybe you can be as copacetic as me." He was prepared this time when Beckham tried to grab him. He jumped out of the way and laughed all the way down the hall.

Normally Beckham had no trouble getting into the zone, but tonight he felt all over the place. When he wasn't thinking obsessively about what it would be like to have a son, he was trying to cloud out the images of Roxie that had taken over his mind. Her skin, her hair falling down her silky back. Her breasts in his hands and mouth. Her whimpering his name. The look on her face when she shattered around him.

Ever since being with her, his body craved her. How had everything gone so haywire?

His body ached. His head hurt. His throat had a solid lump in it that wasn't going away. Maybe he was coming down with something. If thousands of people weren't counting on him to show up, he'd cancel the show. There was no way he could get away with that, not this late.

Sierra found him in the dressing room. He knew she'd heard about what happened. She didn't say anything, just came over to where he was sitting and hugged him.

Nate came in a couple of times and walked back out each time when he saw they were still sitting there.

"What are you going to do?" she finally asked.

"Find out the truth and take him to Italy with us."

She leaned back. "*If* he's yours, you mean. And even if he is, you can't just take him from her, Beck."

He heard what she was saying and he knew she was right, but ... if she'd really kept him from his son all these years, he was absolutely going to make sure he spent the rest of his life making up for lost time. Whatever it took.

There was a brisk knock on Roxie's hotel door. She opened it to find Anthony standing there, holding up a dress. "Here, put this on. We've been waiting on you. The show starts in thirty minutes!"

Her eyes widened. "Beckham still wants me to do the show?"

"You know the saying—it must go on, baby!"

"This is all too much." She shook her head. "I'm not ready," she told him. "And I told you earlier I'm not doing it."

"You can throw on more makeup on the ride over. Suzanne and Coco can't even help you now."

"Whatever happened to Tracy? She did my makeup the best. I miss her."

"She *was* the best, but she flaked and didn't show after her little sick break. You only get one chance with me."

Roxie lifted an eyebrow.

"Besides you, I guess." He rolled his eyes. "Come on, hurry up. We don't have time to dilly-dally. Beckham sent me over to get you. I told him about your concerns and he said he was taking care of more security."

"You guys are insane, you know that, right?" She scowled at Anthony and then looked at Chloe and Leo. "I really just want to be with them. It's been a crazy day. We were going to hang out together..." Her eyes filled with tears. "If he manages to somehow take my son..." she whispered. "Leo is *not* his, Anthony."

"Then there shouldn't be any problem," he said simply. "We'll take them to my bus. It's all planned out."

"I don't know. I'd rather him not..." Roxie crossed her arms over her chest.

"Put the dress on and let's all go. I will personally keep Leo and Chloe company tonight," Anthony promised.

"Yay!" Leo said. "And Beck said I needed to visit his bus!"

Roxie bit down on her tongue to keep from yelling. She changed into the dress, brushed her teeth, and they took off.

It'd be interesting to see what kind of show they managed to pull off under such chaos.

Roxie crawled into bed that night, exhausted. They were still on Anthony's bus. Leo had fallen asleep before the show was over, and Anthony thought it would be best for Roxie if they all stayed put. Nate usually stayed on this bus too, but they never saw him. She figured he had moved to another one for the night.

Being with Beckham on a normal night was already like playing Chutes and Ladders—colorful, making progress then sudden drop offs, and having to go back to the beginning just when you got close to the end—but tonight had been a thousand times that. She made a mental note to throw the game away when she got home.

She kept thinking of his face and felt her insides tremble. He'd looked like he wanted to murder her and devour her all at once. And then to make things worse, they'd been carted off during the intermission to get their mouths swabbed, making her feel like a guest on *Maury*. The more she thought about it, the more she felt very justified in her growing outrage at Beckham, not to mention the non-stop news shows that were discussing the possibility of Leo being Beckham's love child.

She'd made the mistake of turning the TV on to see what they were saying and had seen a picture of her dancing with Beckham five and a half years earlier. How had they managed to find that? And one of her 'friends' from school was giving interviews about how obsessed Roxie had been with Beckham Woods throughout high school, making her sound like a star-crazed groupie who had conned Beckham into impregnating her.

Even more uncomfortable, everyone was mad at her. She'd been on the other bus during intermission and they'd taken their turns at saying their piece. Vanessa was hurt that she didn't tell them about Leo and was in disbelief that he was Beckham's. Brooke just sat at the table and scowled at her, the fury palpable from across the room. The guys were mad at her for the tension she'd caused. The bus had never felt so small.

She didn't bother defending herself. The test results would take care of that. She walked out, stunned that everyone had been so quick to lash out.

And Sierra ... it broke her heart that her new friendship with Sierra had been reduced to quiet distrust. She'd tried to pull Sierra aside to tell her the whole story, but Sierra had just said she needed to stick by her brother on this one. She seemed sorry, but resolute.

She couldn't imagine ever being any more humiliated than this. It stirred up the hurt from years before that she'd thought she was finally beginning to get past. Her heart hurt all over again, the way Beckham had looked right through her, not having a clue what he'd taken from her. It was just a repeat, five and a half years later. Why should this time surprise her? She'd become hardened overnight once before. Innocence lost was *never* pretty, though—no matter how many times the lesson had to be learned.

Next stop: Atlanta. They drove all night and were there by mid-morning. Anthony told them to make themselves comfortable and to plan on staying on his bus for the rest of Chloe and Leo's trip. He'd made sure an assistant picked up some necessities for Roxie since all of her things were ruined. Instead of hanging around the crew at dinnertime, the three of them went out, walking until they found a sushi place. Johnny and Al were always nearby.

"I've missed you so much, Leo. I'm so glad you guys got to come for the last few days. I needed my peoples."

He looked up at her and began swinging their hands as they walked.

"I've missed you too. Really, really bad." He looked at Chloe then. "Auntie and I have been having lots of fun too," he assured them both. "This is my favorite, though. And I can't wait to have sushi!" His face split into a huge grin.

It took Roxie's breath away when he smiled like that. She leaned down and covered his face with kisses. He laughed and finally moved away to catch his breath.

He loved sushi, although he wasn't as crazy about 'wathabi' as she was.

They had just ordered, when she felt eyes on them. She looked up and Beckham was looking at Leo. He wore a fedora low over his eyes, but she could see how his lips curved up as he watched Leo. Oblivious, Leo was chatting about the fish in the nearby tank and didn't even notice Beckham.

Roxie's blood boiled. When Beckham walked to their table she wouldn't look at him.

"Hey, buddy," he said to Leo.

"Beckham! Hi!" Leo said excitedly. "Sit down! We just ordered some major sushi!"

Beckham laughed. "Thanks! I believe I will." He sat down by Leo.

Roxie's eyes cut to him and he stared at her, daring her to try and stop him.

"Did you follow us here?" she snapped.

"I might have." He shrugged.

Her eyes flashed; she was livid. So it seemed they were going to act like children—fine, if that's the way he wanted it.

The waitress came to the table to take Beckham's order and didn't even try to hide the fact that she was checking him out. It didn't seem like she knew who he was, just that she liked what little she saw. He never fully lifted his face into the light. Roxie was learning his tricks. She wondered what other sneaky skills he had lurking.

"So, we'll have a whole day off in Atlanta tomorrow," Beckham cleared his throat, "and I'd like to take Leo to ride the SkyView Ferris Wheel. Would that be okay?"

"Yeah! That sounds *great!*" Leo agreed. "What is a SkyView Ferris Wheel?"

"Well, it's really, really high and was once in Paris and…"

"Hey, hold up. Those are the kinds of things you ask *before* … not while he's right here," she scolded Beckham. "And you can't just take him … I've missed him so much." She tried to give him the rest of the message with her raised eyebrows and at the same time not show Leo how much she despised Beckham.

"It's not every day he can ride the SkyView Ferris Wheel," he replied.

"Fine. But not without me."

"Rox, what do you think I'm gonna do—hijack him?"

"Take it or leave it."

"Okay, you can come. Also, I've arranged for you to be on *my* bus while Leo and Chloe are here. So you'll have more room, and so I can visit with him. We can also extend their stay…"

"Can I talk to you for a moment?" Roxie stood up, glaring down at Beckham.

He jumped up, his face as thunderous as hers.

Roxie heard Chloe chattering about all the sushi they were going to eat as she walked away.

"This is craziness. What are you even thinking?" She put both hands on her hips and glared up at him. "I don't know what you're envisioning, Beckham, but you can't just pretend like he's yours because you *want* him to be. He's not." Roxie took a deep breath before she continued. "Just let me see my son. I'm not fighting you with the testing. He's already been swabbed too, and now the decent thing would be to just let me have a nice time with my boy."

"You will. I just don't want to miss any more time with him if he *is* my son."

"If you get his hopes up in *any* way, whatsoever, I will destroy you," she said under her breath.

He heard her loud and clear. "You've already said that, and I'm done being bullied by you, Roxie Taylor."

She threw both hands up and wanted to throttle him. Her chest rose and fell as she tried to regain her composure before she turned and walked back to the table. He was on her heels. When they sat down, his brows were drawn together, but then he looked down at Leo next to him and his face lit up.

"There's this phenomenal restaurant we'll visit, too. You're gonna love it, Leo. They have these amazing crepes."

He went into a long explanation of what crepes were and how the chocolate oozes out of them. Leo sat there, spellbound.

Roxie rested her forehead in her hands and tried not to cry. She'd always wanted Leo to have a dad, but nothing was worth the fear of losing him. Beckham seemed so determined for Leo to be his, she wasn't sure a test result would settle it for him one way or the other.

18 DEPARTURE

Ian looked around and settled onto a stool. He had arrived at the hair and makeup trailer before Suzanne and Coco, which was a first. It was usually bustling in there by the time he showed up. He looked at his watch—oh, he was way *later* than usual. Maybe they'd assumed he wasn't coming ... sometimes he didn't.

The bright lights showed the sun he'd gotten the other day. He hadn't realized he'd gotten that much. He noticed skin peeling around his right eyebrow and started pulling it. *Damn.* That made it worse. He looked around for lotion or something that might help.

He found lotion and squirted some—a huge glob filled his hand.

"Shit!" He jumped up and looked around for a paper towel. He didn't see any on the counter, so he opened a couple of nearby drawers. Nothing but hair products, makeup, and pain medication.

"Ian?"

He turned around and saw Coco standing by the door.

"I got way too much." He showed her his hand. "Thought I might find some paper towels."

"You can wash it off in the sink."

He nodded. "Should've done that in the first place," he said.

She leaned down to shut the drawer. "Been waiting long?"

"No. First time I've been the only one in here, though."

"I was a-about to lock up. Thought you weren't coming."

"If you could just put some junk in my hair to get it to stay—it's getting too long and I'm out of the good stuff."

"Sure."

He watched her grab the hair paste. As she got closer, her hand shook, and he felt bad if he made her nervous. They'd never really talked much. He knew she was shy and usually Suzanne was available when he walked in.

She fixed his hair and studied him when she stepped back. He lifted his eyebrows and she turned around and got lotion, getting the perfect amount out and putting it above his brow.

"Thank you," he said. He looked down. Her hands had a few painful-looking cuts. "Oh wow, doesn't that sting your hands? What happened?"

"Got a bigger pair of scissors than what I usually cut hair with … d-didn't work out so well for my hands." She blinked and gave him a shy smile.

"Oh, thought you were gonna say the oven or a flat iron." He cringed. "Scissors, ouch!"

"F-flat iron doesn't like me much either," she agreed.

Poor girl. She really was awkward. Surprisingly good with hair though. He stood and walked toward the door, trying to get out of there before he gave her a heart attack.

"Thanks for the hair," he said, with a wave.

She held up a hand. "B-break a leg tonight," she said.

He had almost reached his bus when he heard his name called. He turned around and Coco was walking toward him holding out the hair product.

"Had extra. You take it."

His hand accidentally brushed hers when he took the container. He felt her stiffen and he quickly pulled his hand away. Her eyes were wide when she looked at him.

"That's so thoughtful. Thank you," he said. "I'll make sure to replace it when I get a chance."

"Not necessary," she said slowly. "Haircut next time." She gave him a big smile and walked away.

"Okay then."

He was shaking his head when he got on the bus.

"What's the matter?" Sparrow asked.

"I've met someone clumsier than you," he teased.

She frowned and jabbed his side. "Oh yeah?"

"Yeah," he said against her lips. Before he could feel her up, she backed away. "Aw, come on, I didn't mean it. Kiss me."

She smiled but shook her head. "Who is it? You didn't fall in love with their clumsy ways, did you?"

He snorted. "No, definitely not. You know Coco, hair and makeup girl?"

Sparrow scrunched her nose. "You've actually had a conversation with her? I've never heard her say a word. She's pretty though." She jumped when he tickled her side.

"You think so? I haven't noticed."

"Oh please." She rolled her eyes.

"I'm not kidding even a little bit."

"She's strange, but obviously, *pretty*."

"The 'strange' I picked up on." He held up the hair paste. "Got this out of the deal."

"Aw, someone's got a crush on you…"

He tickled her harder and she fell into his neck, laughing.

"Stop," she wheezed, "I don't want Journey to wake up yet."

"You didn't tell me she was asleep." His eyes got hazy as he reached under her shirt and tweaked her nipple. He leaned down and kissed his way up her stomach until he reached her bra. "Why aren't we naked yet?" He unsnapped the bra and grinned up at her when it fell to the floor.

"Someone came in all distracted by clumsy girls," she said.

"I don't know what you're talking about." He lifted her skirt and turned around to sit on the couch. "Mmm, this is gonna be good."

"You're supposed to be onstage in twen—ohhhh, mmm…" She grabbed his hair and held on.

"I've been off all day," he said. "I just need a little taste."

By the time they were done, he'd had more than a little.

She giggled when he pulled out of her.

"I wrecked your hair," she said.

"I'm gonna leave it like this for the show … that way you can look at me and know that I'm still enjoying the taste of you."

He sauntered off the bus, still buttoning his jeans, even though he was about to be late.

After the show, Ian was worn out and headed back to the bus.

"Ian, wait up!" Beckham called.

Ian turned and waited for Beckham to reach him.

"Hey, you killed it tonight, man," Ian said.

"You think so? Thanks. I expected tonight to be hard, but it helped to get out there and let out all my frustration. Now I'm wiped out." He put an arm around Ian's shoulder. "I feel like I've learned more working with you the last few months than I have the last ten years of touring. Your musicianship ups the quality of every player out there—we all do better. I'm *so* glad you're here."

Ian squeezed Beckham's shoulder. "Grateful you feel that way. It's been a kick. I'm loving it. You've spoiled me, you know that, right? I'm not gonna want to tour without you now."

"I've been so burned out. You almost make me never want to quit."

Ian laughed. "I'd say it was meant to be then!"

"I've been meaning to ask you something—should have long before now. Besides what happened with Sparrow spraining her foot, has Brooke given you any reason to think she's violent? Roxie thinks she was responsible for that. What do you think?"

"I don't trust her…"

"But do you think she hurt Sparrow on purpose?"

"I don't know—her apology surprised me. And she's backed off since then," he admitted.

Beckham blew a long breath out of his nose. "Okay. I'll try to get to the bottom of it."

Beckham had agreed that Roxie, Chloe, and Leo should stay on Anthony's bus when he remembered his mom was coming the next afternoon. In all the havoc, he'd completely forgotten about her visit. He was so glad he hadn't told her about Roxie yet—relief did not even begin to cover it. That had been the cosmos finally aligning right there.

He'd sat in on the questioning of Brooke. She swore she didn't damage Roxie's things, said she'd never liked her but that she'd never done anything like that. By the time she was done talking, all five of them in the room had been fairly certain it wasn't her. Just in case, Beckham and a detective friend he'd called just to scare her, made sure they put the fear of God in her to not step near Roxie or her things.

The next morning was an unusually bitter cold day in Atlanta. He'd talked up the Ferris Wheel so much, there was no getting out of it. The ride was about to close due to the weather when they showed up, but Beckham convinced them to keep it open for one more ride. They froze. Leo gasped when the ride started and the air felt even colder. He looked at his mom for reassurance, but when she cuddled him closer he smiled the rest of the ride. It was worth it.

When they got off and walked to the Jeep, Leo started squealing and pointed to his nose. Apparently his nose had started to run and froze mid-stream. Leo looked terrified, but when Beckham and Roxie laughed hysterically, he nervously chuckled too. Roxie pulled Kleenex out of her purse and got the gross icicle off, making him give his nose a good blow while he was at it.

They'd picked up Beckham's mom together, despite Roxie arguing all the way that he needed to go get her alone. Under his breath, he made a deal with her to not say a word about Leo, but said the deal was off if she'd heard about it on TV.

Leo was a hit with Sophia. Actually, she was immediately taken with both Leo and Roxie. Beckham realized his mistake in bringing Roxie as soon as his mom's eyes lit onto the three of them together.

By that night, Leo had managed to tell the whole crew about his 'icicle boogies' and was still getting laughs out of everyone he told, so he made the rounds a second time.

Beckham noticed how Roxie always kept an eye on Leo, even when she let him roam around a room. She knew where he was at all times. It was obvious from how they interacted with one another that she was a really good mother. As angry as he was with her, deep down he knew she was protective of her little boy. Looking back on his history, all the things she'd probably heard in the press, he could *somewhat* understand why she'd want to keep Leo from all of that. He'd never completely understand why, but when he saw her with Leo, it almost softened him toward Roxie again. Almost.

He just knew Leo was his. There could be no other explanation for the bond Beckham felt with him. It had been immediate and he only felt the connection growing.

Somehow he'd have to work past the former feelings he'd had for Roxie and the new mixed-up ones and move forward so Leo would have the best possible upbringing. Beckham was determined to make up for the years they'd lost. He was thankful Leo was still young enough that he wouldn't hold it against Beckham for not being around before now. At least that's what he hoped.

As for why Roxie would continue to insist that Leo wasn't his, he couldn't figure that out. Maybe she was afraid he'd try to take Leo from her, but every child needed both parents—he had to remind himself of this at least a hundred times a day since he'd found out about Leo. As much as he wanted to steal away with him, he knew he could never take his son from his mother.

A couple of days went by and Beckham thought for sure they'd have the results back by the time they arrived in Washington, D.C., but no such luck. Nate called and told Beckham to let him know the minute he knew anything. Cleveland and Boston went by, and still no word.

They arrived in New York and would only be in town a few days for two shows and the late night circuit. Then they'd all fly to L.A. for the Grammy Awards for a couple of nights. Without a concert every night and staying in a hotel, it would almost feel like a break, even though it'd still be hectic.

He tried to get Roxie to come to the hotel too, with Leo and Chloe, but she insisted on staying on Anthony's bus. She was so stubborn.

He stretched out on his bed for about an hour and slept. As soon as he got up, he felt restless. The hotel room felt claustrophobic. He missed them. *Leo.* He missed Leo. He swallowed his pride and called Roxie.

She answered on the second ring.

"Roxie? Hey."

"Hey, Beckham. What's up?"

He couldn't tell for sure if she was any more annoyed with him than usual.

"I was wondering—would you guys meet up with me at the Rockefeller ice skating rink?"

It was quiet on the other end.

"You still there?" he asked.

"No."

"Sounds like you're there."

"Well, yes, I'm here, but no, we're not going skating with you."

"Rox, I promised Leo I'd show him a good time while he's on this trip. Let me do that."

"He's having a great time, believe me."

"Lighten up, okay? It's just one afternoon."

"Don't tell me to lighten up! Beckham, look ... I know you won't believe he's not yours until you have proof, but that being said—I don't have to hang out with you. And I don't have to make sure Leo is around you all the time right now either. When you hear what you need to hear, you can come find me and give me the apology I deserve. Until then, I'll see you onstage."

There was a long pause until he said, "Come on, Roxie. Just come skate with me. I'm sorry I've been such a jerk. Truce for a day?"

She was quiet. Finally: "You've been an asshole, Beckham."

He laughed in spite of his embarrassment. "Fair enough. I'll dial back my asshole for the day."

Silence.

"Roxie?"

"Okay. I guess."

She hung up on him and he scrambled around the room, throwing on a shirt and sweater. He pulled on a knit cap, sunglasses, and took off, not sure when she was even coming.

He skated about twenty minutes before he saw them, getting on the rink. They both were wearing bright blue and looked like a vision. Leo was talking and Roxie was laughing at whatever he was saying. Her hair was down, the long waves looking like gold against her blue jacket; it always took his breath away when she wore it like that. Her smile faded when she saw him and he felt a sword jab directly into his heart.

His body and heart kept betraying him where Roxie was concerned. Giving his hat a tug, he groaned and plastered on a smile. *Just have fun,* he thought. *Don't let her suck you in and don't even look at her lips. Or ass. Or hair.*

"Hey, you two! Thanks for meeting me out here!" he said. Funny, he felt extremely happy to be with a girl who was twisting him in knots. "Leo! You're looking pretty good—you look like a pro already!"

"Mom and I go skating a lot," Leo said proudly. "She's really good. I don't do the fancy stuff like her, though."

Roxie and Leo's cheeks had two red circles in the center of them. It made their eyes even brighter. Beckham stared at them for a moment and thought: *This is exactly what I want. Right in front of me. Both of them.*

To his mortification, he felt a knot in his throat. His eyes watered, but he hoped he could attribute it to the brisk air. *What the hell is happening to me?* He cleared his throat and gave them both a lopsided grin.

"You gonna show us whatcha got?" Roxie said lightly.

He could tell she was trying hard to be polite and he was relieved.

They did a lap around.

"Do a twirl, Mom!"

"Oh no, that's okay." She laughed. "I'm not really feeling the twirls today."

"Come on, I wanna see!" Beckham pointed to the center of the rink. "Right out there."

"I'm hungry already," Roxie said.

"No changing the subject!"

"Oh, okay," she huffed, "but just a couple. I'm not kidding about being hungry!"

She began skating to the center of the rink. Leo and Beckham stopped, both watching her every move.

"She's beautiful," Beckham said to Leo. "You know your mom is beautiful, right?"

Leo nodded solemnly. "I know. I see her."

"I see her too, buddy. You've got a good one."

They looked at each other, having a moment. When they looked up, Roxie was going around the rink, turned backwards and did a double axel. They both clapped hard.

"That was perfect!" Beckham yelled. "Do another one!"

"One more," she said, "and then food!"

She gathered up speed and as she turned to go backwards, someone skating by sped up and bumped into her, knocking her down. There was a sickening thud as Roxie fell hard. Beckham and Leo rushed over to her, along with a few other people.

She looked up at Beckham and Leo, dazed. "That's what I get for showing off," she said softly.

"It was amazing," Beckham whispered, leaning over her. "Are you okay, Rox? Where does it hurt?" He brushed the ice off of her face.

"You okay, Mama?" Leo knelt down by her.

"I'm okay. I think everything is in one piece..." She tried to joke. She waved at everyone. "I'm fine," she said.

A girl asked if she needed anything and Roxie thanked her and said no. Everyone slowly skated away. She moved her legs and took Beckham's hand, slowly sitting up.

"Ugh. This is gonna hurt." She winced as she stretched her arms. "I'd like to punch the girl who plowed into me."

"Yeah, the thought crossed my mind too." Beckham looked around the rink. "She didn't even stop to see if you were okay."

"She just came out of nowhere! I didn't even see what she looked like."

Beckham didn't bother telling her that he didn't either, because while she was falling, he'd come to the realization that he'd fallen even harder and would never get over her.

19 YIELD

When Roxie stood up, every muscle in her body hurt. She was used to getting sore from all the torture she gave her body dancing, but this was a little more extreme. She moved tentatively to the side of the rink.

Leo and Beckham both looked so worried about her she had to smile. "I'm okay, really, just … ow."

"Here, let's take your skates off and get warmed up."

They shuffled off of the rink and found their shoes.

"I have an idea. How about you come back to my room and we can order room service. You can stretch out and eat at the same time." His smile was so kind, the ice cubes around her heart began to thaw just a tiny bit more.

"I love room service!" Leo held onto Roxie's hand and reached out for Beckham's.

She was going to get an ulcer, with how nervous it made her to see Leo and Beckham together. Leo liked him so much already. They had immediately bonded and there seemed to be nothing she could do to stop it. She hesitated, but they both had such hopeful expressions that she caved. It would help to have a few days at home soon. She'd get her son unattached to this guy later, something she'd have to figure out for herself too. *Later* being the key word. For now, she just needed to balance out her libido vs. her feelings.

"This must be a really nice room. You keep trying to lure us there," Roxie teased.

"You'll see." He raised a cocky eyebrow at her. "Taxi!"

They had maybe a four-minute cab ride.

"I totally could have walked that," Roxie argued.

"Yeah, maybe if I carried you," Beckham teased back.

"Well, I didn't hear you offering." She looked at him, daring him to come back with something.

He looked down at her lips and subconsciously licked his lower lip. When the taxi driver asked for his fare, Beckham was startled.

"Yeah, thanks, here you go. Come on, let's get you people some food," he yelled.

"Wow!" Leo said over and over as he ran through the suite.

It was gorgeous. She should have known it would be. This was the kind of room she used to imagine Beckham in, back when she thought about him all the time, and okay, even this morning. Royal blue and red with lime green touches decorated the room and it just felt *good* in there. Cozy and cheerful.

"Ooo, I love that!" She pointed up at the mahogany ceiling.

Beckham nodded. "Me too. Here, stretch out on this bed. I'll grab the menu for you."

"Thanks." She sat on the bed and leaned back. "Ahhh," she groaned, "a feather bed. I just *thought* I was tired of my bunk." She laughed. "I could get used to this!"

He walked into the other room and she heard him showing Leo how to start the video games.

"No shoes on the couch, Leo!" she called out.

"They're off, Mom!" he called back and she giggled.

Beckham stopped mid-stride on his way back to her. He saw her watching him and seemed to snap out of it. He came the rest of the way, sitting down beside her. Her hair was fanned out on the pillow and he pushed a few strands the rest of the way back.

Without thinking it through, she reached up and touched his lower lip. She couldn't seem to stop herself— her eyes were always drawn to his mouth. She wanted to sink into those lips and bite ...

She yanked her hand away.

"I'm sorry. I don't know why I-"

He took her hand and put her fingers back on his lips. "Don't stop." His eyes crinkled up when he smiled.

Those chameleon eyes. They looked dark grey and smoky at the moment.

He was sexy as hell. And apparently he would always be her downfall.

Her fingers swept across his upper lip, following the curve and then feeling bolder, she pressed down on his lower lip until he opened his mouth.

His grin was mischievous as he let her touch and then when she was least expecting it, his tongue came out and circled around her finger. She went completely still. He teased her finger a little more, waiting to see what she would do, and then without warning, he leaned down and...

"Beck? My game stopped working. Can you turn it back on?" Leo asked softly. His eyes veered between the two of them. "Whatcha doin'?"

"Oh just making sure your mom ... feels better." Beckham's eyes widened at Roxie, but she didn't try to help him out. He stood up. "What's going on with that game?" They walked out of the room with Leo telling him in great detail how he'd tried to get it working.

Roxie turned on the side that didn't feel as bruised and willed her heart to calm down. She was playing a dangerous game, one where she and Leo would be devastated, but today, the pull to Beckham felt stronger than her anger and self-control. She closed her eyes and imagined the kiss he would have given her if Leo hadn't walked in, and fell asleep.

She woke up to voices in the other room. It sounded like Sierra with Leo. She sat up and forced herself to get out of bed.

Leo, Sierra, and Beckham looked up from the couch when she walked in the room.

"Hi, Mama!" Leo said, taking a bite of a hot fudge sundae.

Beckham and Sierra had ice cream too. He looked guiltily at Roxie as he took a bite. "Come here, we'll share. And we can order you one too. Were we too loud?" he asked, bopping Sierra with a throw pillow. "It's her fault!"

"No, it's fine … I can't believe I fell asleep!" Roxie said sheepishly. "You act like me and Chloe … I need to check on her, by the way."

"Hey, Sleeping Beauty," Sierra said, shyly, silently offering up her own truce. "Chloe was having her own fun with Taz. She's fine, trust me." She smiled.

"Looks like I'm missing a party in here," Roxie said with a grin. "I'm not usually around you both at the same time."

"I know! My brother's been hogging you and Leo!" Sierra pinched Beckham. "I was gonna come skating today, but sounds like it's a good thing I didn't—I heard you took a bad fall. You feelin' it now?" Sierra asked.

"I'm so sore," Roxie admitted.

"Beckham texted me and I picked up some Motrin on the way over…" Sierra pointed at the bag of medicine.

"Thanks! Perfect timing." She opened the bottle.

Beckham handed her a bottle of water.

"You guys are quite the team," she said.

Beckham and Sierra looked at each other.

"We've fooled another one," Sierra said.

"Come on, you know you love me." Beckham got in her face. "Come on, say it, say you love me!" Sierra was about to take a bite of ice cream and bumped the spoon so it landed on her chin.

Leo laughed his belly laugh and had to set his ice cream down so it wouldn't spill.

"Oh, you've got someone on your side now, don't you?" Sierra said, laughing. She put a big dollop of ice cream in Beckham's hair.

Leo's eyes got huge and then his laugh took over. He stood up and tried to catch his breath but couldn't stop laughing.

"Wait. Stop! Stop. Can't breathe. Oh my goodness. They're crazy, Mama!"

Roxie was laughing almost as hard. "I know it!"

Beckham stood up. "Oh, you think we're crazy, huh?" He put the whipped cream on Leo's nose. There was so much that the cherry stayed upright in the whipped cream.

Leo started the duck dance, trying to keep the cherry on his nose.

They all lost it then.

Sierra and Leo were playing Mario Kart and Leo kept winning, much to Sierra's aggravation. While they were battling it out, Beckham motioned for Roxie to come in the other room. He leaned against the doorjamb and touched her cheek.

"Are you feeling okay?" he asked.

She nodded. "I'm feeling better."

"Good. I've gotta get ready to go see Fallon in just a little bit here, but I'm wondering … would you want to come with me? I'd love for you to meet Jimmy. He's great. Leo's good here with Sierra. She mentioned earlier she was free to watch him, if we wanted. Or if you don't feel like getting out, would you … stay … here? With me? I'll be late, but we can watch a movie when I get back or something."

"I don't know, Beckham. This is … weird. I probably shouldn't. Things are still not resolved with us, you know…"

"I know. I know." He rubbed his hand over his head, making his hair go every which way. "I promised myself I wouldn't let myself get sucked in by you today, but I just can't … stop." He shut the door and pulled her against it. He rested his hands against the wall and pressed his body against hers. "I've stopped thinking rationally," he said. "I just … as much as I try to fight it, I need you, Roxie. I need to touch you. I need to be with you. I just want you in my space, making yourself at home with my things." His mouth was an inch from hers. "I want to eat your lips. They drive me insane. That thing you do with your hair when you get nervous and you tug on it. I can't take it anymore. And I know, believe me, I know we have a lot of issues to deal with, but when I'm with you, it just all fades away…"

He leaned back to look in her eyes and she couldn't take it anymore either. She wanted to stay angry at him, but she just couldn't. She grabbed his face and brought his mouth to hers. When his tongue touched hers, she moaned and then prayed to God that Leo and Sierra hadn't heard her. She pulled back.

"No, please don't stop. Please," Beckham whispered, kissing her neck.

He went back for her mouth, kissing everywhere but right on her lips. For such sweet kisses, it was so intense. Like drowning without fighting to break the surface again.

Sink, sink, sink.

Let me drown if it means this.

She lived for *more* and when his mouth teased her lips, she stopped fighting it and kissed him with every shred of attraction, anger, and lust she felt for him.

Actually, it felt like a lot more than that.

It felt like breath.

Fuel.

Home.

It took every scrap of strength Beckham possessed to leave her in his hotel room. He could still feel her lips on him. Just a taste and he was ready to move heaven and earth to get another. He couldn't convince her to come out with him, which was disappointing, but he thought he had talked her into staying there, so he was already looking forward to that.

Beckham and Ian had a blast with Jimmy. He knew Jimmy and Ian would hit it off. The three of them were completely in sync and did a segment where they sang everything like Elton John. Everything clicked into place like it was supposed to—improvisation came so easily when he was comfortable. His band joined The Roots, and that was a kick. If every night could be exactly like this one, he wouldn't want to leave the business.

He shut the show down and was saying good-night to Ian and his band, when he checked his messages. There was a missed call from the lab. He called the technician's number immediately and was happy when it didn't go to voicemail.

"Do you have the results? This is Beckham." He loosened his tie, so he could breathe better.

"I do. The results are negative. You are *not* the father."

Beckham leaned against the car, feeling like he was just sucker-punched. He motioned for Howie to unlock the door. As soon as he did, Beckham sat down and leaned his head between his legs.

"You're sure?" he asked.

"We're 99.8% sure," was the reply.

"I guess that's pretty sure," he said softly. "Thank you. I appreciate you letting me know."

He ended the call and put his hands on his head. He didn't know what to think. Part of him wanted to redo the test at least a dozen times, even though that was nonsense. The other part raged for not believing Roxie in the first place. And another, very small part of him, hated her for being right.

He wanted so badly for Leo to be his. Had he imagined everything—the similarities, the bond, the rightness of it all—just because he so desperately wanted it to be? Was he that fucking lonely?

"Drive around, Howie. I can't go back yet," he said.

He was so ashamed of how he'd treated her. He couldn't believe she'd had anything to do with him after he'd been so hateful. He imagined her earlier that night, pressed up against him, as hungry for him as he was for her. At least it had seemed that way. But he didn't know what to believe anymore.

They drove for hours. He wanted to go in every single bar they passed, but instead gripped the edge of the seat so hard it hurt.

"You 'bout ready to call it a night, Beck?" Howie asked.

Beckham hadn't spoken in at least a half hour.

"I guess so," he said.

He went in the back entrance of the hotel and said goodnight to Howie at his door. He walked in quietly, hoping he didn't wake up Leo and Roxie. Everything was neat and tidy. All the mess from the ice cream had been cleared out. He peeked in the bedroom, and they weren't there.

He cursed, frustrated that she'd left, but really it was probably for the best. There was no telling what mood he'd be in tomorrow. He needed some time before seeing her again.

The guilt that he'd stayed out so long weighed him down. How long had she waited for him? Shit. It was 3:30. He wouldn't blame her for being mad at him. He deserved it.

He sat on the edge of the bed and dragged his hands through his hair.

This was just all so fucked up.

He didn't leave his room or talk to anyone until it was time to start the show the next night. The sound check had been taken care of without him. Nate and Anthony both called a few times, but he didn't talk to either one of them. He'd stared at the mini bar until 6 that morning and finally fell asleep. The only person he'd called was his sponsor, Troi. They agreed to talk a few times every day, at least until Beckham felt stronger.

He felt the hurt emanating out of Roxie as she danced that night. It was his fault and he couldn't stop it. She'd let herself be vulnerable with him the night before and he'd crushed it. But his own pain was just under the surface too. He was riding on the edge of self-destruction and didn't want her caught in the crossfire.

The next day was a repeat of the day before. He had an early morning talk show to do and then his show that night. He stayed in his room until it was time to perform and came back the minute it was over. He'd asked the front desk to make sure the mini bar was cleared out, so he wouldn't have that staring him in the face when he got in that night.

He stayed up late, packing for his flight to L.A. the next morning. He should have just stayed up, because when the alarm went off at six, he'd only gotten two hours of sleep. His head pulsed with pain as he rode to the airport. They'd chartered a private flight for his crew and Roxie was the first person he saw when he got on the plane. She was sitting next to Sierra. He knew she saw him, but then she hadn't looked at him again.

Sierra called out, "Hey, you're the last one on ... was starting to wonder if you were gonna show. Late night, little brother?"

He nodded. "Hey, Rox," he said softly. "Where's Leo?"

"Chloe and Leo flew out already. My parents are meeting them and they're going home with them for a day or two." She looked like she was going to cry and looked out the window.

"I wish I could have told him goodbye," he said softly. And then under his breath, "I got the results back."

"I know," she said just as quietly.

He waited for her to say something else, but she didn't look at him again.

"Roxie, I'm sorry."

She nodded but kept looking out the window and didn't say a word.

Dejected, he sat down a couple rows ahead of them and buckled his seat belt. He didn't think he'd be able to, but he fell asleep not long into the flight and slept most of the way. Before he'd opened his eyes all the way, he stretched an arm out and bumped into someone.

"Oh, excuse me," he said, looking to the side. "Hey..."

Coco sat facing him, holding a pillow.

"How are ya?" he asked groggily.

"Tired. S-sorry. It was noisy in the back and I ... saw you sleeping up here. Thought maybe I could sneak in a nap too," Coco said. "I'll go back now," she said shyly.

"Don't worry about it. I need to get after this." He ran a hand through his scruff and grabbed his bag. He smiled at Coco. "Go ahead and stretch out."

She nodded, put her pillow on his side, and laid down. He got up to shave and brush his teeth before they landed.

The flight attendant followed him into the bathroom. It was barely larger than most airplane bathrooms.

"Uh, what are you doing?" he asked.

"Just seeing if you need any assistance," she said, running her fingers along the back of his neck.

"I'm good, thanks," he said.

"I've heard," she whispered seductively in his ear.

He took a step away and held up his razor. "Excuse me while I shave."

"Just let me know if you need me. Now or anytime," she said.

"I'll be sure to do that," he replied, shaking his head no to say otherwise. "Go ahead and shut the door behind you."

"Do you mind if I just stay here and watch?" she asked.

He shrugged his shoulders and started shaving. "Knock yourself out."

It was like he had a flashing sign pointed at him, saying, *'Eat the apple.'*

When he came out, the girl was practically on his heels. Ian flashed him a look, and then Beckham realized how suspicious things seemed. He looked at Roxie, and thankfully, she was asleep, leaning peacefully against her window. Coco wasn't asleep, but watching him from her pillow. When she saw him looking at her, she sat up and moved her pillow, making room for him to take his seat.

"Thanks," he said.

She didn't answer, but her cheeks turned pink.

He could have sworn he'd never seen the girl blink.

The weather was perfection in sunny California. Seventy-two degrees and warming up later in the day. Beckham took out his sunglasses and shed his scarf and sweater. Everyone got their luggage and he noticed Roxie taking flip-flops out of her bag. He smiled in spite of himself.

Everyone was excited to be back in California and planned to either stay home or to check into the Beverly Hilton. Sierra, Brooke, and Vanessa were talking about how happy they would be to sleep in their own beds for a couple of nights.

Ian and Sparrow were going to check on the progress of their house and then come over. Beckham had invited them to stay at his place so they could get a break from their bus, and they'd agreed. He gave them the code to get inside, just in case it was late.

He looked around for Roxie. She was standing next to Brad and Shelton. Most of the tension had faded between her and the rest of the group. He guessed they'd heard about the test results too, and imagined they all felt bad about the way they'd treated her. A cab came up and she waved as Brad and Shelton got in and drove away. He moved beside her.

"I should've called," he said.

She shrugged. "It's okay. I figured you'd..." she trailed off.

"It's not okay. I'm embarrassed, Rox. I don't know why I latched onto the idea so hard of him being mine. I've just—I've never clicked with a kid, or even many adults, the way I have with Leo."

She nodded. "He's special, and so are you. It doesn't surprise me. And I never thought I'd be telling you this, but ... watching you with him ... I really wish he *was* yours, Beckham." She looked at him then and her sincerity nearly knocked him over.

"Thank you," he said, choked up. "Roxie. I don't even ... *thank* you," he said.

"It's the truth." She looked over his shoulder. "My cab should be here any minute. See you tomorrow night!" she said lightly.

"Wait. Come home with me, Roxie. Please?" He raised both hands. "We'll just hang out. The Sterlings are staying too. It'll be fun. I have several bedrooms you can choose from…"

"Beckham," she sighed, "I can't keep doing this manic thing we have going. It's wearing me down. I know you just got caught up with things, but now that you know Leo's not yours, you can move on from me too. We have too much baggage. Let's just leave it at that."

A cab pulled up. She got in and didn't look back.

20 SHRIVEL

She wrapped her hands with gauze and ignored the familiar pain. She'd been experimenting with acetone and hydrogen peroxide for the last few weeks. Making ammonal wasn't as difficult as she'd expected—she finally had the mixture of ammonium nitrate and aluminium powder down pat. The fun part was testing to see which measurements caused the best results. However, it was becoming more and more difficult to hide the burns from all her experiments.

She tested her limits, careful to not get too close when detonating, but then seeing how long she could endure smoke, the length of time her skin could taste the heat before it became unbearable.

She was ready.

What she was having a hard time getting past was the fact that Leo wasn't Beckham's son. And just when she'd made her peace with him having a child and come around to wanting him, too. It just didn't seem fair.

Maybe this was all for the best. Beckham was vulnerable right now. And soon, she would be the one to give him the child he so desperately wanted. He would never want anyone but her again.

Tonight. It had to be tonight.

She'd waited for the perfect timing, and she knew there would be no better opportunity than this. It was risky, but she felt confident it would work.

Beckham would forget about Roxie when she wasn't constantly in his face. And getting rid of Roxie would finally pave the way for her.

The difference between a successful murder and a botched one was all about planning and patience. She'd done her time and research.

It was now or never.

21 DOWNWARD FACING DOG

It felt strange to be in L.A. without their bus or even their old place. Ian knew it would be nice at Beckham's house, but he wanted to make sure Journey didn't keep them up all night like she sometimes did when they were in a new place. So he took Sparrow and Journey to Beckham's as soon as they left the airport, made sure Journey went down for her nap on time, and then left to run errands.

Tomorrow was their second wedding anniversary and also the Grammys, so he wanted to make tonight special for Sparrow. Sierra would be watching Journey at her mother's house while he took Sparrow out for dinner to Providence. Sierra had offered to take her to her place overnight, but Sparrow wasn't quite ready for that yet. They hadn't really had babysitters, being on the road together, so it would be interesting to see how it went.

He couldn't wait. As much as he loved his little family and loved hanging out with everyone on the tour, he needed this time alone with Sparrow. He picked up her present—a Tiffany jazz ring in platinum with diamonds. She loved her wedding ring, but he knew she'd love this, too. It looked like her, unique and exquisite.

He had one more stop to make. The instruments they'd be playing at the Grammys had been sent to the warehouse to store overnight and one of Ian's guitars had accidentally gotten in the mix. It wasn't crucial that he get it today, but he was close and he'd feel better having it on hand to practice the next day.

He pulled around the back and unlocked the door to the storage room, going straight for his guitar. He glanced at the clock at the end of the hall. There was plenty of time—he should beat the traffic. Something made him look up again and when he did, he went dead still.

She was staring at him, equally shocked to see him. His mouth was hanging open, and he closed it and shifted the guitar to his other hand. She moved slowly toward him and he had the thought that he should run, but he wasn't sure why.

"What are you doing here?" he asked.

Her face was covered with something powdery and her black hair went every direction. It hadn't been that long since he'd seen her on the plane, but she'd obviously been busy since then. She moved until she was standing beside him but still didn't say a word.

"Coco?" he said softly.

"Can you help me carry a few things to the car?" Her voice was different when she finally spoke. Measured and monotone.

He wondered if she was on something. Something seemed off about her. Really off.

"Are you okay?" he asked.

"Yes. I have to get this stuff to Suzanne. It's in one of the closets on the other side." She pointed behind her. "It won't take long."

He hesitated, but he really wanted to get out of there, so maybe the sooner he helped her, the sooner he could leave. "Uh, okay. I'm in a hurry, so as long as we're quick. Did you park out front? I didn't see a car."

She nodded and gestured for him to come with her. He set the guitar down and followed her. They walked down the hallway, through the rooms where they'd eaten and rehearsed, and through another hall on the far side that he'd never noticed.

She stopped at the last door and unlocked it. They stepped inside and he looked around. The room had a table and chairs and a door on the other side.

"It's just through that door, to the right," she said, motioning with her head.

He sighed and moved forward, regretting ever stopping at the warehouse in the first place. He opened the door past the table and stepped inside.

"What should I grab?" He turned around to make sure he knew what she wanted, and she had a crowbar raised in the air, coming straight for his head.

He heard talking and whimpering when he woke up, but he was so out of it, he thought he might be dreaming. He was lying on the floor, face down, but his arms were ... were they broken? They were stuck in such an odd angle. Once he started trying to move his arms and feet, he realized he was tied up.

Coco.

He lifted his head and the pain nearly made him pass out again, but he didn't. She was staring at him from across the room. She muttered something over and over, it almost sounded like a chant, but it took him a while to make out what she was saying.

"He was nice to me. I never planned to kill him. He was nice to me. I never planned to kill him. He was nice to me. I never planned to kill him. He was nice to me. I never planned to kill him. He was nice to me. I never planned to kill him. He was nice to me. I never planned to kill him..."

When it registered, he looked her in the eye and spoke in his calmest voice, right over her chanting.

"Do you mean me? I'm not dead. See? I'm okay." He had to repeat it a few times and she finally stopped and her eyes focused.

"For now," she said.

She wiped the tears from her face and smiled a tiny, shaky smile that made his blood run cold. Holy shit, he was with a psychopath.

She picked up the bottle of pills sitting next to her, popped one in her mouth, and stood up. She walked to the door then turned to look down at him.

"Where are you going, Coco? Let's talk. Tell me what's going on. I can help you. Coco, please." The words sped out of his mouth and he knew they weren't doing any good.

"I'll have to deal with you later," she said, calmly. "I can't let you get in the way of my plan."

"What plan? I can help you, if you tell me what you need."

She shook her head, all quick, jerky movements.

"I don't need help," she said. "I have a plan and you showing up here was not part of it." She leaned against the wall and when she spoke again, her voice was softer. "You're a really nice guy and if I didn't love Beckham, you're the only other guy I've ever met who I'd even think about being with."

"Beckham is a great guy," Ian said. His head hurt too bad to look at her anymore, so he stopped trying and rested his head on the floor.

"He's the best," she said.

"Have you loved him a long time?"

"Since I was 12."

"Is that when you met? When you were 12?"

"No, I met him when I was 15."

"Does he know you love him?"

Coco's cheeks flushed. "Oh no." She shook her head. "I've always been too shy to tell him. Soon, though." She leaned forward, her eyes suddenly bright with excitement. "I have a plan," she whispered.

A chill went down Ian's spine.

FACE TO
Red

"So you said. Wish you'd let me in on that plan. I want my buddy Beckham to be happy," he said with a smile.

He had no idea what to do, but stalling her seemed like the best option until he could get the rope loose.

"I can make him happy. I know I can. He likes my eyes. He said I remind him of Zooey Deschanel." She nodded and opened her mouth like she was going to say something else but didn't.

Yeah, Zooey on a deranged, psychopath day, he thought. *I'll never look at her the same way again.* In the next second he was kicking himself. *You're about to die here and you're cracking jokes to yourself? Idiot!* And the never-ending, underlying thoughts that wouldn't stop running through his mind were, *Please let me live to see Sparrow and Journey again. Please protect them. Please let them know how much I love them.*

"Well, I've chatted long enough. I need to go get rid of your car." She opened the door. "I'll be back soon. Don't go anywhere." She laughed at her joke and left.

He tried to fight it but fell asleep while she was gone. When he woke up the next time, he felt more out of it than before. He had the sensation of motion ... things were passing in a blur. He tried to focus but his vision kept going black, and then everything came to an abrupt stop.

She'd either hit him again and knocked him out or drugged him. He blinked and tried to focus, but the floor tilted. He couldn't tell what was real. *Get your head together, Ian!* He tried to shake himself. He heard Sparrow's voice. *Don't let this girl outsmart you, babe.*

When he came to again, he was in a room with a thick leather band looped around his waist. His feet weren't tied, but his hands were. A chain hooked onto the leather band and was attached at the other end to a metal bedpost. He could see a toilet in the small bathroom connected to the bedroom, and it looked like he'd be able to reach it. He just couldn't reach the door out of here.

The cottage was so quiet without Chloe and Leo, Roxie didn't know what to do with herself. She showered, did laundry, and video chatted with Leo a few times. He was excited to be at Grammie's house and had to show her how the house was still the same without them. Grammie also still looked the same, and so did his rock collection.

She threw on a pair of shorts and a tank and opened all the windows. The breeze drifted through the windows as she did Pilates. She blew out all the negative thoughts and breathed in peaceful ones. Her nerves calmed and she felt better. Except for one huge bruise on her thigh, her body was healing from the fall. And as close as she had come to losing her heart again, she felt like she'd taken a step in the right direction. She wished she could blow Beckham Woods out of her brain as easily as a puff of air, but she knew that was impossible. His music had always been deeply imbedded in her, and her fantasies of him had long ago played out and backfired. Now that she'd gotten to know the real guy, though, she found that he'd penetrated her heart far deeper than she imagined possible.

She'd waited for hours in his New York suite, laughing her head off at him and Ian on *The Tonight Show*. The three of them had been magical that night. Beckham looked and sounded better than she'd ever seen him. The thought actually crossed her mind that maybe it was her kisses that had given him that extra spark. She allowed, in those quiet moments after Sierra left and Leo fell asleep, to think that maybe she could have that life. Maybe she could have *him*.

When he never came back and she saw that she'd missed a call from the lab, she realized what had happened. She carried Leo out of there, got a cab, and they crawled into the bunks on the bus. Beckham's distance after that further solidified that she'd temporarily lost her sanity. There was no future with Beckham.

And then if she'd had any doubt, seeing the flight attendant follow him into the bathroom and then not come out for a while ... it was obvious he was getting her out of his system. She had to pretend to be asleep so she wouldn't be bawling when he came out.

Why he then invited her to stay with him made no sense, but nothing about Beckham Woods had ever made sense when it came to her. As much as she wanted to believe they could have something, it just always ended up in disarray.

It stung, but she was a big girl. Yes, she'd cried more times than she could count, but that would eventually stop. She'd gotten over him before, she'd be fine this time too.

No more feeling sorry for herself. And no more daydreaming about what could have been. It was time to move on.

She heard something outside and looked out the window. She'd told Johnny to go home. There was no need for him anymore. She thought he was probably still out there though. He seemed to think he didn't have to answer to her.

While she did a few more stretches, the breeze picked up and she felt chilled. She slowly stood up and went to shut the windows.

She screamed when she saw someone standing outside her window. They turned and ran. The gauzy curtains made it hard to see any features, but she felt certain it'd been a girl. Shaking, she opened the door and looked around.

"Hello? Johnny?" she called.

No answer.

Creeped out, she shut the door and locked it and then closed all the windows. She didn't see any signs of the girl or her bodyguard. Still shaking, she told herself to calm down and called Jill, the owner of the house. She looked out the window again to see if they were home.

"Jill? It's Roxie," she said as soon as Jill answered.

"Oh hey, girl! How's the tour going?" she asked politely.

"It's been great. I just wanted to let you know I'm back for a couple of nights. I should have let you know I would be back, so you didn't think someone had broken in out here." Roxie laughed nervously.

"Thanks, that's probably a good idea!" Jill laughed.

"You didn't just come by, did you? I saw someone outside my window a few minutes ago."

"Weird! No," she said. "I'm actually not home right now, but I can have Eddie take a look around if you're nervous."

"I'm sure it's nothing. Just thought I'd check. Maybe I'll see you before I head out again."

"That'd be great. Let's have coffee or something."

They hung up and Roxie took another look outside but didn't see anything out of the ordinary. She dialed Johnny.

"Johnny here," he answered.

"Hey. Did you finally listen to me and go home?"

"No, I'm coming back. Silly girl. You can't get rid of me that easily. Boss would kill me if he knew I left, though."

"It's fine. I won't tell."

"Thanks. I'm close. I needed a 4x4, animal style, and backup hadn't come yet. Al's supposed to be working tonight. Want anything?"

"Mmm, that does sound good. I'll have a double meat, animal style ... wait—make that without the onions though. But everything else. Please," she added.

"You got it. Fries?"

"Pfft. Yeah!" she snorted.

This was going to change her whole day. She hadn't had In-N-Out since before the tour started.

Johnny knocked on the door ten minutes later and handed her the bag. She wanted to hug him.

"Thank you!" she said, cramming her mouth with fries.

"Don't mention it."

"Hey, it's probably nothing, but someone was here earlier, looking in my window. I think it was a girl." She pointed at the window closest to the door.

"What?"

"Scared me to death. I screamed when I saw her and she took off."

"Why are you just now telling me this?"

"I did call to see where you were and got sidetracked by this." She held up her burger.

He glared. "I'll take a look around the perimeter." He suddenly stepped into bodyguard mode and backed out of the front door. "Before it gets dark…"

"Thanks, Johnny. I'll go ahead and make up the couch bed for Al. And I'll sleep with Leo, so you can have my bed."

"No, don't worry about us. We'll take turns sitting up. I'm about to set up the tents. Really," he raised his hands when she began to protest, "I'm looking forward to being outside. So is Al. We've been cooped up too long. I know this'll be good for me," he said with genuine enthusiasm.

She laughed. "Okay. If you're sure. I can give you some extra blankets."

"Thank you."

The iPad mini dropped into her lap at least five times before Roxie gave up and stopped trying to read her book. She turned her light off, put in her ear buds with soft music playing, and closed her eyes. Her dreams gave her permission to think about Beckham Woods.

The girl in the window. A car backfired and the ground shook. Kissing Beckham. His eyes. His touch felt real. They were in her bed. He leaned down and kissed her bare skin. She tossed and turned, then shook the covers

225

off. It was so hot. She reached for the covers again because the girl was watching from the window.

"Let me see you," his voice echoed in her dream.

"Why is it so hot in here?" she asked him.

"Wake up," he whispered. "Wake up!" The voice got more urgent.

She opened her eyes and her room was so full of smoke, she couldn't see anything. She got down on the floor and crawled toward the door. She yelped when her hand touched the doorknob. Wrong thing to do. She snatched the blanket off of her bed and put that over the doorknob. She was shaking hard. Nothing was moving fast enough. Her eyes burned and her body felt sluggish. Maybe this was part of the dream too. Some of the kitchen walls were missing and the table was in pieces. She turned to the closest window and crawled out of it, stretching out on the grass.

Shaking. She woke up to someone shaking her. An oxygen mask was put over her nose and mouth. She looked up and she was in an ambulance. She tried to sit up.

"Hold up. Take it easy. How are you feeling?" one of the EMTs asked.

"I don't know what happened," she said in the mask.

"We're gonna take you to the hospital, get you checked out. You're really lucky you got out of there."

She looked past the two men and out the open doors of the ambulance. The cottage was black in places and the smoke still filled the air. She couldn't see the main house.

"Are Jill and Eddie okay?" she croaked, lifting the mask.

"I see a couple being checked out over there." He tilted his head to the left. He shut the doors and said something to the guy driving. "Is there someone we could call for you? We're gonna be on our way now."

She shook her head as they started driving. "Johnny will call my parents. Wait! Did you see Johnny and Al?" she asked. She tried to sit up. "Sleeping outside."

They both tried to get her to settle down and keep her mask on, but she kept pushing it back and coughing. "Where are they?" she repeated.

Her head was pounding and her eyes wouldn't stop running from the burn.

"We'll have to see when we get to the hospital," one said softly. "It's important that you stay calm. You inhaled a lot of smoke. Keep the oxygen on."

22 RETREAT

When Roxie got into that cab and didn't look back, Beckham knew he'd lost his chance with her. He should have gone home, worked out until he couldn't think straight, or asked Sierra to not let him out of her sight. But he didn't. He told Howie to take the day off and not bother coming around until they drove to the Grammys the next night.

Another cab pulled up and the flight attendant from earlier stepped beside him and opened the door.

"Need a ride?" she asked with a smirk.

"I need a drink." He squelched down the bile that threatened to come up and welcomed the dark spiral he was diving into headfirst.

"I can arrange that," she whispered.

Anything to forget. He'd do anything to wipe it all out for just one night. It was pulsating with every heartbeat that Leo wasn't his. Everywhere he looked was a reminder that Roxie didn't want anything to do with him. *You deserve a relapse*, he told himself, and he stepped into the cab with her.

His cell phone vibrated and fell off of the nightstand. He grabbed it, crawled out of bed, and tried not to wake up Flight Attendant—what was her name? Morgan? Megan? Megan sounded right...

Stumbling over an empty Jameson bottle, he made it to the bathroom and turned the light on, nearly falling again over the brightness. He held onto his head, trying to push it into his neck. The room wanted to go sideways.

It's not like you're in a relationship, he told the bottom of his chin. He couldn't venture up to his eyes.

What's wrong with you?

He ran his hands over his face and through his hair.

You didn't do anything wrong ... but you may as well have. This is who you've always been. And this woman wanted you. No baggage there.

A beautiful woman that he never wanted to see again, much less, *touch.*

She was all he could see. *Roxie. Roxie. She's not Roxie.*

Relationship or not, he loved Roxie. If he'd doubted it before, he was sure of it now. He'd hoped to put her out of his mind and had only succeeded in realizing he was in love with the woman.

Megan had been all over him the night before and he'd been all over the Jameson. When she unzipped his pants and got on her knees, he let her. But when he looked down and focused on the dark hair beginning to bob up and down on him, he'd yelled at her to stop.

She'd stared up at him in shock when he told her to get out. She wouldn't leave and he was too drunk and exhausted to force her out.

It doesn't matter that you didn't have sex with her—you still went too far, you filthy fuckin' loser.

He gagged over the sink, fisting the mirror and cursing every ounce of Jameson that still sang in his veins. He rinsed his face with cold water, put the phone in his pocket, and walked out of the bathroom.

Megan leaned up on her elbows when he went back into the room and watched as he tried to button his pants.

"Come back to bed, let me finish what I started last night..." She had smudged mascara circling her eyes and he felt his stomach heave at the sight of her.

His phone buzzed again. He took it out of his pocket as she said, "Ignore it. Come here."

He took her hand off his hip. "If I didn't want you when I was drunk I sure as hell don't want you when I'm sober."

He didn't even hear the rest of what she said. He gathered what little he had with him and got out of there. Finally glancing down at his phone, his gut curled when he saw he'd missed twelve calls.

He didn't listen to any of his messages, but called Nate. "What's going on?"

"A lot. Meet me at Cedar Sinai. There are already reporters, so find a way in without being seen."

He texted Nate when he was close and Anthony met him at one of the back entrances. Anthony came to an abrupt stop when he got a good look at Beckham.

He shook his head. "Beck..."

"I know. Believe me, I know I screwed up."

"Follow me."

They walked as fast as they could and Anthony talked quickly.

"Nate will meet you upstairs. He's talking to the police right now. It's Roxie. An explosion went off by her cottage—they're monitoring her closely."

"What?" He stopped walking and Anthony tried to keep him moving.

"I'm taking you to her. Just keep walking. Beck, have you heard from Ian at all? Since yesterday at the airport?"

"No, why? Is Roxie okay?"

"I think she will be, but she's been through a lot. Like I said, they're really watching her closely, so I think there's still concern about all the smoke she inhaled. You're sure you don't know anything about Ian? He's been missing since yesterday."

"Missing? What the hell is going on?" He wanted to punch something.

"He took Sparrow and Journey to your house, left to run errands, and never showed up for their anniversary dinner."

Beckham drew a sharp breath. "Something's wrong. He'd never do that."

"I know. Howie and Matt have been looking into it."

Roxie woke up and looked around. Beckham was sitting by her, with a tight grip on her hand.

She blinked and tears ran down her face.

"Rox," he breathed. "I'm here. I'm so sorry. Are you in pain? You scared me so bad..." he paused and took another breath. "I'll get the nurse." He pushed the button behind her.

"My eyes are on fire," she whispered.

A nurse hurried into the room.

"Fastest service ever. Celebrities have magical powers," Roxie croaked. "Where am I?" Her voice barely came out; she sounded like a million fires had settled down in her lungs.

"Cedar Sinai," the nurse said, smiling at Beckham.

"You look rough," Roxie said.

Beckham's heart dropped. The nurse laughed. He didn't.

He brought her fingers up to his lips and kissed each one. He'd nearly lost her. This was all his fault. If he had been with her and not ... oh God, what a fucking idiot. He squeezed his eyes shut and held her hand to his cheek and kept it there.

She was so shaken, she let him.

When he opened his eyes, both Roxie and the nurse were staring at him.

"How bad is the smoke inhalation?" he asked the nurse. "Is there anything we can do to make sure it doesn't get worse in her lungs?"

"We're starting a brief course of steroids and will be watching her for at least 24 hours, possibly longer. Sometimes symptoms can worsen later, and with all the smoke she took in, we just need to run some tests and keep a close eye on her."

Beckham nodded. "I plan on doing that too."

"You need to go get ready!" Roxie protested. "You're not missing the Grammys for me..."

"I'm not going anywhere. Nate's taking care of it. He let them know we had an emergency and that we won't be there." He looked at the hand that was bandaged. "Does your hand hurt?"

"Yes. Very much. But, Beckham, you *have* to go. You're up for ... what—8 Grammys? You can't miss that!"

"*I don't care,*" he enunciated each word. "I'm not leaving you."

She closed her eyes and let the tears fall. "Can Ian cover it for you?"

He shook his head but didn't tell her about Ian.

"Have you seen Johnny and Al?" she whispered right before the medication took her under.

Nate came into the room a little later. Roxie was still sleeping and Beckham hadn't moved. Nate's eyes narrowed when he saw Beckham.

"How is she doing?"

"She was awake for just a few minutes earlier. They've got her pretty drugged up. What about the guys? How are they?"

Nate shook his head and put his hand around the back of Beck's neck. "They ... didn't make it, Beck."

"*What?*"

He shook his head again. "They're pretty sure both died instantly. A bomb went off around 12:30 a.m., looks like it did the most damage outside. There's a small crater where their tents were."

"A bomb?" Beckham got up and walked to the window, his fist softly pounding the wall. "How the hell does this happen?" He turned around to make sure he hadn't woken up Roxie.

"I don't know much yet. They'll probably question Roxie pretty soon. I saw the police with the owners of the house earlier. The guy called the fire department and got out there with a hose before the fire got too out of hand."

Beckham pressed down on his eyes and squeezed. "Johnny and Al ... I can't believe it. Does Howie know?"

"He's outside waiting to see you."

"Ten years we've been together. They've been through it all with me. I just can't ... believe it. Roxie will be devastated too. She already felt bad that they were-" He looked at the ceiling. "I can't believe she got out of there."

"She had a guardian angel tonight, that's all I know. It's hard to even process about the guys ... it's gonna take a while." Nate bit his lip and looked away.

They leaned against the wall and didn't say anything for a few minutes.

"And Ian? You think it's related at all?"

"I don't know what to think. You know him better than I do, but I can't picture him abandoning Sparrow on their anniversary. There's been no sign of him. Sparrow is out of her mind with worry." Nate cleared his throat.

"I'll call her in a little while. Can't imagine what's going on in her head, with what's happened to Roxie and the guys."

Nate nodded. "We have guards at the house with her, and she's been checking on Roxie practically every half hour." He shook his head. "Poor girl's spooked." He put his hand on Beckham's shoulder. "You watch your back, do you hear me? And listen, I've made sure you're completely free of everything tonight. The police are guarding this floor, so you shouldn't have to worry too much about cameras or anything else. Don't you even think about anything but this one right here." He looked at Roxie. "Be with her." He leaned closer to Beckham's face and jabbed his finger into Beck's chest with each word: "Don't. Blow. This."

"I already have," he whispered.

"Well, I can see that. Fix it, dammit. Do you hear me? Go clean yourself up. Stay *away* from the Jameson. Call Troi. Do whatever you have to do. She nearly died tonight. You don't have time to have a breakdown. Not if you want a chance with her."

Nate clapped him on the neck and pulled him in for a quick hug before he left. Howie walked in next. Neither of them said anything, but they grasped each other by the arm and had a moment. They didn't move until Beckham sniffled and cleared his throat.

"This just can't be right," he said.

"I'm gonna find who did this," Howie said. "Fuckers need to pay."

"I'm with you there, but we're gonna need help. Have you talked to Dion yet?"

"Yeah, and you know he'll do anything for you," Howie said. "He's still the best in the business."

"He handpicked you guys for me—I trust him. Can you get him on this? I'll meet with him too, whenever he's available. We've gotta find Ian too. I don't have a good feeling about that."

"On it." Howie gripped Beckham's shoulder and left.

Beckham sat down and watched Roxie sleep. The hand that wasn't wrapped up looked perfect. He placed it carefully in his, grateful that from what he could tell, her body seemed undamaged. If she had been anywhere else in

235

the house, or outside, it would be a completely different story. The thought made his blood curdle and his eyes drip with the tears he'd been fighting since he saw her.

Roxie woke up just as her parents rushed into the hospital room. Beckham jumped to his feet and Roxie waved a hand groggily.

"Mom and Dad, Beckham. Beckham, Mom and Dad, uh, Rachel and Daniel…"

Their eyes turned to Beckham and they gave a quick nod before turning their focus back on Roxie.

"Oh honey. Are you okay? What happened? Did any of your skin get burned? What about your lungs?"

"Mom, breathe. I'm okay." She gave a faint smile. "I inhaled a lot of smoke but was really fortunate to get out of there when I did."

"She has third degree burns on her hand," Beckham interjected.

"I'm okay," she rasped. "Where's Leo? Is *he* okay?"

"He's in the waiting room with Chloe. We didn't tell him everything yet. We wanted to see how you were before we brought him back here. You sound really hoarse…"

"I want to see him. Would you get him?"

Her dad kissed her forehead. "I'll get him right now. Love you, honey. So glad you're okay … you scared us to death."

She nodded and brushed the tears off her cheeks. "I'll be fine. My eyes are bugging me more than anything—they haven't stopped burning yet. Do I look bad? I don't want to scare Leo." Her breathing came in quick, shallow bursts.

"Your eyes are really red and puffy," her mom whispered, her eyes filling with tears as she took Roxie's hand.

"I'll be okay, Mom."

"You always say that." She shook her head and straightened Roxie's blanket.

The chair scraped the floor when Beckham sat down, and the noise startled Roxie's mom. She jumped and smiled.

"I'm sorry. I forgot you were here," she said.

"More important people to think about," he said. He smiled at Rachel then rested his elbows on his knees and stared at Roxie. "Can I get you anything?"

"I'd kill for a Coke," she whispered.

He jumped up.

"Ooo, with hospital ice!" Her voice perked up. "The only good thing about the hospital."

"You got it." He kissed her cheek before leaving the room.

Rachel and Roxie both watched him walk away. Roxie let out a long sigh without even realizing it and her mom laughed.

"I can see why you have it so bad for him," she said. "He's gorgeous." She laughed and fanned herself. "When you're feeling better I want you to tell me every detail about how you won the heart of *Beckham Woods*." She leaned forward to whisper his name and looked behind her shoulder to make sure he wasn't back to hear.

"We're not together, Mom." Roxie closed her eyes. It was hard to tell what was making her cry more—the fact that her eyes felt like they were on fire, or the grief that sat on her chest.

There was a little rap on the door and Leo peeked in the door. Her dad and Chloe stood behind him and Chloe gave Leo a nudge.

"She's awake. Go ahead, bud."

"Hey, little man," Roxie held out her hand to Leo.

He ran to the bed and put his head on the bed, patting her stomach. Roxie ran her hands through his hair while they both cried.

"I'm so glad you're okay," Leo kept saying, between hiccups.

"And I'm so glad you and Aunt Chloe weren't there. So glad. I'm gonna be fine, okay?"

Everyone in the room was crying when Beckham came back in the room.

"Aw, hey. I need to get in on this crying session." He put his hands on Roxie and Leo's back. "It's all gonna be okay," he said softly. "You need to be using the oxygen, though." He put the tubes back in her nose.

Roxie lifted her head and saw that he had tears in his eyes too. She wiped her eyes and sniffled. "Johnny and Al? How are they?"

He shook his head and a tear dropped down his cheek. She turned her head into his chest and cried harder.

She began coughing and couldn't stop. Beckham pushed the button and asked a nurse to come in right away. She panicked when she saw how much she was scaring Leo. He wailed as Chloe carried him out of the room.

Her lungs felt like they were closing in on her and she had to fight with everything to not panic. She coughed harder. Beckham pushed the nurse button again frantically when her blood sprayed across the white blanket. An alarm went off on the monitor when her O2 levels dipped too low.

The nurses and a doctor rushed in.

"We're going to intubate," she heard someone say, "And we'll give her a cobinamide antidote to reverse her toxicity levels. You should leave the room for this. We'll let one or two of you back in when she's stabilized."

And that's the last thing she heard for a while.

She woke up several times in the night. It was scary to have a ventilator breathing for her. She hated it.

Her parents and Beckham were there whenever she opened her eyes. In a different part of the room each time. Sometimes Anthony sat beside her and held her hand. It could have been hours or days, she didn't know the difference.

Eventually she woke up and felt more coherent. She stayed awake for a while and her mom said her levels seemed to be steadily improving. The doctor came in later and took her off of the ventilator and removed the tube.

Her throat felt like a million knives were piercing her at once. She cringed with every swallow. Beckham held one hand and her mom held her arm above the bandage. Her dad held onto a foot. She tried to smile even though she wanted to cry.

"Leo?" she whispered.

"He's with Chloe. They're in a hotel. Chloe will bring him as soon as you're ready."

Roxie nodded. She wanted to see him right away.

"How are you feeling?" Beckham asked.

She nodded again and held her throat.

"Is it killing?" he asked.

She nodded. He looked so sad, she couldn't stand it.

"Your throat will be sore for a few days." A nurse spoke from the end of the bed.

"No kidding," Beckham snapped. "Sorry! I'm sorry," he said to the nurse before she stepped back nervously. "We're just all on edge here, I apologize."

The nurse nodded before escaping the room.

"You need to go get some rest, Beckham. You too, Mom and Dad," she whispered.

"They've given us a room on the floor below that we haven't taken advantage of—perks of knowing a rock star." Her dad winked and patted her foot. "We should probably go get showers there while you're having tests done. We're smelling up the room," her dad said. "Well, at least that one is." He pointed to Beckham. "You know your mother doesn't stink."

Roxie giggled and then cringed. She wanted to yank her throat out for a while and put it back when it stopped tormenting her.

"Do that, please. I'll feel better if I know you're comfortable," she said. "And take a nap. You all three have dark circles. Please. Go rest. I'm already sleepy again." She looked up at Beckham, who was gazing at her as if she was the only woman he'd ever seen before.

His eyes filled as he stared at her. "I never want to come *close* to losing you again. Ever, Roxie."

"I'm here," she said. "I'm not going anywhere."

He kissed her hand. "When you're out of this hospital, you know I'm not letting you out of my sight, right?"

Roxie made a face. "This doesn't give you permission to be *any* bossier than you already are."

"You've always been the boss of me and you know it," he whispered.

Her parents laughed. Her dad stood up and looked at her mom and Beckham. "I'll just step out and check with the doctor on call to see when they're taking her down for tests." He looked at Roxie. "Maybe I can go grab something besides hospital food for you?"

She shook her head. "Everything sounds too hard to swallow."

"Hospital soup it is, then."

Her dad came in with the new nurse on shift a few minutes later.

"Sounds like," he looked at the nurse's name tag, "Claire here has the paperwork, so you're going down to radiology with her."

Her mom and dad patted her shoulder and Beckham put both hands on her cheeks.

"I'll be back before you are," he said.

She nodded and smiled up at him. Claire stood next to the bed and they both watched Beckham walk out of the room until the door shut behind him.

"You are one lucky woman," she sighed. "He is so hot. Anyway, I'm not telling you anything you don't know," she took a breath, "but seriously, he's always been on my list of free passes. My husband would die if he knew I actually met him because, you know, that list is supposed to be so hypothetical. You know, *the* list?" She looked at Roxie and her eyes got huge. She gulped. "That just came out. Not something I should be telling the girlfriend, right? Right. Okay. So. I have to get a wheelchair and we'll be set." She paused for a quick breath. "We didn't have any on the floor just as I was coming to get you." She backed out.

Roxie leaned her head back. "Thank you," she whispered.

She'd dozed off when she heard a creaking wheelchair. The room was even darker than it had been before. Roxie groggily sat up but felt so limp she relied on help getting into the chair. Something was said as a cool cloth was placed over her eyes, but they sounded so far away. Her eyes still burned, so she held the cloth in place as they rolled down the hall. They got in an elevator and Roxie's head jerked back as she dozed off.

Disoriented, she tried to hold up her head, but it felt like a bowling ball. Everything was blurry. The cloth was placed over her eyes again and held down.

"I don't feel right," she slurred.

A muffled voice responded, but she couldn't hold onto consciousness long enough to hear it.

23 HUNCH

Ian had crawled into the bed at some point in the night. It smelled musty, but he didn't care. He felt like he'd been out for days, but surely not. He'd be hungrier if it had been that long. He finally thought to look at his watch. 2:01 a.m.

He couldn't stand to think of Sparrow worrying. She'd be frantic by now. She knew he'd made big plans for their anniversary, but he hadn't given her any details. She didn't know where he'd run the errands, but maybe the car had shown up somewhere and given them clues.

In one of the other rooms, someone was making a racket. He wondered if it was Coco or if she had help. Maybe she was angry or didn't want him to sleep. He sat up in the bed and swallowed away the nausea. Not many musicians could brag about concussions. From a stalker. It probably didn't count since she wasn't even stalking him. He'd just been in the wrong place at the wrong time. She wanted Beckham, which meant Ian's chances were slim.

He was about to get up and look around when the noise stopped. He heard steps coming toward his room and waited. Coco burst through the door and turned on the light. She looked manic.

"Tonight backfired," she said, pacing near the bed. "Literally. I should have done it at least an hour later, but I was too wired to wait. The placement was perfect—close to the guards, so they couldn't save the bitch. And the bomb worked just as I hoped, but it was so loud the owner came outside and hosed it down before the fire could even burn much of the cottage!"

She talked faster and faster, while his panic grew.

"Whose cottage, Coco?"

She looked at him and frowned, shaking her head back and forth. "I just have to get a new plan," she said. "It'll be okay. I'll do better next time."

"What did you do? Why don't you sit down and tell me about it?" he asked.

She sat on the floor for a second but quickly jumped up and kept walking. "I can't sit still right now." She shook her head faster.

"That's okay. Just tell me when you can."

She nodded. "Okay."

Her eye twitched and she rubbed her face. Her hands shook.

"I-I can't tell you," she said. "I have to kill you soon."

"All the more reason to tell me," he said. "You know that saying, *I can't tell you or else I'd have to kill you*? You may as well tell me since you're already planning on killing me." He smiled and she stopped pacing and stared at him.

"Are you making fun of me?" she yelled.

"No! Not at all. I promise."

Her face softened. "Okay."

"Have a lot of people made fun of you?"

"Always," she said. "But not Beckham. He knows I'm just shy. And you don't either. You're nice to me."

"Has anyone made fun of you on the tour?" Ian asked, frowning.

"School," she corrected. "I get made fun of at school."

"Oh yeah. What year are you?"

"Sophomore."

"How old are you?" He thought she was probably in her late twenties.

"Fifteen."

Holy mother. She was all over the place. No way she was anything close to fifteen.

"Do you know Roxie?" he asked.

Her face darkened. "I tried to kill her tonight and she survived. How does someone survive a bomb like that?"

His pulse quickened. Roxie was okay. Oh God. He was scared to mention Sparrow. She didn't seem to be on Coco's radar, but he had to know.

"Were you able to get rid of my car?" he asked.

"Oh yeah. I pushed it off a cliff not too far from Beckham's house. I stayed until it went underwater." She held up her hand. "You'll be glad to know this didn't go to waste." Sparrow's new ring was on her finger.

Rage hit him so hard his body physically burned. The knot in his chest grew and he swallowed hard before he spoke again. He knew he was walking a tightrope.

"Smart. You're staying a step ahead. I can't believe you were able to drag me to this place. I'm a heavy bastard." He struggled to keep his tone light.

She smiled. "I've had a lot of time to work on this. You have to be prepared for every scenario. Surprises. You were a surprise, Ian."

He took a deep breath. She was so fuckin' creepy. *Flippin'.* Flippin' creepy. Sparrow and her crazy penchant for words had played through his head for years now. Even now she wrecked him from cussing properly. If he made it out of here alive they'd have a good laugh about that.

"Do you have family nearby? Do they know you love Beckham?"

Her smile curled and her expression turned in an instant. "No. They didn't understand. They never understood."

"Sometimes family doesn't," he agreed.

She studied him. "I like talking to you. I've already talked to you more than Beckham." She twisted her fingers and laughed nervously. "I hope I can talk to him this easily when we're together."

"Of course you can. And you're getting good practice with me," he added. He was making himself sick being so agreeable, but it seemed to be working for now. She was responding.

She nodded. "It *is* helping." Her eyes widened and filled with tears. "It's gonna be really hard to lose you."

"Lose me? You don't have to lose me," he said, sliding his teeth over his chapped bottom lip. "I don't have to go anywhere." He shrugged.

She didn't blink and a fat tear dropped. "Beckham wouldn't want to share me," she said.

He wasn't sure what to say to that. This was so twisted. He leaned his head against the metal headboard and gulped back the manic laugh building in his chest. He had to get the hell out of there.

"Everyone needs friends," he finally said.

Before Coco left the room, she turned off the light. Pitch black. No windows. He worked his hands, trying to loosen the rope around his wrists. It took a while, but the rope gradually gave; he held onto it. He stood and felt along the wall until he found the light switch and flipped it on. He half expected Coco to jump back in the door if she saw the light on. All was quiet.

He inspected every inch of the room that he could reach. The door was the only way out, and if he stretched his foot as far as he could, the tip of his toe almost touched the doorknob. The thick leather around his waist wouldn't budge. The part of the headboard that he was chained to was secure, but some of the posts seemed like possibilities. He'd work on loosening them...

The bathroom had a sink and toilet, no shower. He leaned against the wall, feeling a wave of dizziness. His head was pounding a rhythm that would drive him mad if he let it. *Think*, he repeated over and over. Like a rush, it came to him. It was a slim chance, but he didn't see anything remotely better. He made his way over to the bathroom, then took the lid off the back of the toilet and whispered relief that the flush lever was metal and not plastic. He unhooked the chain and tried to unscrew the nut holding the lever in place. It was old and rusted, so it didn't want to move. He kept working at it, barely feeling it through his calluses. It was an hour before it budged and he could unscrew the handle off of the toilet. He'd have to keep Coco from noticing it was missing, but he'd worry about that later. He sat on the bed and dug into the leather with the lever. It was a frustrating angle and he gouged his stomach again and again, not bothering to be careful. Drips of blood gathered on the sheets.

Ian woke up sweating and sat up, panicked. Coco stood in the doorway with a tray of food. Her hair was pulled back and she looked tired. She set the tray on the floor. Her skin was washed out and the rims of her eyes were red. She reminded him of a mouse.

He didn't know what to make of her this morning; her demeanor was completely different. She wouldn't make eye contact and seemed almost sullen.

"Thank you," he said.

He adjusted the rope so it was loosely twisted around his wrists and slowly stood. If she'd just come a little bit closer he'd wrap it around her neck. He went as far as he could go, but she stayed just out of reach. The leather dug into his skin and he turned so she wouldn't see the progress he'd made on the restraint.

She nodded briskly and backed out of the room, closing the door.

The air rushed out of him and he leaned over, his fists and forehead against the wall. Everything hurt. How could he let himself fall asleep? He pictured Sparrow and Journey waiting for him and energy flickered, bolstering his resolve. He wouldn't stop until his arms were wrapped around them.

He picked up the tray, smelled the water and oatmeal she'd left for him to eat like a dog, and decided to only drink the water out of the sink. He wouldn't have thought Coco could go through with poisoning him, but something about her today, in just those few moments, scared the living hell out of him.

There were no outside noises giving him an indication of where they were. Without the sounds of traffic or ocean or people, it didn't sound anything like the L.A. he knew. He strained to hear Coco moving around the house and occasionally thought he heard footsteps. About a half hour after she'd come in the room, he heard a garage door. And then silence.

Beckham took the fastest shower of his life, partly to make sure he didn't take all the hot water from Roxie's parents, but mostly so he could get back to Roxie as quickly as possible. It was painful to see her suffering like this. He hoped to God there was no lasting damage to her lungs. He'd never forgive himself. He had to know the son of a bitch who did this. Not just for Roxie's sake, but also for Johnny and Al. He owed them that.

"I'm heading back to the room," he said as he was walking toward the door. Rachel was sitting at the small table and Daniel was still in the shower.

"We'll be right there." Rachel smiled and Beckham's heart lifted.

It sank just as quickly. He'd bonded with Roxie's parents but didn't feel he deserved it. If they ever found out where he'd been when Roxie was nearly killed...

He couldn't forgive himself for it; he didn't expect Roxie to.

He rounded the corner and saw Claire rolling the wheelchair toward Roxie's room. When she saw him, she turned bright red.

"Just getting her now," she said.

"Oh, okay. Well, let me kiss her before you take her away." He smiled at Claire and she turned an even brighter crimson. "Are you okay?" he asked.

She fanned her face. "Oh yeah. So hot ... in here."

Beckham nodded at the police officer standing outside Roxie's door. He thought the guy barely looked old enough to drive. There had been a steady rotation of officers guarding the room, and Beckham was grateful they were keeping the press away and taking the threat to Roxie seriously.

Claire backed into Roxie's door and turned on the light. "All ready?"

Beckham stepped in and looked around. "Roxie?" Her bed was empty. He looked at the nurse then called out. "Are you in the bathroom, Rox? You were supposed to call a nurse to help..." He smiled at Claire.

"I'll check on her. She shouldn't be up by herself." Claire walked to the door and gave a little knock before barely cracking the door to ensure Roxie's privacy.

Beckham went and stood by the window to get out of the way. He tapped out a rhythm on his leg.

"Roxie? I'm just out here if you need help," Claire called.

The room was silent. Claire knocked lightly again and opened it wider. She turned back to Beckham, a look of confusion on her face.

"She's not in here!"

"Did someone else take her to radiology?" he asked.

"Must have." She picked up Roxie's chart and frowned.

He walked toward the door and motioned Hernandez inside. "Where is Roxie and why aren't you with her?"

"A nurse took her to radiology, said I couldn't be in there," he said.

"And you listened?" he snapped. He held his hands up and tried to soften his tone. "You're here to guard her. Make sure one of us is with her when she leaves the room next time, please."

Hernandez swallowed and nodded.

Claire walked past them. "I'll be right back. I'll find her and see how long she's been gone. Why don't you stay put until I can call down there? She might already be on her way back up."

He dragged a hand over his face and reluctantly agreed. His phone dinged.

> **Sierra: Is now a good time to visit Roxie?**

> He texted back: **I'll text you when she's back in the room**

> **Sierra: Need food?**

> **Coffee**

> **Sierra: Done.**

He paced the room, eventually ending up in the hall. Roxie's parents looked surprised and then concerned when they saw him. Claire returned before he could explain anything to them. She stopped in front of Beckham and avoided looking any of them in the eye. A long, spiky icicle of fear lodged in his throat.

Claire took a shaky breath and began talking at super speed.

"I've talked to radiology and she hasn't been down there. I'm the only nurse who has been in her room this shift. Hospital security is looking for her … putting guards at every exit. Someone will also be coming any minute to talk to you…" She ran out of breath. "I'm sure she's fine," she said, her voice slowing down and becoming softer with each word. "Oh, there he is now." She let out a relieved sigh and motioned to the guard. He introduced himself, and Daniel and Rachel began talking at once.

Beckham looked over at Hernandez. "Wherever the hospital keeps the surveillance footage—that's where I need to be right now. I don't want to wait for any hospital protocol bullshit. Pull whatever strings you can. She was taken on *your* watch."

Hernandez gulped and stood up taller. "I'm so sorry, Mr. Woods. I'll do whatever I can to get her back to you."

Beckham's jaw ticked and it took everything in him to not take the guy's head off. He gave an infinitesimal nod to Hernandez, but it was enough to get the cop moving.

Every minute Roxie was gone meant she was one step further away from him.

Hernandez spoke into his walkie-talkie and motioned for Beckham to walk with him as he listened. They got in the service elevator, went down several floors, and as soon as they got out, Beckham called Howie. He picked up on the first ring.

"I need you back at the hospital. Someone took Roxie. Can't wait for a meeting with Dion—if he's helping us, we need him now."

"Already with him and we're not far. Be right there, boss."

A security guard met them in front of the door leading to the room with surveillance monitors, and indicated with a shake of his head that Beckham couldn't enter. Hernandez gave him a guilty look as he went inside.

Beckham put his fist to his mouth and stared at the guard. "I need to get in there and see what's on the cameras. Now. *Please.*"

"I'm afraid I can't let you in there, Mr. Woods," the guard said.

"I need a moment with Mr. Woods and then you'll let him inside, Charles." A booming voice resonated through the hospital corridor. Dion walked just ahead of Howie, looking ready to pounce.

Charles ducked his head. "Yes, sir. Take your time." He unlocked the door, and Howie went ahead, leaving Beckham in the hall with Dion.

"I trained that kid to do security—he ain't giving me that mess, don't you worry," Dion said with a grim smile. He shook Beckham's hand and pounded his back. "I'm sorry to be seeing you under these circumstances, son."

"Me too. Just relieved you're here," Beckham said.

"We'll get to the bottom of all of this. I promise you that. I wish I had better news for you about Ian," Dion said.

Beckham's hand dropped from Dion's.

"A possible lead came in about a car sinking—some surfers reported seeing one that fits the description of Ian's. Police are working on getting it pulled up as we speak. We'll know if it's his car soon. Not too far from your house…"

"Shit." Beckham closed his eyes and leaned against the wall. The thought of Ian drowning out there was a nightmare. Why Ian and Roxie? Why not him? He felt a jolt of panic and stiffened. "My mom and Sierra. I need to make sure they're okay."

"Already have someone on them. You know I've always had a soft spot for your family. Think I'd let anything happen to your mama?"

Beckham sagged against Dion's arm. "Thank you. I didn't even think past Roxie. I can't believe any of this is happening."

FADE TO
Red

"Let's not jump to any conclusions yet. One thing at a time. Right now we need to find your girl." Dion forced Beckham to look at him. "We'll find Roxie *and* Ian. Okay?" He turned and knocked on the door before opening it.

"Right." Beckham rubbed his face and followed Dion.

The room was not very large to begin with, but when the door shut behind them, it felt miniscule. Screens ran the length of the walls, showing different sections of the hospital. Hernandez was standing by a guy who faced the screens, and he motioned them to come closer.

"Ty is looking at all the traffic in and out of the exits for the past hour plus. So far, there's been no one who looks like Roxie, but we'll be watching it over and over," Hernandez said.

Ty nodded at them and they all turned to the screens.

Dion spoke up. "Ty, while Howie is watching your footage, can you set it up for me and Beckham to watch from the beginning? They know her looks and mannerisms far better than any of us do." He put his hand on Beckham's shoulder and squeezed. "We'll find her, son," he said to Beckham. His eyes softened briefly when he looked at Beckham, but hardened as soon as he turned to the rest of the men in the room. "Let's get to it."

They sat in front of the screens and watched every frame closely. After fifteen minutes, Beckham shifted in his seat, frustrated that nothing suspicious was showing up. The thought of her out there, at risk in every way, made him *crazy*.

"Beck, come take a look at this," Howie said. He was watching with Ty, about a half hour ahead of the footage Beckham watched.

Beckham looked over Howie's shoulder at the screen. For a millisecond, he saw Roxie roll by in a wheelchair. Her head tilted back briefly and her eyes were closed.

"That's her!" he yelled. His heart raced out of control as he watched her being pushed out of the hospital door.

Ty rewound and they watched the whole sequence again and again. The person pushing the wheelchair had slicked back hair and was wearing blue scrubs and a face mask that covered nearly everything.

"It's a woman," Dion said. "I'll be damned."

Ty slowed everything down and focused on the woman. It was hard to make out any features with the distance and most of her face covered. They watched it a dozen times before Beckham let out a startled groan.

"Can you focus on her feet?" he asked.

It took Ty seconds to fill the screen with the assailant's shoes. They matched the scrubs so well that at first it was unnoticeable. Nothing close to nurses' shoes, these were shoes that he recognized. Blue boots.

24 EXTINGUISH

Before she left the hospital, she took her second dose of meds for the day and felt the calm wash over her. She'd gone too long without them yesterday and by the time she realized it, she'd almost been completely hypnotized by Ian Sterling's charm.

No more.

She couldn't think about his ever-changing eyes and pretty boy looks. His sweetness to her. He'd been interested in what she had to say. It didn't matter. He knew too much and distracted her.

Half of her life had been spent working toward *this*— she was closer to Beckham than she'd ever been. She could finally feel him within her grasp. She couldn't forget her priorities. Not when she'd just stolen the patient right out from under their noses.

She breathed in: Invincible.

Breathed out: Determined.

Roxie was a fighter. It just made this all the more enjoyable. Neither Ian nor Roxie should still be alive, but instead of feeling daunted, the thought excited her. She was up for a little challenge and wanted to prolong the play a little longer. What good did it do to put out the bait and then not enjoy the hunt?

It was all worth it. She put her camera strap around her neck.

Time for some live action.

25 WITHDRAWAL

Roxie came to for a moment—long enough to hear the end of an advertisement and then music. The radio. Justin Bieber. She groaned. Her eyelids were too heavy to open. She wanted to lift a hand to her eyes and pry them open, but her hands weighed a thousand pounds. Her last thought before going out again was that she must be in a car and her head felt like a log.

The next time she woke up, she was able to open her eyes. It was dark, but she could see that she was in a small garage. Arms were wrapped around her ribs, and she was being dragged backwards across the concrete, away from a car. Her lungs and chest ached, feeling as if they were caving in. Fear swallowed her whole, sudden and complete.

What's happening? Her mind screamed, but no sound came out. *Where am I?*

They came to a stop and Roxie heard keys jingling. And then more dragging inside the door. Once inside, she was dropped, her eyes squeezing shut as her head hit the floor. They jarred open again as she was yanked up by her hair across carpet that burned through her thin clothes. Her mind raced as she tried to wake up enough to figure out what was happening. She'd been in the hospital. She was still wearing a hospital gown. Whoever dragged her was silent. Roxie's side slammed into the wall as they turned a corner. *Clump, clump, clump,* her body was dragged down a flight of stairs like a life-sized rag doll. Down the hall and into a room that was bare of furniture, they finally stopped.

Her eyes were still watering, but she narrowed them into tiny slits to make her vision clearer. The walls had pictures covering every inch of space as far as she could see. Pictures of Beckham and Leo took over a whole wall. She gasped and turned as much as she could—her hair was still tight in someone's grip. The wall to the right had about a dozen pictures of her with large red X's crossed over them. Another dozen were pictures that she knew had been her with Beckham, but now she was cut out of them.

She had to get out of there.

Leo. Leo. Leo.

His name ran through her mind on repeat.

She lifted her heavy arms and swung behind her, hitting a leg. That earned her a swift kick in the gut. Her stomach clenched and she began swallowing too fast. She tried to turn her head as much as she could and threw up on the floor. She heard a high yelp and her head was released, but before she could look up she was bashed with a heavy boot that wouldn't stop.

She was too weak to crawl very far, and moving just made the blows come harder. She curled up into a ball and covered her face with her hands. The sharp tang of blood filled her nose as everything faded to red.

When she woke up, a thick cloth filled her mouth and was secured in a knot at the back of her head. Her hands were tied behind her back, and a rope around her neck held her in place. It looped onto the knobs of the bedroom door and what she assumed was either a bathroom or closet door. It was tight enough that if she stood up or leaned forward for very long, it would cut off her circulation. She didn't want to move anyway; every inch of her felt bruised, but she shifted her head slowly back and forth to see if the ends budged at all. It only added to the chaffing on her neck. Her heart galloped through her chest and she felt her pulse nudge the rope around her wrists. She stilled and glanced down. Burned photographs were piled next to her on the floor. Some of them had portions of the picture showing through the torched marks. In a few of them, she recognized her clothes.

She told herself to stay calm, but it was too late. Fear clung to her, as much a part of her as the now drenched hospital gown she wore. She smelled like vomit, sweat, and terror.

Another pile of pictures lay next to the burned ones—everyone from the tour, even Chloe and the guards, and a few girls she didn't recognize. She looked at the walls. The only wall that didn't have pictures was the one to her left—a huge map covered that wall, but she wasn't able to see the places marked by tacks. Directly across from her was one she hadn't seen yet. From floor to ceiling, Beckham at every age looked back at her. She studied it for a long time, seeing some photographs she'd seen through the years in magazines, but a lot were snapshots ... some of Beckham looking really young, and others that she knew were taken recently on the tour. And then the wall with Beckham and Leo ... *Leo.*

God, please keep him safe.

Tears ran down her face and she struggled to swallow. Whoever had her was clearly meticulous. Not to mention, *deranged.* And by the looks of it, had gotten away with following Beckham for *years.*

Roxie heard footsteps and felt the rope around her neck shift as the door opened. She blinked, unable to believe who she was seeing.

"Coco?" she murmured.

All the images of Coco doing her hair and makeup flashed before Roxie in triple time and nowhere in the memories did she see a single hint of Coco doing anything like this—to anyone or anything. Introverted and maybe a little odd, but so ... fearful.

"Clearly I'm a horrible ... judge of character." The cloth in Roxie's mouth made her voice sound like garbled gibberish. Nothing in the sentence came through.

Coco didn't speak, but the hatred in her eyes screamed at the highest decibel. Roxie braced herself for whatever was coming. She was surprised when Coco undid the rope from the door, never turning her back on Roxie for even a second. She went to the next door and undid that side too. It seemed as if she was trying to decide her next form of torture because once she had both ends of the rope in her hands, she just stood and focused her laser beam eyes on Roxie.

That's what was different—Roxie realized that Coco had never made eye contact with her until now.

"Why the rope? I don't have the strength to fight you," Roxie tried to say, but only nonsense came out. She gave up trying to talk—she didn't have the strength. It hurt too much and Coco couldn't understand what she was saying anyway.

Coco still didn't speak, but she stood for a moment longer and then jerked the rope so hard that Roxie lurched forward. She had to follow the pull or choke, a fucking marionette under this psycho's control.

Roxie didn't quite make it upright on both feet, crawling not possible either, with her hands tied behind her back, but one of her legs inched forward while the other tried to catch up. They reached the other door in the room, and Coco tightened her hold on the rope, gagging Roxie as she brought her up to both feet. Roxie's eyes shut and she forced herself to wait to breathe until the rope had loosened a bit. It took every ounce of effort she had to stay standing. Her throat constantly reminded her that a tube had been lodged there, the fact that she should still be in the hospital adding to the fear already camped out in her brain. Being beaten by Coco on top of everything else made her wonder if she'd already died and this was just hell warming up.

She heard a faucet being turned on and opened her eyes in time to see water coming out of the ceiling. It looked like she was standing in a large bathroom that had also been used as a darkroom. Cold water shot straight down onto her head; her bare feet blocked the drain. Cold, yes, her hell *would* be cold. Her nerves flinched against the pelts of water. Coco secured the rope and picked up a pair of scissors, walking toward Roxie with them. She was a little shorter than Roxie, and Roxie blinked back water, but kept her eyes trained on Coco. If she moved an inch, the rope gripped her neck tighter.

I will find a way to make you pay, even if I'm dead. Roxie's eyes promised.

Coco blinked and lifted the scissors to Roxie's chest, pausing for a moment before she cut the hospital gown off of her. She looked Roxie's body over then poured soap onto a hard loofah and scrubbed. The wounds she'd inflicted oozed and still she scrubbed. Roxie didn't make a sound. She wouldn't give the bitch that satisfaction.

Coco turned the water off and rubbed Roxie's hair with a towel, but dried nothing else, apparently a hair stylist to the very end. She didn't bother dressing Roxie, leaving her to shiver in the brisk air as she led Roxie back into the room with the photographs. Instead of tying her up, she kept a firm grip on the rope, clutching it at Roxie's neck and forcing her into the hall. It was like trying to find your way out of the middle of a corn field at midnight, but Coco never faltered, continuing to push Roxie.

They passed a few doors, turned a corner, and stopped in front of what seemed to be the last door. Roxie saw a tiny sliver of light at the bottom of the door and felt her first palpitation toward hope. In the next second it was gone and she feared whoever was in the room might be the mastermind behind her kidnapping.

Beckham called Sparrow on his way to Dion's office. She answered on the first ring.

"Hey, my friend. I wish we were having this conversation in person," he said.

"I'm so glad to hear you. How is Roxie?" she asked.

"You haven't heard?" He was shocked no one had told her.

"No, I'm so frustrated! No one's telling me anything about Ian or Roxie."

"I should have called you sooner. I'm so sorry. I thought someone was with you."

"I've had a full house—the extra guards are here and the police came by to question me, but no one is *saying* anything." Her voice broke on the last word. "It's driving me crazy."

"I'm really worried about Ian, Sparrow. Can you have Matt bring you to see me? I'm talking with one of my friends—he owns the company that provides all of our security. He has some information. We don't know anything for sure yet, so I know no one has wanted to say until they know. I really want to talk to you in person. Can you come soon?"

"You're scaring me, Beck."

"I'm sorry, hon. I'm terrified right now. Someone has taken Roxie."

"Oh my God," she cried.

"I don't want you to do a single thing without having one of the guards with you, understood?"

"Yes," she whispered.

"As soon as you can come," he reiterated.

"On my way."

For the past twenty-five years, Dion had run a successful private investigation agency, opening branches all over the world, the largest one being in L.A. He'd personally offered physical surveillance to presidents, celebrities, and musicians, including the Woods when they first began touring as a family. He'd trained hundreds to work with him and helped the LAPD with more cases than he could count. Once he'd worked on a case, he remembered everything with explicit detail, making him invaluable in his field.

In all the time Beckham had known him, he'd never been to Dion's office. He didn't know what he'd been expecting, but it wasn't this. He sank into a brown overstuffed couch and looked at the walls. The room had murals on every wall, a continuous theme of *Where the Wild Things Are*. He felt like Max seeing all the creatures for the first time when his eyes landed on Dion. Come to think of it, Dion did kind of resemble a Wild Thing, with his big eyes and wide mouth.

Dion gave Beckham a kind smile and reared his head back to howl. Howie sat beside Beckham and snorted.

Beckham chuckled and leaned forward. He'd have to bring Leo here—the little guy would love it. His smile dropped and he felt his chest constrict. *Leo.* It wasn't the first time he'd thought of him since she'd been missing, but he kept being blindsided by the thought all over again. Roxie was *gone*.

"Roxie has a little boy," he said in a choked voice. "He can't lose her ... I can't lose her. How do we find her?"

"I have people looking into Coco's background and we're questioning everyone on the tour. I'm recording this meeting—you've already met all the men who will be listening. I'll be typing directives to them and they'll jump on anything they hear that could be a possible lead to follow. Do you agree to this?"

"Yes."

"It's my understanding Coco replaced someone named Tracy. Do you know why?"

Beckham shook his head. "I'm not positive. Tracy's been on several tours with us, but I think she got sick and then never met back up with us." He paused. "Do you think Coco had something to do with that?"

"Remember how I said to not make any assumptions about Ian? Let's do the opposite with Coco—let's assume the worst until we can prove it wrong. Let's assume she did have something to do with Tracy not coming back. What would her motive be?"

"She'd take her place," Beckham answered.

"Yes. Was there any sign that Coco was unstable?"

"No."

"Does Roxie have enemies?"

"I don't know who, but yes," Beckham groaned. "Someone kept messing with Roxie's things on the tour. Twice that I know of. Once her blanket and books were cut up and then her outfits were burned."

"When did that start?"

"I think … it was after news came out about Roxie and me. Pictures were all over the place of us kissing and then she spent the night with me on the bus. Roxie thought it was one of the other dancers, but we questioned her pretty thoroughly and I don't think it was Brooke." Beckham stood and started walking. He was beginning to feel like a Wild Thing himself.

"So she tried to scare Roxie off and when that didn't work, she tried to kill her. What would her motive be and how does Ian fit into that?" Dion's fingers trailed over his computer keys.

Beckham couldn't get past his first sentence. "Do you think she's killed her?" He stopped breathing while he waited for an answer.

"I think we need to find her as soon as we can," Dion said. His face looked like steel. "Had you ever met Coco before the tour?"

"Not that I know of. I don't remember even hearing her last name. She did sorta look familiar to me when I first met her, though."

Dion nodded. "Good. Phil, look into records of all his past employees and people he might have had encounters with over the years." His mouth settled into a firm line and he looked down at his desk. "I apologize that it's going into personal territory, but we've gotta go there, Beck. Is it possible that you've had a sexual relationship with this girl?"

Beckham stood still and looked at the floor. "It's possible I wouldn't remember if I did," he admitted. "I didn't know I was capable of that, but yeah, turns out I am." He put his fingers on the bridge of his nose and squeezed. "That stretch where I was high more than not ... I very well could have."

"Thanks for your honesty. And for the record, I'm proud of how you've gotten your act together," Dion said gruffly.

Beckham could hardly see past the shame. It was filling him up, the longer this nightmare lasted. If he'd trusted Roxie and hadn't been such a fool, she'd be safe. They'd be together right now.

"Anything else you can think of regarding Coco?" Dion asked.

He remembered coming back to his seat on the plane. Something about her eyes staring at him when he'd come back from the bathroom ... a cold shudder went through his body.

"I think she was getting bolder. She was usually so quiet and shy anytime I was around her, but the last time I saw her, the day of the fire, I think she might have been making a move and I was too blind to see it."

They talked for another ten minutes or so before Dion's secretary paged him.

"Sparrow Sterling has arrived," she said.

"Send her in."

Dion opened the door and Sparrow stood there holding Journey. Matt was just behind them.

Beckham moved past Dion and hugged Sparrow. She looked a wreck. When he pulled away her hands trembled.

"I'm so sorry that I haven't seen you before now," Beckham said.

"Please don't apologize. My only consolation in not being there with Roxie was knowing you were with her. How long has she been missing?"

"It's been about five hours now."

The tears fell down her cheeks and she gave up trying to wipe them all. "I love that girl. I know you do too. We have to find her."

He grasped her hand. "We will," he said. He was about to tell her about Ian's car, but Dion stepped in then and took her hand.

"Ms. Sterling, thank you for coming. And look at this little beauty," Dion said, smiling at Journey. She smiled and her dimple deepened, causing him to grab his heart. "Oh, she's gonna break a thousand hearts."

Sparrow gave a wobbly smile and sniffled. "What do you know about Ian?"

Dion cleared his throat. He led her to a chair. "Please sit down. I'll tell you all we've heard so far." He went behind his desk and sat down, opening his file on Ian.

26 STOOP

Ian had worked through about four inches of the leather band and had another inch to go. His hands and stomach were bloody and scratched up, but he wouldn't stop until it was off. He hadn't seen Coco in a while and it made him nervous to think of her out there, on the loose.

He paused, thinking he heard something and situated the ropes quickly around his wrists. He pulled the blanket up over the leather and lay back, breathing hard. He held the metal lever in one hand. The door opened slowly and Ian sat up, pushing the lever underneath the covers.

A battered girl stood naked in front of him. Her skin was bruised and raw, hair wet. Pink droplets fell to the ground, water mixed with blood. Her mouth was gagged, and a rope pulled taut around her neck made her step carefully into the room. Her hands were behind her. Coco pushed her forward with the hand not clutching the rope.

It took a moment before he realized who it was. Holy fuck.

"Roxie!" He jumped up and went as far as the chain allowed.

She went completely still when she heard his voice. She blinked and tears dropped down her cheeks. Her eyes narrowed. *"Ian?"*

She tried to turn and fold into herself to keep him from seeing all of her, but Coco pushed her toward him.

"Coco, why would you do this?" Ian asked. "Beckham will never forgive you."

"He won't see. I have a new idea," she said. "Get back in the bed, Ian."

She pulled the gag out of Roxie's mouth and gave her a hard push forward. Roxie stumbled and ran into him, and still Coco pushed until Roxie was falling forward and he was falling back on the bed. He heard click, click, clicking and could see over Roxie's head that Coco was snapping pictures.

"This isn't gonna work. Sparrow and Beckham both know we'd never do this to them," Ian said.

"Do they? I think I can make it look pretty convincing," she said.

Coco looped the rope around the doorknob, and as soon as Roxie felt the rope give enough for her to move, she scooted back toward the headboard, putting her knees against her chest. Ian moved to the other side of her and pushed the covers up with his knees. Roxie got far enough under the covers and lay down.

Coco nodded and snapped pictures. "Good. Ian, lie back and kiss Roxie."

He stared at her. "No."

"I dug up a little dirt on you last night, Ian. And I know all about Roxie here. Both of your pasts will make this so easy. Everyone is just waiting for you to fail." Her voice sounded hypnotic. No stutters and shakes now. "You need to both do as I say, and I'll be a lot nicer when I kill you," she said under her breath. "Let me see your face, Roxie."

Roxie's head was turned away from Coco and facing Ian, but she wouldn't look at him. Coco stayed by the door, not budging from her safe spot. Ian looked down at Roxie. He leaned in and heard her gasp. She was scared of what he might do and it killed him. He kissed her cheek and then kissed his way to her ear. Coco clicked away.

"It's gonna be okay, Rox." He kissed her ear again but turned his head so Coco wouldn't see his mouth. "I'm gonna hit her," he whispered.

Roxie's eyes shifted to his. He kissed his way over to her other ear.

"I can't see your faces," Coco said.

Roxie gave a barely-there nod. She turned to face him and he laid on his side. The only way Coco would get a shot that showed who they were was if she stood right over them. He found the lever and stared at Roxie. They didn't move.

"No, that's not gonna work," Coco said. "Roxie, your turn. Give Ian some love. We need to see you." She giggled.

When neither of them moved, they heard her move and Ian leaned closer to Roxie's face. His hands were free of the rope and he was ready to pounce the second Coco was near enough. Instead, everything happened so fast. One second he was leaning in, and in the next, Roxie was yelling and grasping her throat. Coco yanked the rope and moved Roxie into position on top of him.

She rested her forehead against his and cried.

"Roxie … just breathe, sweetheart." Ian closed his eyes. All of the fury he suppressed was ready to explode into a bloodbath. He took a deep breath. "We can make this look better if we have our hands, Coco. At least let Roxie's be free so she can wipe her face. Won't look very sexy if she's obviously crying."

Coco was quiet. Agonizing minutes ticked by. And then Ian's stomach dropped. She was inching closer. He and Roxie didn't breathe. Coco edged near the bed and instead of untying the rope, she lifted the blanket to wipe Roxie's face. Roxie rolled off of him. He grabbed a fistful of Coco's hair, and, in that split second, her eyes grew wide when she saw something coming toward her. She didn't have time to move before he lunged forward and stabbed her in the side and stomach with the jagged edge of the lever. Blood painted the room in red streaks and polka dots.

Coco's screams rattled Ian's conscience. He wanted to kill her. He really did.

Instead, he pulled her hands behind her back and shoved her facedown onto the ground. He was eye level to the rope on the bed. Just out of reach. With his knees digging into her back, he stretched out his arm. Roxie used her knees to scoot the rope closer to him.

He wrapped it around Coco's wrists and tried to make it more secure than his had been. If she got loose he was afraid he *would* kill her. She sobbed hysterically and he grabbed the gag that had been in Roxie's mouth and tied it around Coco's. He didn't doubt the wounds hurt, but she'd inflicted a lot more pain on Roxie and Roxie wasn't howling like a two-year-old.

He stood up and pressed his foot into her back, making sure she didn't try to move. Her camera was on the floor across the room.

He looked at Roxie and motioned for her to come closer so he could undo her rope. She turned around and he was able to get it undone quickly.

"Get the camera and start taking pictures of her and this room," he said. "I'm gonna finish working on this." He pointed to the leather around his waist.

Roxie wrapped the blanket around her and tied it under her arms. "Forget everything you saw, Ian Sterling," she said weakly as she walked toward the camera.

"Don't know what you're talkin' 'bout, Roxie Taylor," he said.

He worked on the leather and Coco gradually quieted. The click of the camera echoed in the room. Roxie pointed the camera at Ian just as his restraint fell to the floor.

He closed his eyes for a moment and enjoyed the relief. Roxie touched his arm and he opened his eyes. She had the chain in her hands and handed it to him.

"Can we get this to work still?" she asked.

When he moved his foot off of Coco, she turned over, kicking and bucking her head like a woman possessed.

He never dreamed he'd pummel a woman, but he did. When she stopped fighting, he stopped hitting. He shook when he looked down and saw that she had passed out. He studied his hands in shock. All the strength drained out of his body instantly, like the explosion that comes after a fat water balloon pops.

He forced himself to move; he picked her up and put her on the bed, looping the chain around and around and around her and the posts until it was secure. When he finished, he stumbled to the wall, leaning his head forward and gasping for breath.

This is not who you are. Not who you are. You are not this man.

His father danced across his mind, laughing at him. Taunting him. *You thought you were so different from me? That you could rewire who you are? Like father, like son.*

He felt a hand on his shoulder and he jumped.

"Ian?"

He rubbed a hand across his face, trying to wipe the tears, but only smearing the mixed blood on his face.

He turned around and Roxie stood there, eyes full of concern.

"Are you okay?" she whispered.

He swallowed and slowly nodded. He reached out and hugged her.

"We need to get out of here. You ready?" he asked.

"So ready."

"Hang onto your blanket. Beckham's gonna kill me for seeing your boobs."

She elbowed him in the gut and they both winced.

"Too soon to joke about," he said with a nod.

"You better be glad you saved my life, or I'd so kick you in the balls right now."

He backed up and gave her a huge grin. "I'm so glad you're feeling better. Got your sass back. Good."

A choked laugh came out of her, surprising them both. She laughed until she cried big gasping sobs.

He looked at her with tears in his eyes. "Let's get out of here, Rox, before we both get sucked so far into Crazy Land we can't find our way out."

"I hope it's not too l-late."

He looked over his shoulder at Coco, who was still knocked out and opened the door.

Roxie's eyes didn't adjust right away and she bumped into the walls, yelping each time. The loofah and whatever Coco had poured onto it had inflicted worse pain than everything else put together. Roxie could hardly think straight. They opened door after door, but each led to another bedroom or storage space.

Finally, a door led to stairs. They went up quickly and opened the door at the top, blinded by the brightness. The house had been beautiful once, but was now dirty and reeked. Heavy draperies were ripped and some of the formal furniture toppled over onto its side. A thick layer of dust coated the tables and the high ceilings had a tinge of grey.

"Let's find the garage," Ian said.

They moved through the rooms until they found the kitchen. Roxie gagged—the smell was repulsive. Dishes with leftover food had been left out on the countertops. Maggots squirmed in a mixing bowl. Coco had been on tour for months, so the mess was at least that old.

Ian moved past her, opening doors.

"Bathroom. Laundry. Pantry. Garage! Come on, Roxie!"

She followed him into the garage and looked at the row of cars. Five of them.

"Do you have any idea what she drove?" he asked, looking in each car.

"No," Roxie answered.

"I think I could ... oh wait..." He looked in the windows of the white BMW and moved to the trunk. "Jackpot," he said, holding up the toolkit. He opened it up and found a valet key.

Roxie shuffled to the car and got in. He started the car and pressed the garage door opener. They pulled out quickly. The house was a sprawling mansion.

Ian whistled. "Do you see the address?"

A huge rock out front had the house number.

"4257 Windhill Drive," Roxie repeated over and over.

When they drove away, the shakes took over. Ian turned the heater up.

"Make sure your seat warmer's on," he said. "I ... have no idea where we are..."

They saw one other house not too far and then a mountain stood between the other houses. They drove through the canyon, toward the valley. It was ten minutes before they saw a gas station or restaurant.

Ian pulled into the gas station. "I just want to find out where we are and call the police," he said. "Keep the car locked and start honking if anything goes wrong."

Roxie nodded but wanted to chase after him so she didn't have to be alone. She huddled under the blanket. A car pulled in the parking lot and Roxie ducked, but then peeked carefully over the seat to see if it was Coco.

She was chained up and knocked out cold. She couldn't have gotten out of there so quickly, she told herself. The police would get there before Coco could get out of those chains. But Roxie's heart wouldn't stop pounding. A man got out of the car and walked past her to go inside. She let out a rush of air. Ian was talking to the older man behind the counter; they turned to look at her and kept talking. Her body shook uncontrollably and she felt like she was gonna be sick. She opened her car door in time to throw up on the asphalt.

She heard Ian, but his voice came from a tunnel far away. Cutting in and out.

"Need—her—hospital—how—"

She felt him in the car beside her and wanted to reassure him that she was okay, but she remembered telling Beckham she wasn't a liar. Her vision had black smudges dusting around the edges. She gave her head a good shake and the dark swallowed her up.

Disjointed dreams.
Fragments of reality.
Nightmare and fantasy.
Jumbled.
Collision.
A song.
Leo.
Coco.
Beckham.
Coco.
Leo.
Beckham...
Wishes.
Truths.
Rope.
Bright lights.
Explosions and poison.
Shades of white.
A perfect dance.
Burning.
Book shreds.
Dirty words.
Lullabies.
Pretty dresses.
The dark.
Kisses and hope.
Scissors.
Ice Cream.
Muscled skin.
Running.
In a trunk.
On a bus.
Counting seconds.
Ripped photographs.
Toes in the sand.
Naked.
Cold.

Love.
Consuming.

Beckham.

Beep_____

27 PASSAGE

Beckham was sick of waiting. He felt helpless listening to Dion drone on about what little they knew regarding Ian's disappearance. Dion's phone buzzed and he held up a hand.

"Excuse me. I should take this."

He was on for a few minutes and when he hung up, his expression was grave.

"They've confirmed it *is* Ian's car," he said.

Sparrow gasped and covered her eyes with her hand. Journey fidgeted on her lap, but she was quiet.

"They're searching the water too but haven't found anything yet," he added.

Sparrow's phone vibrated. She lifted her hand and Beckham cringed at the anguish on her face. She was all splotchy and the tears just kept spilling over.

She swiped her screen and stared at the phone before dropping it.

"Sparrow?" Beckham moved toward the phone and picked it up. A picture filled the screen and long blonde hair caught his eye. He held it closer and felt the wind get knocked out of him when he saw the whole picture.

Roxie was on top of Ian, naked. Her hair was wet and she looked beautiful. Beckham's vision clouded and he blinked, trying to focus. Her breasts were on Ian's chest; her hair splayed out through his fingers. *Ian and Roxie?*

Sparrow stared at him with haunted eyes. He gulped.

"We don't know what this is," Beckham said. "We don't know." He reached in his pocket and pulled out his phone, feeling it vibrate. His picture showed Ian leaning over Roxie, kissing her face.

"Let me see," Sparrow said.

Beckham hesitated to hand it to her.

"Let. Me. See."

Dion stood up and took a look at both pictures. "Have either of them given you reason to suspect they were having an affair?"

Both were quiet, thinking through the past few months.

Beckham spoke first. "Not at all."

Sparrow shook her head. "No. It's never once crossed my mind…"

"Do you recognize this number?" Dion asked.

Sparrow sounded dejected when she answered. "It's Ian's number."

Beckham nodded.

"The good news is they probably won't find Ian's body in the water," Dion said, lightly.

Beckham and Howie glared at Dion and the older man had the decency to look remorseful.

"I think this is all Coco," Beckham said. "Sparrow, look at me. I know this looks bad, but just think about it. Neither of them would do this to us. Well, I don't have any claims on Roxie, but she wouldn't do this to *you*," he clarified.

Sparrow's eyes glistened with tears. "You're right. She wouldn't. He wouldn't. I trust them." And then softer: "I do." She shifted Journey onto the other hip. "I don't know how he'd have time to have an affair…" She tried to smile.

"We can't let this distract us from finding them." He looked at Dion. "You've already run a track on Ian's phone?"

"Yes. I'll run another, though, see if anything new turns up."

Dion made a few phone calls, and Sparrow walked in front of the window, back and forth, until Journey fell asleep. She sat on the couch and looked exhausted herself. When her phone went off, she jumped and nearly dropped the phone while trying to answer it.

"Baby?"

Beckham could hear Ian's voice through the phone. He raised his head to the ceiling and took a deep breath. *Thank God.*

"Ian?" she cried.

Dion stopped talking and everyone stared at Sparrow.

"Okay. Okay, we will. I'm with him right now." She glanced at Beckham and stood up. "They're together," she told Beck. "Mission Hospital. We need to go now."

Dion nodded and got on his cell, while they all walked out of Dion's office.

Sparrow sniffled. "Are you okay? Is she?"

The tears kept falling down her cheeks. Beckham was divided between making sure she was okay and snatching the phone out of her hands to hear what Ian was saying.

Sparrow was quiet, listening. Then she put her hand on Beckham's arm, her eyes wide. "Roxie's unconscious— she was beaten pretty badly," she said.

"What?" Beckham paused mid-step then rushed forward when Sparrow gripped his arm.

Howie held up the keys and Beckham nodded.

Sparrow shook her head and choked up. "I can't believe it." She paused. "We're on our way. We'll get there as soon as we can." She could barely get the words out. "I know, babe. I'm not gonna let you out of my sight." Her voice shook. "I love you."

She hung up and Beckham stared at her.

"He hung up? I need to talk to him," he said.

"I know, I'm sorry—the police got there," she said.

Will stepped up. "I'll take Sparrow and Journey," he said.

Beckham nodded. "Did he say anything else about Roxie?"

She shook her head and wiped her face. "Just that he's worried about her." She opened her car door and squared her shoulders. "She'll be okay, Beckham. We have to hurry so she knows we're there with her and that she's safe."

Both cars drove at breakneck speed to get to the hospital across town. Howie and Dion flanked either side of Beckham as they rushed to the ER.

"Can you tell me which room Roxie Taylor is in?" Beckham asked the receptionist. "Miss, please?"

Her shiny blue nails clicked on the keyboard as she finished typing whatever she was working on. Finally, she looked up at him in annoyance. Her mouth dropped.

"Roxie Taylor?" he repeated.

"I'm a big fan of yours," she said. "Like, the *biggest*." She scrolled down the screen. "She's been moved to ICU." She pressed a button on her phone. "Can you cover the desk? I'm taking a break." She looked at Beckham. "I can take you to her room," she said softly. She didn't look at the people in line behind him.

Several made a commotion about her walking away, but she didn't respond. When the whole group moved with Beckham, she turned and frowned at Sparrow and the baby. "Only one person at a time."

Beckham sighed. "She's here to see her husband. We're not sure if he was admitted. If not, he's probably with Roxie. Ian Sterling?"

"If Ian *Sterling* is here, I'ma throw a hissy that I didn't hear about it." She looked at the hulking men staring her down and took a deep breath. A code alert went over the sound system and seemed to jar her into moving. With a flick of her hand, she motioned them back and they walked through the double doors. When they reached Roxie's door, it was open and the room was full of doctors and nurses. The receptionist looked alarmed and backed up.

"You'll have to stay out here for now," she said. "I'll take you to an empty room, so you can be close."

"What's going on?" Beckham asked. "Please." He was stunned by all the doctors around Roxie's bed. Her body rose and fell beneath the CPR. "No," he whispered. "Roxie!" he cried louder. "I'm here."

Leo.

Beep—beep

Beckham.

Beep—beep—beep—beep—beep

Beckham was pulled away and taken to a nearby chair. Sparrow clutched his hand and they watched as activity continued to be hectic around Roxie. An officer stood nearby and Dion began talking with him. Howie and Will stood like a barricade close to Beckham, Sparrow, and Journey. A nurse stopped when she saw them.

"Are you Sparrow?" she asked.

Sparrow nodded and the nurse smiled.

"Your husband has been describing you in great detail to anyone who would listen." She looked Sparrow over. "He was right on the money." She leaned in closer and whispered. "He's a little *happy* on some meds right now. I can take you to see him whenever you're ready."

"Thank you!" Sparrow glanced at Beckham. "Can you tell us about Roxie Taylor?" she asked.

"Yes, I'll see what I can find out," she said.

Beckham put his hand on Sparrow's back. "Go be with him. I'll text you when I hear something."

Sparrow gave him a quick hug. "I'll be close—I'll check on Ian and come back."

The sound from Roxie's room seemed to shift, a flurry of white lab coats and green scrubs exiting the room. Beckham stood up and moved closer. He stopped one of the nurses walking out.

"Is she okay?"

She seemed startled but nodded as she pressed the antibacterial foam hanging on the wall into her hand.

"And you are?" she asked.

"Her boyfriend." *I hope.*

She nodded. "The gentleman who brought her in said you'd be coming. She's stable. I'll have the doctor who's in with her now come talk to you as soon as he can."

"Thank you."

It was some time before the doctor came out. Roxie's parents arrived in the meantime and they sat together, trying to piece together what little they knew of the kidnapping and what she'd been through with Coco. The doctor introduced himself and launched into his update.

"Roxie is stable. Because of a broken rib, she had a tension pneumothorax, which caused her to code. A chest tube relieved the pressure and she's breathing a lot better now. I'd still like to see her saturation levels come up. After speaking with Dr. Herring at Cedar Sinai and also Mr. Sterling, we know her lungs were under duress before the kidnapping. What her body endured after that…" He shook his head. "She is a *fighter*. We'll keep a close eye on her. She seems to be responding well to the oxygen now. We've given her something to help with the pain, so hopefully she can rest well tonight. You should get some rest too."

They all had questions and he answered them patiently, but really the bottom line was that they'd have to wait and see…

They were allowed to sit with her and when Beckham got his chance to hold her hand, he whispered into her ear.

"Hey, Rox. I'm here, and I'm not leaving you for even a second. Doc says you're a fighter and I have never been happier hearing those words about you. I love my kitten with claws." He leaned in closer. "Do you hear me? I love you, Roxie." His voice caught in his chest and he sagged into the chair by her bed, still clutching her hand. Her parents were sitting on her other side.

He looked down at the hand he was holding and his heart plummeted. What the hell had happened to her? The hand that had been hurt in the fire looked infected and the one he was holding looked raw and exposed.

She was covered with bruises and cuts and blood. One side of her face looked normal, but the other side was puffy and shades of blue, purple, green, and pink. The pictures of her with Ian seemed even more strategic now that he saw her. She'd been photographed on her good side.

He'd never wanted to kill anyone, but the thought crossed his mind that he didn't care whether Coco lived or died, just as long as she didn't get away with this.

The day stretched on, endless, and late that evening, Roxie was moved to a different room. The nurses allowed Beckham and Roxie's parents to stay with her. Beckham was grateful—he couldn't stand the thought of leaving her. Daniel left around midnight so he could be with Leo and Chloe the next morning, but her mom stayed. They were hoping the staff would let Leo visit Roxie. Her levels had been good for a few hours. They encouraged them to keep talking to her.

Beckham did just that, pouring his heart out to Roxie, and in the process, her mother, Rachel, also got an earful.

"I hope you can hear me. I want to start over, not forgetting what we've been through, but having a clear slate from here on. I've made so many mistakes, and you've paid for a lot of them. Some that you don't know yet, but I'll tell you everything, I promise. I don't want any secrets."

He looked at her mom. "I know you heard about the paternity test. If I'd just trusted Roxie when she told me the truth, it would have saved us both a lot of pain. I just wanted him to be mine so badly. That kid is ..." Beckham smiled faintly, "something special. Like his mom." He looked at Roxie, lying there so helpless, and felt his heart break. "I want both of them more than anything. My life felt complete for that brief amount of time when she let me in." His voice broke. "Please wake up, Roxie. Come back to me. I'll get it right this time. You're the only one for me." He leaned his forehead on the side of her bed. "I will live every day trying to deserve you," he said quietly. "Let me show you how much I love you."

Rachel blew her nose and cleared her throat. Beckham looked up at her, startled from his heart-to-heart.

"If you say half the things you've said to her when she's awake, I don't see how she can refuse." She smiled and dabbed her eyes.

A nurse brought in a few extra pillows for them and Rachel eventually fell asleep. Beckham kept talking and faded with the sunrise.

28 DISINTEGRATE

She hadn't been this angry in a long time.

Three years.

This might even surpass that anger ... in fact, she was sure it did. Loving Beckham had cost her something. It had not been easy. She'd made sacrifices, lost years of her life, and the people she loved ... she'd risked *everything* to have him.

She shook the chain and felt it cutting into her skin. Tears rolled down her face.

Her parents tried to stop her.

When they realized she wasn't going to let anyone stand in her way of getting Beckham Woods, they threatened to put her away, lock her up.

"You can't stop me," she screamed.

Her parents had forced her to kill *them*. She'd lost part of herself that day. It hurt. The rage nearly sunk her. It wasn't fair. They'd been decent parents—older and reclusive. She still missed them every day. They were 'building wells in Africa' and other exciting things in remote destinations. She periodically went through their email and had 'them' touch base.

She should be able to have whoever she wanted and still have her parents around to enjoy it with her. In a way they were. They weren't far.

It felt like poetic justice somehow.

One day, when he moved in with her, it would be complete.

But this was the worst—two people who had everything, *everything* handed to them, and they still stood in her way. Ian had a successful career, a beautiful wife and daughter. Roxie could have a dancing career anywhere in the world and she had a perfect little boy. And they couldn't let her have Beckham?

She screamed and cried and twisted and shook until she felt the chain begin to loosen. One hand got free. She shut her mouth and focused in earnest then to escape.

29 DEFER

Melissa, Ian's nurse, came in the room and smiled. "You ready to break out of this joint?"

Sparrow roused out of her place on the couch and sat up.

Ian grinned. "So ready. You letting me out of here?"

"Dr. Michaels is on his way to tell you when, but like he said earlier, your scan looked fine." Melissa took his temperature. "You'll be sore for a while, I expect, but we'll send some meds home with you. Temp is normal." She wrote on her chart. "The police are wanting to speak with you again. You up for that?"

"Sure," he said. "You'll be glad to see me go. Grand Central can slow down."

He looked over at Sparrow and Journey. When Sparrow wasn't checking on Roxie, she'd been in the crowded room with him for hours, along with a revolving door of other people. He'd talked to Dion and several guys from his team, three police officers, doctors, nurses. Between answering questions and having tests run, he felt he'd hardly gotten to talk to Sparrow.

She'd been quiet and looked exhausted. Journey had finally settled down after a long stretch of being restless.

"I'll be back shortly with a prescription list," Melissa said.

Ian turned to Sparrow. "Have you gotten any sleep at all since ... everything?" he asked.

"No." She laughed lightly. "I'm a mess."

"You've always been a thousand kinds of beautiful," he said. "Inside and out. My Little Bird of a thousand and one faces."

Her eyes filled.

"I made it out of there—I'm fine." He lowered his head but kept his eyes on her. "I can't imagine what it's been like for you, not knowing where I was. I was going crazy not being able to get to you."

Her tears spilled over. "Right before you called, we'd gotten word that your car was found in the ocean. The thought of you being in that water..." She shook her head. "I don't think it's all hit me yet, everything that's happened. I've imagined every worst-case scenario since you didn't make it home for our anniversary dinner."

He groaned and picked up her hand, kissing her knuckles. "Happy Anniversary. I want a do-over. I had a ... it doesn't matter." He touched her cheek. "We'll have our celebration. I need a date with you. Bad." He grinned at Journey sleeping next to Sparrow.

Sparrow looked down at her hands. "I need to ask you about something."

There was a long pause. "Okay..."

"Beckham and I got texts of you and ... Roxie..." She looked up at him then.

He stared back at her, his heart pounding. "You *saw* those?" He sat up higher and winced. "Why didn't you tell me?"

Sparrow leaned forward but didn't come as close as he wanted, so he shifted his legs off the bed and pulled her closer.

"Baby, come here. Coco is sick in the head. *Sick.*" He shuddered. "You've seen how awful Roxie looks. I'm guessing that didn't show in the pictures? And Beckham saw that too?" He made a face and leaned back against the pillows. "I'm sorry you saw that. I ... really hoped you wouldn't. That crazy bitch forced us into those poses."

"Beckham didn't believe it was real. He talked sense into me," Sparrow said.

"So you believed it?" He couldn't hide the hurt he felt over that.

"No. For a moment, I was ... uncertain. It did *look* real. But I knew I could trust you."

Ian's shoulders sagged as he exhaled. "You can. Always."

Someone knocked and a police officer leaned in. "Mind if we ask you a few more questions?"

Ian shook his head. "Come in."

Two officers walked in. One had a folder in his hand and opened it up to show Ian a picture. "Do you recognize this room?"

Ian's eyes narrowed. "Yes. It's where I was locked up, and where I left her chained to the bed." He swallowed. "Did you find her?"

The officer looked down at the picture. "There was no sign of the suspect. We have a team searching every inch of that property. Her picture is already up on every news channel. We *will* find her." He closed the folder and stood with his arms crossed. "The fact that Beckham Woods' girlfriend was kidnapped makes this already a high-profile case. But add you to the mix, and the public is in an uproar. No one is going to let her get away."

Ian looked at his wife and little girl and wished to God he'd made sure Coco couldn't walk out of that house alive.

"God help us," he said.

After Ian was discharged and assured Sparrow he was fine—a little sore, but *fine*—they went to Roxie's room. The hospital was willing to bend on the rules a little bit for him. He didn't have to leave in a wheelchair. No one was quite sure where they should go anyway, with Coco still out there. It seemed like more guards had accumulated outside his door during the night, and when they reached the outside of Roxie's room, it was also fully secured.

Dion smiled when he saw Sparrow and Journey, and he shook Ian's hand.

"Good to see you up and around. You had your wife worried sick," he said, patting Sparrow on the back.

Ian cringed and leaned over to kiss Sparrow's temple. "Not my finest hour," he said.

"I was just getting ready to head to your room," Dion said. "We need to talk."

Ian bit his bottom lip and nodded.

"Any word on Roxie?" Sparrow asked.

Roxie's dad stepped out of the room, looking exhausted. He introduced himself and apologized in the same sentence.

"Sorry I'm leaving ... I'll be right back—gonna pick up Chloe and Leo to come see Roxie. Just wanted to see her before I brought Leo..." His voice cracked at the end. "You should check on Beckham. He hasn't left the side of her bed all night."

Beckham leaned his head back and his neck and shoulder blades made a loud protest. When he righted himself, he looked at Roxie and she was staring back at him.

He gasped and stood up then quickly sat back down.

"Roxie!" He wanted to wrap his arms around her, but he was afraid of hurting her. "How are you feeling?"

She swallowed and sounded hoarse when she finally spoke. "Like I've been beat up." One side of her mouth lifted and she briefly closed her eyes. "You look so tired,

Beckham." It seemed like it hurt for her to even talk. "How long have you been here?"

"Ian let us know you were here yesterday afternoon. I came as soon as I heard. Not leaving you," he said with a smile.

"How is Ian?" she asked.

"He's doing well. In some pain, but Sparrow texted that he'd be discharged soon. They've been asking about you every ten minutes. When you see all the texts on my phone, you'll see how popular you are," he teased.

He remembered the text from Coco and his smile dropped. He pushed it down. It didn't matter.

"I'm ... so sorry, Roxie. I can't imagine what a nightmare that was."

Roxie's eyes filled and she leaned her head back on the pillow. A tear dropped on her cheek. "Yeah."

"I need to let your mom know you're awake. She just went to grab coffee. She hasn't left your side before now."

"Has Leo been here?"

"Your dad said he was gonna bring him in a little bit."

"Good," she whispered. Her eyes closed and she dozed for a few minutes. She jolted and her eyes were huge when she opened them.

"You're safe. I'm not letting anyone near you," he said.

He stood and leaned over her, kissing her hair, the one spot on her that didn't look hurt.

The nurse came in and thoroughly examined Roxie. Beckham watched in amazement as she didn't flinch even once. His insides cringed just looking at her bruises. And the broken ribs—she had to be in so much pain.

"The doctor is on his way to see you. He was pleased with the way your night went, but he'll want to see you now that you're awake," the nurse said with a smile.

She looked at the tray of food that Roxie hadn't touched. "Can you try to eat a little something?"

"I'll try," Roxie said.

"Good. Time for meds. Why don't you try some of that juice?"

After the doctor had been in, Dion arrived. Roxie was taking a nap and Beckham stepped toward the door and held his hand up to keep it quiet. Dion was in full business mode, so much so that Beckham was about to tell him to come back later, when he brought up leaving the hospital.

"Once Roxie is physically out of danger, I think we should get you both out of here. The Sterlings too. We can hire full-time care until Roxie is feeling 100%, but I'm not comfortable with this…"

Beckham got in Dion's face.

"*They haven't found Coco?*" Beckham snapped. He tried to clear his head with a shake but just wanted to punch the wall. "What have you guys been *doing* all this time?" He knew that was a bit of a low blow, but he couldn't seem to rein in his rage.

Dion lowered his head and nodded. "Trust me, I understand your anger. We're going to find her *and* we're going to protect you in the meantime. We've been questioning Ian on this, since he has more insight on the house and Coco's state of mind. And I know you've needed to concentrate on her. Now that we know she's going to be okay, we need to talk about the next plan."

Beckham took a deep breath.

"One of my men took pictures of the scene and I'd like you to go through them. I tried earlier, but you were in no state of mind to look then. Are you up for it now?" Dion asked quietly.

Beckham swallowed and rubbed a hand over his scruffy jaw. "Yes." He suddenly felt all the energy eke out of him.

Dion held up a folder. "You sure?"

"Yes. I'm sorry for blowing up."

"No apologies necessary," Dion said.

He handed the folder to Beckham. The first picture showed a room with photographs on the walls. There were so many it was hard to tell what the pictures were. He flipped to the next one. It was a close-up of one of the walls. He took a step back and dropped some of the pictures. Different shots splayed out on the floor, the charred ones of him with Roxie shocking him the most.

Dion helped him pick up the pictures and handed him one of a bedroom. "Do you recognize anything in these pictures?"

"Other than the pictures of me that I never knew she was taking? No. Some of these are from when I was a *teenager.* Family events ... who is this girl?"

He went through dozens of pictures and then reached a photograph of the outside of a house. His blood went cold.

"I recognize this house. I ... know who she is." The truth hit him like a brick. "Oh my God. She's been watching me for at least half of my lifetime. How is that possible?" He stumbled back and sat down in the chair by Roxie's bed.

He was fifteen and had been going out with Lana Redley for about a month. She was a few years older and already had her own car. She'd sneak into his bedroom late at night and they'd make out for hours. She was a little reckless for him, but he liked her.

His first time had been with Lana. He didn't want her to leave afterward, but she had to work early the next morning, so he walked her to her car that night. Someone jogged by and stopped when they saw him.

"B-beckham? What are you doing here?" she asked.

Beckham could barely see her in the dark, but he recognized that awkward voice. He'd met her at school and every time he saw her he tried to be friendly—she was such a loner.

"Hey, Colette! I live here. What are *you* doing here?" He laughed.

The night was brisk, so he put his arm around Lana and pulled her closer.

Colette made a weird sound and he looked at Lana, wondering if he'd imagined it. She gave a subtle shrug.

Colette coughed. "Oh w-wow," she said. "I live right there." She pointed at the house next to his, their only neighbor for miles.

"So crazy!" he said. "I had no idea."

Distracted, he turned to Lana and gave her ponytail a tug. He nuzzled his nose into her hair, and if Colette hadn't been around, he'd lean Lana against this car and go again.

Colette coughed again.

"I've gotta go," Lana said, backing up. "Thanks for the best-" She leaned in and said the rest in his ear.

He laughed and kissed her. When she got in the car, he closed the door for her and stood staring at the car after she'd driven away.

"She your girlfriend?" Colette asked.

For a moment, he'd forgotten she was there.

"I think she is now," he said, smiling. "Night, Colette!" He jogged backwards, waving at her before turning around and going back in the house.

Lana was found dead two days later. She'd hung herself with a rope in her bedroom.

Beckham could never reconcile the fun-loving girl he'd known with a girl who would kill herself, but everyone had their own theories about her being depressed and not having the greatest family life.

He'd started drinking shortly after that.

"Beckham?" Roxie called.

Beckham turned, dazed. *How many other casualties have there been?* He looked at Roxie. She was looking at him with concern.

"We have to get you somewhere safer," he whispered.

It was a few more days before the hospital was comfortable releasing Roxie. Although she was still sore, she was breathing much better. Her hand hadn't been infected, just needed cleaning. Once it was treated, it improved. The bruises and cuts still looked awful, but she was moving around better and never complained about how she felt.

She was a wreck from missing Leo though. He'd visited once, but she hadn't gotten to see her family or Leo in the last two days. It was taking its toll on her. Once Dion had a plan in place, their families and the Sterlings had gone to a safe house.

Tonight, after her release, they'd be able to see everyone, and Beckham loved how excited that made Roxie. She needed her family and normalcy more than ever.

He breathed much easier when they were safely out of the hospital. Their leaving was very covert, and they both sagged against the seats in relief when they got in the back of the car. Howie and Dion were in the front seat.

"I can't wait to get my hands on Leo," Roxie said, looking out the window. "I don't want to go another day without him ever again. In that house ... seeing his face kept me going..."

"You won't have to, not if I can do anything about it," Beckham promised. "I wish I'd known how miserable you were without him on tour."

"I wanted to remain professional and provide for him—dancers don't get to bring their families on tour. I knew that and still chose to do it." She looked out the window. "We made the best of it, but ... I don't think I can do it anymore." She bit her lip and wouldn't look at him.

There was an awkward shift in the air. For the first time since she'd woken up in the hospital, he felt unsure about what to do. His hands ached to hold hers. He wanted to put his arm around her and to kiss her. It had seemed natural in the hospital to take care of her and do some of those things, but now that she was out, it seemed like it reminded them both of where their relationship had been before she was kidnapped.

He put his hand on hers anyway. She turned and looked at him, eyes serious.

"I know nothing is really resolved with us, Roxie. I haven't forgotten that you were done with me. And I know I deserve it. But ... I've never been more sure of what I feel for you. I-"

She touched his arm.

"Beckham ... thank you taking care of me in the hospital the last few days," she interrupted. "You've been wonderful. And I know we need to talk. Can we just-" She leaned her head back. "We don't even know..." She groaned. "I can't make sense of my thoughts right now," she admitted. "I ... see Coco in my dreams and around every shadow. All I can think about is getting to Leo. I think the last few days are the longest you and I have ever gotten along and that might have something to do with the fact that I'm doped up."

"Not true," he protested.

She laughed and held onto her ribs. "You know it is."

He stared at their hands. This talk wasn't going how he'd hoped, but at least she wasn't telling him no.

It was nearly an hour before they pulled into the parking lot of what appeared to be a small, outdated apartment complex. Howie pulled around the back and went through the open garage door.

Beckham helped Roxie inside. They walked through a hall and then it opened into a huge open space with vaulted ceilings, plush couches, and a big screen TV. The inside was much nicer than the outside.

"Mama!" Leo yelled and ran toward Roxie, coming to an abrupt stop before he reached her.

He leaned his head on her arm instead of hugging her, gazing up at her face. She wrapped her arms around him and pulled him closer.

"I'm okay, little man. I'm sore, but I have to get a hug from my boy." Her tears dripped on his head and she laughed. "I might cry for a few days. I'm just so happy to see you. All of you!"

Ian put his hand on Beckham's shoulder and squeezed. "Glad you're here."

Everyone was there—Roxie's parents, Chloe, Leo, Ian, Sparrow, Journey, Beckham's mom and Sierra. They took turns hugging them, maneuvering around Leo since he wouldn't leave his mom's side. It was strange to see everyone acting like old friends.

"A lot has happened since I've been in the hospital," Roxie said, smiling.

Chloe put her arm around Roxie and they put their heads together. "We've made the best of a horrible situation," she said. "Good thing is that everyone gets along."

Beckham's mom laughed. "If we have to be locked up, this is the place to be."

Beckham watched when Ian and Roxie hugged. She'd been so out of it when he visited her in the hospital. She put her forehead on his shoulder and sobbed. He patted her back and looked at Sparrow. She was crying too and put her hand on Roxie's shoulder.

"I don't know what I would have done without you," Roxie said to Ian when she lifted her head.

"You were so brave—you would've gotten out of there. I'm really glad we were together, though." His eyes were agonized as he looked at Beckham and then he put his hands on either side of Roxie's shoulders. "I've talked to Sparrow and Beckham about the pictures. They understand what happened."

Roxie looked at Sparrow in alarm and cried harder. "I'm so sorry," she said to Sparrow.

"I know that was all Coco," Sparrow said, touching Roxie's cheek. "I'm just sorry you had to go through any of it."

Dion interrupted. "Can I have your attention while we're all here? I want to let you know I appreciate all the ways you've cooperated with us. None of you have complained—at least not to me—about having to give up your phones and Internet access. I know you must be having withdrawals, but I appreciate you not taking it out on me." His shoulders shook as he chuckled. "The fact that Coco is still out there is heavy on all of our minds. Beckham and Ian are already aware of our next step. It won't be easy, but I hope that it will draw Coco out and we can get you back to your homes safe and sound. I ask for your patience for a few more days. My team will be happy to get anything you need ... within reason." He chuckled again.

When it seemed like he was done, Daniel spoke up. "I'd like to hear how you plan to draw Coco out..."

Roxie's eyes shifted to Beckham's and he felt his pulse quicken. She wouldn't like this. At all.

Dion nodded. "For now I'd like to fine-tune it, if that's okay. If all of you can just continue to be patient. Roxie and Beckham, so you know, no one leaves this house or calls anyone. There's an emergency phone here, but I want it only used for emergencies." He motioned to Howie and Will. "They'll be able to reach me or let someone on my team know if we need to re-stock any supplies."

He looked around. "Any questions?" No one spoke. "Okay, Beckham and Ian? Word with you upstairs?"

30 TAKEOFF

Roxie tucked Leo in and sat on the edge of his bed.

"Are you going to sleep too?" he asked.

"Soon. That bed over there is looking really good, but I want to stay right here until you fall asleep."

He smiled and nestled deeper into the covers.

The place was huge. They were in a room with two twin beds. Everyone had their own bedroom and there were still more rooms left. It was like their very own commune.

"I don't want you to be away anymore, Mama," he said quietly.

Her eyes filled. "I won't be away from you anymore, baby," she whispered. She wiped her tears before they fell on him.

"But what about Beckham?" His mouth trembled.

She wiped her nose. "I don't know what will happen next, but I do know you and I will be together."

He touched her cheek. "That girl is a very bad girl what did this to you."

She couldn't help but smile. Now and then he still mixed up a few words and she didn't correct him. She wanted to hang onto those childish phrases just a little longer.

"Very bad," she agreed. "But Ian gave her a few bruises like this too."

"Good! I wish I could!" He sat up. "I'd make her ribs hurt too, since she hurt yours."

"I don't want to be anything like that girl, and I don't want you to be either," Roxie said. "But I do hope she goes to jail and never gets out."

"Me too! I hope that too!" he said, his brows furrowed.

She kissed his cheeks. "Okay, lay back, little man. Time to stop our thoughts and start our dreams."

He smiled and lay back. "I like that."

"I like *you*."

Chloe stuck her head in and smiled at the two of them. "Love you both. This place is awesome!" She came in and pushed Leo's hair back, kissing him.

Roxie leaned into Chloe's side. "Auntie makes everything fun, doesn't she?"

"Yeah." Leo smiled sleepily at both of them. "I want to live here. Grammie and Gramps and Beckham and Soph and Journey and Sierra and Sparrow and Ian and Will and Howie..." He took a breath. "If Uncle Joey was here it'd be perfect."

Roxie was overwhelmed with gratitude for her people who kept her little boy so protected that he was excited about hiding from a kidnapper.

"Does this place have board games and cards?" Roxie asked him.

He inhaled an excited breath. "I don't know! Tomorrow let's play all day if they do!"

"We can pretend like we're snowed in and make hot chocolate with huge marshmallows." She leaned down and kissed him.

"Yeah," he whispered. His eyes shut for a second then he opened them quickly. "Just seeing if you're still here," he said.

Her heart clinched. He'd been so worried about her.

"I'm not going anywhere, love," she said. "Sleep now, Mama's right here."

She woke up the next morning and Leo was still in bed, stretching. She saw the clock on the nightstand and yelped.

"It's after ten o'clock! I can't believe you slept so late!"

Leo hopped out of bed and stared at the clock, eyes wide.

"Can we play games now?" he asked.

The others were in the main area of the house, except Beckham, Ian, and the guards. Her mom and dad were eating breakfast. Chloe and Sparrow were reading and Sierra and Sophia were chatting nearby.

Roxie greeted everyone and got a cup of coffee. "Where are the guys?"

"I'm right here," her dad said.

Roxie smiled. "Sorry, Dad. Where are the other not-as-great-as-you guys?"

"Oh them. They're talking with Dion upstairs."

She hadn't seen them upstairs, but didn't argue the point. She looked for hot chocolate after she poured cream in her coffee. No marshmallows, but the can of whipped cream would be a treat. She started making it for Leo and told him to hunt for games.

"You'll both wear bulletproof vests and no one will even be able to tell," Dion told Beckham and Ian.

He held the vests up and handed one to both of them. Ian and Beckham started talking at the same time.

"Why would she shoot me if she wants to be with me?"

"What happens if she tries to shoot somewhere other than the vest?"

"What makes you think she'll even come to the show?"

Dion lifted an eyebrow. "I think she's desperate. I have no idea if she'll try to hurt anyone, but I do think she'll show up and possibly try ... who knows what? It's worth a try to draw her out. We'll make sure the news covers that you *are* still performing tomorrow night in L.A., a special acoustic show, despite having to cancel the last several dates. Just hear me out, and hopefully she'll come."

Everything was still on hold with the tour. Dion and Ian knew what Beckham wanted, but they were the only ones.

Dion tossed beanie hats in their direction. "The outside of these have the same material as bulletproof glass, and the inside is like a wet suit. Wear it low enough on your forehead for more coverage. Oh, and don't get shot anywhere else. That's all I got."

Beckham put his hat on first.

Ian sighed. "I'm not gonna look as good as you. I don't look good in hats."

"Oh please, you're the Sexiest Man Alive. You look good in anything."

Ian put his hat on and stared at Beckham, both eyebrows raised. Beckham choked and then laughed hard.

"How is that possible?" he asked, wiping his eyes.

"Told you." Ian shrugged.

"Are you guys done playing dress-up?" Dion asked.

"Geez," Ian mouthed to Beckham over Dion's head.

"Saw that," Dion muttered.

Ian and Beckham laughed. Dion shook his head, but his mouth twitched.

"Shall we walk through it again?"

They nodded, the gravity of the situation pulling them back to the moment, and he went through the plan from the top.

Once Dion had gone through everything and grilled Beckham and Ian backwards and forwards, they joined everyone else. The rest of the day felt like a vacation. Sophia and Rachel stayed busy in the kitchen, making tons of food: hoagies, queso and chips, brownies, lasagna, salad, garlic bread, and cheesecake.

Roxie and Leo kept the board games going. They were a good team. Beckham got a kick watching the two of them interact. They were both competitive and talked a fair amount of smack ... with everyone but each other. They were both so partial with each other that several times they were called out for not being fair.

Leo shrugged. "If I can't win, I want *her* to win."

Roxie laughed. "And if he can't win, *I* want to win."

"Maybe Beckham could win sometime though, once or something," Leo said a few beats later.

If life were always as sweet as this...

Beckham loved the way the little guy looked at him—like he was eleven feet tall.

Roxie noticed Beckham smiling at her and Leo and her eyes warmed. It might take time to prove to her how much he loved her but when he remembered how she'd responded during their night together, he knew it was worth it. He hoped he was right and that she loved him too. It'd make what he planned to do go so much smoother if she did.

That night after dinner, he stopped her before she went to tuck in Leo.

"Do you feel well enough to stay up a little longer? I won't keep you up late," he said quietly.

"Sure. I'll come out after Leo falls asleep."

Leo was doing his rounds, hugging everyone. When he got to Beckham, he barreled into him with a huge hug.

"This has been the best day ever," Leo said.

"I hope to have lots more days just like this with you," Beckham said.

Roxie walked out, her hair piled high on her head. She looked like she'd been in a bad fight and lost, but she was more beautiful and graceful to him than she'd ever been. It reminded him of the first time he saw her. He hated that even his thoughts would always be prefaced with the words, 'that he could remember' because for him, seeing her onstage that day in San Diego had changed his life.

She stopped in front of him.

"How are you feeling?" he asked.

"About the same as the other thirty times you've asked me today." She smiled.

He groaned. "I just don't understand how you're up and around like it's no big deal that you were nearly killed. How are you not complaining all day with the pain?"

"I'm a woman," she said and laughed.

He rolled his eyes. "You've got me there."

"Seriously, I am feeling better. Yeah, I'm really sore, but I'm breathing so much better and I'm so happy..." She stopped and looked shy all of a sudden.

"Go on," he said with a grin.

"I've enjoyed this day too. It's been fun seeing our families get along so well."

He let out a whoosh of breath he didn't realize he'd been holding. "I meant what I said to Leo—I want to have more days like this ... with you."

Her lips parted and he had to kiss her. More tentative than he wanted, trying to make sure he didn't hurt her, but it still felt like magic. He stopped before he got too carried away in the kiss, and her eyes were shining. He traced her lips with his thumb, unable to look away.

"I love you, Roxie."

He felt her breath hitch and her eyes widened.

"I know I still have some things to prove to you, but I'm willing to spend the rest of my life putting in the time it takes."

She swallowed and he trailed his fingers down her neck, still looking in her eyes for any hope of a chance.

"You don't have to promise me forever," he said, his voice low and husky. "But do you think ... one day ... you could think about it?"

She took a deep, shaky breath and her eyes fell to his lips. "I already know what I'm too scared to hope for..."

He waited, but she didn't say anything else. "What is that?"

"That you really do mean what you just said." Her eyes shifted to the side.

A grin nearly split his face wide open, and he tried to tame it down before she looked at him again.

"That I *love* you? Because I really, really *do* mean that, Roxie Taylor!" He leaned down and put his face in her hair. "I really do love you," he whispered in her ear.

She shivered and turned her face toward his. Her hands wove through his hair and she pulled him closer, kissing him the way he'd wanted to kiss her—complete abandon. He felt lightheaded and bereft when she put her hands on his cheeks and pulled away, breathing hard.

"Are you okay?" he asked.

She smiled. "More than okay. Just ... catching my breath."

He rested his forehead on hers. "You've given me exactly the answer I hoped for tonight."

The next morning, he had to leave before she woke up. He was still flying high on her kisses from the night before. By tomorrow, he hoped to have the fear of Coco far behind them.

Beckham and Ian were in the conference room at Dion's office. Beckham wasn't even sure who everyone was—he wondered for the hundredth time if he should even be putting his trust in all these people. He trusted Dion and Howie, but this was a little much. One of his friends from the LAPD walked in and his tension eased.

"Did you tell Sparrow what we're doing?" he asked.

Ian frowned and swiped his hand across his jaw. "No. And she's gonna have my head for it, too."

"Might need to wear that hat around her too, then." Beckham smirked.

"And lose my swagger status? Nuh-uh. I don't think so," Ian said, shaking his head.

"*Swagger* status? Do I even want to know?"

Ian smiled. "Just something Sparrow says…" He drifted off, lost in thought.

Beckham chuckled. "Right."

Howie sat down beside him and Dion began the meeting.

Before they went onstage that night, Beckham stopped Ian.

"I just want to give you another chance to get out of this. I'm already so grateful that you got Roxie out of that house. You don't have to go out there tonight."

Ian's brows creased. "I'm not letting you do this alone, man. I want to see her locked up as much as you do." He put his fist out for Beckham to bump. Beckham came in for a hug. "All right. That's cool too." Ian laughed. "Come on. Let's do this. Maybe we'll even have some fun out there."

Beckham gave him a weak smile and they went out together. The crowd went wild.

The night went without a hitch. As in, *nothing happened.*

Musically, it was one of the most fulfilling shows they'd done together. There were thousands of people there, but it still felt intimate. Between songs, they talked with each other the same as they did offstage—like best friends with the same quirky sense of humor—and the audience at it up.

When they walked offstage, Beckham looked at Ian.

"Is it crazy that tonight was my favorite?"

Ian pounded Beckham on the back.

"I think it's fitting. Honored to be out there with you, Beck."

Beckham glanced up at the ceiling and swallowed his emotion.

"Thank you," he said. He looked at Ian and nodded, knowing Ian got all that he wasn't saying too.

Howie and Will flanked Beckham and Ian as they walked through the back halls of the stadium. Two guards in front and back joined them before they reached the doors. When Dion stepped out to walk with them, he looked apologetic.

Beckham nodded in greeting. "I don't regret a thing about tonight," he said.

The doors opened and there wasn't the usual huge burst of flashes and people cheering, but a small crowd had been given access. Beckham and Ian waved and smiled, stopping to sign a few autographs, but moving quickly toward the limo.

Beckham sensed it before it happened. He lowered his head and kept walking. A loud shot rang out.

PING.

He felt like he'd been hit with a baseball bat.

He heard screams in the distance and his eyes blurred as he looked over his shoulder at Ian.

The second shot gutted him and he went down.

313

Concrete.
Ambulance.
Syringe.
Black.

"We've just received word that pop star Beckham Woods was pronounced dead on arrival tonight by hospital officials, after suffering two fatal gunshot wounds outside a downtown Los Angeles venue where he was performing earlier this evening. Ian Sterling was with Woods at the time but appeared to be unharmed.

The two stars have been through a lot in their short time as friends, with Beckham's girlfriend, Roxie Taylor, and Sterling being kidnapped by Colette Williams earlier this month. Williams' location has still not been identified, and at this time we have no evidence suggesting she was part of the shooting.

Police are requesting anyone with information regarding this case call the hotline. The number will be shown at the bottom of the screen for the remainder of this broadcast.

We will greatly miss the performer who has entertained us for nearly two decades with his award-winning songs and playful personality. The world has lost a star whose light will never go out."

"This news just in: The home of Colette Williams, the alleged kidnapper of Roxie Taylor and Ian Sterling, burned to the ground last night. Neighbors from the nearby house heard a loud explosion and called 911 at 11:59 p.m., but the house was leveled by the time the fire department arrived. The remains of three bodies were found, but at this time, they have not been identified.

Colette Williams allegedly stalked the newly deceased Beckham Woods for many years. It is still unknown whether or not she was responsible for his death."

31 CURVATURE

The emergency phone line rang, and Daniel moved to pick it up.

"Don't answer that!" Will shouted.

Roxie and Sparrow stared at the guard. Daniel paused by the table and frowned. Mild-mannered and quiet, it was the loudest they'd heard Will speak.

Will answered the phone and said very little. He agreed with whatever was being said and hung up.

It was late. Leo and Journey had been in bed for hours, and everyone else was tired but concerned about Beckham and Ian.

"Okay, what's going on?" Roxie asked. "Beckham and Ian have been gone all day. We're really getting worried."

Will seemed nervous. "Pack your things. We're leaving in an hour."

"Tonight?" Sierra asked.

"I don't want to leave without Beckham," Roxie said, folding her arms.

His mom and sister agreed.

Will mumbled and then looked at them. "Dion will explain it all when he gets here. Get whatever you want to take with you, otherwise it will be left if it's not packed within the hour."

Sparrow's eyes were wide. "Wow," she said, glaring at Will. "I don't know why we've been kept in the dark all day about … whatever's going on … but there's no need for you to be rude." She immediately went splotchy, her signature embarrassed face, and Roxie walked over and put her arm around her.

"What she said," Roxie said, squeezing Sparrow.

They split up, each hurrying to their rooms. Chloe decided to take a quick shower since she didn't have much to pack. It took Roxie a while to get everything together because Leo had spread out his toys in their room. She was waiting until the very last minute to wake him up.

She'd had a bad feeling in her gut since that morning. After the sweetness of the night before, it had been a blow to not see Beckham all day. And for there to be no word about him or Ian—it just did not sit well with her.

Dion was all business when he came to the safe house. It was past midnight and he didn't want to answer any questions about anything. It was infuriating.

"We'll be taking two vehicles and we ask you to remain patient for a little while longer."

"Ian and Beckham aren't going with us?" Daniel asked.

"The guys asked me to see you safely to the next location," was all he would say.

All the warm feelings about Beckham that Roxie had been soaking in throughout the day turned. She wanted to kill him. Wring his neck for making her worry like this.

The vehicles pulled into an airplane hangar out in the middle of nowhere. The plane sat at the other end.

"This is all very cryptic," Roxie whispered to her dad.

He was carrying Leo and nodded, shifting Leo to his other hip.

Ian walked down the steps of the plane. Everyone breathed easier seeing him. Sparrow rushed to him and they hugged before he took Journey from her.

"Come on, it's a nice plane," he said to the rest of them with a smile.

Roxie walked as quickly as she could and went up the steps after Ian and Sparrow. When she got on, she looked around but didn't see Beckham.

"Where is he?" she asked.

Ian motioned for her to follow him and took her to the back of the plane. He rapped on the door twice and opened it. Beckham was lying on the bed, asleep.

"Is he okay?" she asked, moving toward the bed.

She sat down and took his hand, looking at Ian when Beckham didn't move.

"He's fine. He was given a sedative—poor guy couldn't handle getting shot twice with a-"

Roxie gasped.

"Bulletproof vest on underneath…" he finished.

"You have a lot of explaining to do," she said.

Ian nodded. "It went a lot differently than we expected, but I think it still worked. Hopefully he'll wake up soon and tell you everything, but if he doesn't, I've got strict instructions on what to say."

Roxie frowned and motioned for him to keep going.

"I'm gonna cut out the flowery crap even though I love it," Ian laughed, "but I know you'd rather hear that from him." He looked at Beckham. "Sure wish he was awake. That wasn't part of the plan."

"Out with it, Ian."

"Okay. Bottom line: will you go on a little trip with him? Maybe a long trip, depending on how long the rest of the pieces fall into place?"

"You're talking in riddles."

"Sorry. I know. So … we thought we'd draw Coco to the show tonight, but went with plan B when she didn't show. We'll have to straighten it out, but right now the world thinks Beckham is dead, and we just got news that Coco blew her house up. Good lord, that sounds crazy. And I wish I felt sad about Coco, but I don't." He tugged his hair and bit his lip, waiting for her to say something.

"What?" Roxie's mouth dropped and she looked at Beckham. He didn't stir. "Are you sure he's really okay?"

"Positive. I heard him griping on the fake ambulance."

"I'm gonna need to hear all of this again, but for now, you should check on Sparrow. She's been worried about you all day."

"You should come out here too. If you agree to go with Beckham, you'll want to say goodbye to the rest of us." He put his hand on the door and opened it a crack.

"You're not coming with us?"

"Originally yes, but with Coco gone … that changes things. As much as I'd like to pretend I'm dead for a little while, I'm not quite at that level financially." He raised his eyebrow and grinned.

Roxie laughed. "Come here. Let me hug you first."

He put his arms around her and tried not to squeeze too tight.

"You guys are right for each other," he said. "Don't be too stubborn to see it."

"I'll try," she said. "And we'll see you soon, right?"

"I promise."

There were hugs and tears as everyone told each other goodbye. No one was shy about saying exactly how they really felt.

"You need this time together," her mom said. "Give him a chance. Okay? That man loves you."

"You won't be able to keep me away for long," Chloe said. "Call me when you need a maid of honor." She winked.

"Are you sure you can't all come?" Roxie cried. "You guys are sounding like it's forever!"

"You'll see us soon," Sierra said.

Sophia nodded, patting Roxie's shoulder. Just then, Beckham stumbled out of the door, looking groggy.

Ian was the closest and tried to steady him.

"She said yes?" he slurred, looking at Ian.

"She said yes *to the trip*," Ian said, giving Beckham a look.

Beckham smiled. "You're the best friend I've ever had," he said, leaning his head against Ian's.

Ian's eyes crinkled when he grinned. "I love you too, man. Best friend ever."

Beckham lurched forward. "Take me to Roxie," he said, turning to Ian.

Roxie giggled and walked toward Beckham. "I'll come to you. You've been through a lot tonight," she said, pressing her lips together. "It's hard getting fake shot."

Beckham looked wounded. "I wasn't fake shot! I'll have you know the bulletproof vest doesn't make it not *hurt*. It feels like being repeatedly hit with a mallet."

She nodded. "I'll take care of you," she said.

"You will?" He gave her a sleepy smile.

She kissed his cheek and said softly: "Wanna go on a trip?"

"Very much." He nodded.

His mom and sister came forward and hugged him.

"I love having new material to tease you about," Sierra said.

"Shut up," he groaned.

Everyone took their turns saying goodbye, and before they knew it, it was just Dion, Howie, the pilot, a flight attendant and the three of them on the plane.

"I've had my men check your location thoroughly. Call me if anything doesn't feel quite right—whether it's security, house, decor, you name it—and I can send someone from over there to help," Dion said.

"Thank you for everything, Dion," Beckham said, sounding more like himself.

Dion pounded his back and Beckham looked like he wanted to hit him. Roxie choked back a laugh. Dion must have hit a sore spot. She knew how that was, having extreme huggers for family and friends.

When Dion got off the plane, they made sure Leo was still okay buckled up in the bed.

"This plane is better than Elvis's," Roxie said.

Beckham reared back to look at her in shock. "There's no gold-plated *anything*."

"But Leo has his own room and so do we!"

He nuzzled into her hair. "You are making me so happy right now."

"And did you see the little kitchen?" She was giddy. "Where are we going anyway?"

EPILOGUE

FOUR MONTHS LATER

Italy was even more beautiful with Roxie and Leo by his side. He'd thought they were coming to test out Italy for the future when they flew away that night, but they'd gotten there and never wanted to leave. Beckham woke up every morning excited about what adventures the day held, and went to bed excited to make love to the woman who had him by the heart.

After Dion reassured him that Colette had died in the fire, he'd given a private interview explaining why he'd gone into hiding. He didn't give any hints about his location or that Roxie and Leo lived with him, but he knew that people occasionally recognized him. Word would eventually get out everywhere.

He couldn't respond to the questions about the crowd who saw the shooting, the ambulance, and the reporter who had announced his death on the news team, but as he'd told Roxie, they were either employees of Dion or part of the FBI. It felt good to know they both had his back.

Roxie was finally beginning to shed the fear. He'd taken her to see a psychologist, who'd diagnosed her with PTSD, but their sessions were helping. She wasn't as jumpy and didn't seem to be looking over her shoulder every moment. It had given them such peace to know that they didn't have to worry about Coco anymore.

She walked outside and set a cup of coffee by him. "You sure are in deep thought," she said. "Sitting out here having second thoughts about marrying me?"

He put his hands on her backside and pulled her closer to him. "You know I'm not." He lifted her sheer blouse and kissed her smooth skin. "Any second thoughts about me?"

"None," she said, leaning down to kiss him.

Later that morning, their family and friends would be flying in and he was going to marry Roxie tonight outside their villa by the water.

"Come on, take a shower with me. Leo's still asleep..." Roxie said, pulling back.

She looked over her shoulder as she threw in a little extra sway to her walk.

Ian insisted to Beckham that they'd take a cab when they arrived, since he knew they'd have their hands full with wedding details. Of course Beckham didn't want to listen to him, so he hadn't even let him know exactly when their plane would land. They were all three in the wedding. Journey would probably steal the show in her fluffy dress.

"I can't believe we're finally here," Sparrow said, smiling at him. "It's exactly how I pictured it!"

They were on their way to the villa and Sparrow was beside herself. Italy and Roxie ... she'd talked on the whole plane ride and she wasn't usually such a talker.

"I like excited Little Bird," he said into her ear. "One of my favorites."

She gave him a quick kiss and turned back toward the window, pointing out a quaint colorful building.

The tour had been great for his career—even if it was cut short—and he was already planning his next project. He hoped Beckham would collaborate on some of the songs with him. Maybe he and Sparrow would even get Beckham and Roxie back on another tour with them eventually.

"Think we could move here someday?" Sparrow interrupted his thoughts.

His eyes grew wide. "You already know you love it that much?"

She nodded, her eyes bright. "We could get a little shack on the water and have sex on the beach every night."

"Done!" he said.

"You look like so beautiful, Roxie," Chloe said.

"Like a vision," her mother added, waving a hand in front of her face. "Don't cry, don't cry—just fixed my makeup for the third time!" When she got a grip, she walked closer and put her hand on Roxie's cheek. "I see contentment in your eyes that I've never seen. As a mother, you know that's all we ever want for our children."

Roxie's eyes spilled over. "Now you've got me crying!" She leaned over and kissed her mom's cheek. "You were right when you told me to give him a chance. He makes me so happy. And Leo—the way they love each other is … oh, I'm not gonna be able to stop in a minute." She carefully wiped her eyes with a tissue and looked at Chloe,

Sparrow, and Sierra. "I'm so glad you're all here. I've missed you so much."

They huddled around her and hugged her one at a time. Chloe went last and held her extra long.

"Roxie, is it okay if we come in?" Daniel asked, knocking lightly on the door.

"Come on in, you two," she called.

When they came in, a whole new round of tears started.

Chloe finally shooed everyone away from Roxie and helped touch up her makeup.

"It's time to get you married off, Rox." Chloe kissed Roxie's cheek and then gave it a final dusting of powder.

"Thanks, Chlo-bo. Let's do this!"

The wedding was everything she'd hoped it would be—she felt like a princess in her dress, the twinkle lights and candles overlooking the water was stunning, and the man she was marrying looked at her like she was all he ever wanted in life.

It was a dream.

But the best part was after they said their vows. Beckham and Roxie turned to Leo and asked him to come stand between them. Beckham knelt to eye level with him.

"I feel so lucky today, Leo, because I'm not just marrying your mom, but I get to have *you* as my family now," he said. His face crumbled a little, but he took a breath and regained his composure. "I have papers here for your mom—our marriage license—and I have papers for you, that if you agree, say you are now legally my son. Your name can even change from Leo Taylor to Leo Woods, if you'd like. "

Leo's mouth dropped and he looked like he was going to jump up and down but remembered he had on a fancy suit. He nodded his head over and over again instead.

Everyone laughed and wiped their eyes while Beckham hugged Leo. He stood and Leo smiled up at him.

"Does this mean I can call you Dad?" he asked.

"Absolutely."

"Yes." Leo pulled back his fist and held out his lisp extra long.

When they were pronounced husband and wife, Beckham tilted Roxie back and kissed her until she felt weak.

"You ready to dance?" he asked, lifting her back up.

"With you? Always," she said.

DEAD AGAIN

She clicked the camera with her left hand. She'd lost her right hand in the explosion. A casualty of playing with fire. Can't play too long and not get blown to bits eventually.

Thankfully it hadn't been her time quite yet.

Next time she might not be so lucky.

She adjusted her long-focus lens and scoffed when she saw the cream wedding dress. The bitch deserved nothing even related to the white family.

When *she* married Beckham, *her* dress would be pure white as the snow.

She click, click, clicked until her left hand throbbed and then she watched the dancing through her telescope.

She was too tired for a plan just yet, but she'd found them. That had to be enough for now.

ACKNOWLEDGMENTS

There are so many people to thank that I'm terrified of leaving someone out! Please forgive me if I do.

I'd like to thank Jesus for not letting me *completely* lose my mind.

Huge thanks to my husband and kids who still love me after I went missing this summer to finish this book. I will do my best to make up for it. I love you so much it hurts.

Thanks to my dad for being the best. Thank you to my brother and sister-in-law for being happy for me! I love you all so much.

Special thanks to all of you who forced me to write this book. I wasn't sure I'd ever finish. Melissa Perea, Calia Read, Darla Williams, Priscilla Perez, and Morgan Scheer, thank you!

Thank you to everyone who has begged for more of Ian. I resisted, but he (and you) won out. I have to give special thanks to Jennifer Mirabelli, MJ Fryer, Maria Milano, Soreonne Spellman, and Savita Naik for the extra-EXTRA Ian love. The five of you have my heart forever.

Thank you for the massive work you did on this project, Marie Piquette. I love you so much and thank God every day that you're in my life.

Thank you to my betas for the help and encouragement! Couldn't do it without you! Staci Frenes, Tosha Khoury, Courtney Shutes, Calia Read, Melissa Brown, duo Riley Mackenzie, Rebecca Espinoza, and Melissa Sutherland.

Tosha Khoury, you're in here a lot and that's because you do so much to help me with each book release, signing, staying sane, making life fun, etc, that I can't thank you enough. Ever. I love you.

Thank you, Linda Russell, for holding my hand through the process of releasing this story. I live for your stickers.

Thank you, Jovana Shirley from Unforeseen Editing for the beautiful formatting! You're awesome.

Thank you, Aaron Cota and Jeanette Abell, for graciously letting me use this picture!

Special thanks to Blade for taking the picture and making even more magic happen. I love you.

Thank you, Susan Finesman and Rebecca Friedman, for your direction. I appreciate you both.

Thank you, Steve and Jill Erickson, for always being up for whatever is next. Life with you both makes our lives richer and better. Love you. And the puglets.

Thank you to all of you who hang out with me in my street team and Facebook group. You make it fun to wake up, my lovely flowers! (Asssssters)

Tosha Khoury, Ashleigh Still, and Courtney Nuness— TAWC here, haha—I don't even know where to start. You each deserve a book of gratitude and devotion, but you're already all over the place in this one. :) My heart is too full. Weddings and funerals give perspective and we've survived multiples of both together, stronger than ever. Love you madly. For life. And then some. Amen.

Thanks to my loves in the Safe House.

Savita Naik, love you, my sister friend.

Special thanks to Maryse, Natasha (is a Book Junkie), Kell Donaldson, Lisa Ashmore, Christine Estevez, Kelly Moorhouse, Laura Wilson, Leslie Fear, Jodie Stipetich, Jennifer Diaz, Talon Smith, Heather Monahan, Kendra Kirby Haneline, Bobbie Jo Kirby, Kimberly Kimball, Robin Segnitz, Kathryn Perez, Mimi Abraham, and Dawnita Kiefer for the love and for being especially wonderful to me on a regular basis.

Darla Williams and Priscilla Perez, I have to say your names again just because I'm so crazy about you both.

Love you, Claire Contreras! You make me happy. That goes for you too, Mary Elizabeth, L.B. Simmons, and Leylah Attar!! XO and so much love, Christine Brae.

Thank you to ALL the wonderful authors I've met in this process. Thank you for taking time to care about my books when I know you're busy working on yours. It means so much!

Thank you to anyone who has read my books. If you don't like one of them, feel free to try another! I appreciate you more than I can say.

Thank you, Tarryn Fisher, for telling me when to live like an animal and also when to stop. I love you more than all the books in the world ... times a million.

If you want to know how Ian and Sparrow began, read this!

Growing up in an idealistic home, Sparrow Fisher is sheltered and innocent. When she meets Ian Sterling, a musician who is rising in popularity, she instantly falls for his charm. They run into each other over the next few months and eventually begin an unconventional relationship.

At different places in their lives, Sparrow is off to college in New York, and Ian is traveling the country with the band. When they see each other, all seems wonderful and lighthearted, but when they're apart, Sparrow is left to wonder if Ian really cares about her the way he says he does, or if she's just another pretty face to him.

Once their relationship steadies, they're both happier than they've ever been, and it's hard to not get caught up in the magic they have together. Until something so devastating comes to light that threatens to shatter everything they've built with each other.

True Love Story is about the real highs and lows that come with a relationship—happiness, pain, angst, and finding out if love really is enough.

For more information about Willow Aster
and her books, visit:

http://www.willowaster.com/

Facebook:
https://www.facebook.com/willowasterauthor

Goodreads:
http://www.goodreads.com/author/show/
6863360.WillowAster

Instagram:
https://instagram.com/willowaster1/

To be added to the Willow Aster Facebook Group (we
have lots of fun in there and talk about things I don't talk
about anywhere else):

https://www.facebook.com/groups/870978829643191/

Reviews mean the world to authors! If you enjoyed this
story, please take the time to share a line or two.
It makes all the difference.

XO, Willow